Julie Shackman is a former journalist and writer. She lives in Scotland with her husband and sons.

 twitter.com/G13Julie

Also by Julie Shackman

A Secret Scottish Escape

A SCOTTISH HIGHLAND SURPRISE

JULIE SHACKMAN

One More Chapter
a division of HarperCollins*Publishers* Ltd
1 London Bridge Street
London SE1 9GF
www.harpercollins.co.uk

HarperCollins*Publishers*
1st Floor, Watermarque Building, Ringsend Road
Dublin 4, Ireland

This paperback edition 2022
1
First published in Great Britain in ebook format
by HarperCollins*Publishers* 2022

A catalogue record of this book is available from the British Library

ISBN: 978-0-00-853894-1

Printed and bound in the UK using 100% Renewable Electricity
by CPI Group (UK) Ltd

A tale of regretting what you haven't done...
not what you have...

Chapter One

"What the hell is this?! This isn't the shade I asked for!"
Her mahogany fake-tanned face edged closer to mine.

I glanced at the stream of pretty olive ribbon the bride was flapping about in her hand. "Ms Carberry… er… I mean… Mrs Carberry-Joyce," I corrected myself, as the wedding guests stumbled around us, slopping champagne and braying loudly. "That was the shade you requested for the favours."

Her pale cat-like eyes narrowed. "Indeed, I did not." Her frothy veil protruded from her head like a volcanic eruption. "I wanted parakeet-green."

"Darling," soothed her new husband from behind. "Can't this wait for now? Bunty and Seb are having to leave early. They have a red-eye flight to Gstaad."

She threw off her groom's pale hand. "Can't you see I'm busy right now?"

I slid my folder out from underneath my arm and riffled

through a few pages, which listed, in every minute and painful detail, the demands of Misha Carberry-Joyce.

Everything was there in Arial font, from the release of a dozen pink canaries in the hotel ground to the sculpted, entwined hearts she had commissioned to be made out of two blocks of ice.

As the reception was in full throttle, with swaying guests, glowing chandeliers and bodies throwing shapes on the dance floor, I couldn't help but notice that the elaborate iced sculpture was now beginning to surrender to the heat and lights. It reminded me of a melting waxwork in a horror movie.

I tried not to stare as it slowly crumpled in on itself, growing ever closer to their six-feet-high lemon and chocolate ganache wedding cake. That melting statue was how I felt right now.

Jerking my attention away from the vanishing sculpture, I located the sample of ribbon Mrs Carberry-Joyce had brought with her months ago inside my folder. Well, when I say folder, it more resembled a phone book. It seemed like two years of my life had been devoted to organising this bloody wedding.

I pushed my growing resentment to one side. *Hold it together, Sophie. Only a few more hours and then this living hell will be over.*

I had sealed the section of the requested ribbon in a small plastic pouch for safety. I slid it out and handed it to her. "Can you confirm this is the sample of ribbon you asked me to ensure was on the favours, Madam?" I attempted to conceal my burning resentment. I had thrown everything I had at this

2

wedding, working late and pulling in favours from contacts. Yet had I received so much as a thank you? Not a chance.

Behind us, the classical quartet had vanished, to be replaced by a plummy-sounding DJ by the name of Astor.

As the strains of Pharrell Williams struck up, the confrontational bride's eyes drank in the piece of ribbon. She shifted in her spikey heels and swallowed. "You must have got them mixed up with someone else's. I'm going to complain…"

Her accusatory voice trailed off, as I turned over the sheath of glossy satin. Written on the reverse, was *"Olive for my favours,"* in her spidery handwriting.

Two flashes of colour bloomed in her cheeks.

I waited for an apology, but she just fidgeted in her swathe of white meringue and struggled to speak.

"Is everything all right, Ms Harkness?"

My stomach dropped to the floor. *Oh great. Just what I needed.*

Heston Cole, the manager of the luxurious Castle Marrian and my boss, materialised at my shoulder without making a single noise. How did he do that? I could understand it when he traversed some of the hotel's plush carpets, but the floor in the Great Hall was polished cherry wood.

"Everything is fine, thank you," I trilled, willing him away.

Ignoring me, Heston turned his smarmy smile to the complaining bride. "I hope everything is to your satisfaction, Madam."

Her smile was tight. I could see her deliberating. She shot me a look. "Yes, thank you. Everything is … satisfactory."

Satisfactory? Was she joking?

The ice statue, the pink birds, not to mention the Ed Sheeran look-alike who'd serenaded them as they walked down the aisle and the jewel-encrusted rose gold limo which had been booked for later on this evening to whisk them away on honeymoon ... and that was just for starters.

I could feel my blood bubbling in my veins. Months organising this sodding wedding had pushed my stress levels to warp drive and meant I very often went home with a migraine. Today's shindig had made the dozens of weddings I'd previously organised here at Castle Marrian look like two-hour kids' birthday parties.

Sensing my seething fury, Heston swung his sharp features to face me. "Why don't you call it a night, Ms Harkness? I can attend to Madam's needs for the rest of the evening."

My fists balled up at my sides. I could barely bring myself to look at Misha Carberry-Joyce.

A ghost of a smirk crossed her lips.

I fixed on a smile and marched out of the wedding melée and along the chequered, portrait-adorned hallway to the patio doors, which led out onto the hotel grounds. They were flung open, displaying this Saturday April evening in all its spring-fresh splendour. Further across the lawn were a couple of guests, wrapped around each other in a clumsy embrace.

I dumped my folder down beside me on the gravelled path and stood there in my rumpled navy suit and pointed heels. I took in several sharp breaths, savouring the zing from the mint garden and the tinkling from the mermaid water feature, which sounded like Christmas bells.

I had been so ecstatic and excited when I had secured this

job after working in the PR department at the local council. It was a relief to leave behind the drafting of press releases about local authority spending and fire-fighting questions about a dodgy councillor who was juggling his wife, mistress and fairy-tale expenses.

But gradually, the dazzle of coming to this sprawling luxury hotel with its turrets like whipped ice-cream and acid-green lawns, not to mention its high-profile clientele, began to fade.

I soon found myself run ragged by the stream of ludicrous requests from couples; in particular, the monied brides.

My growing reputation for getting things done had spread amongst the society brides-to-be and I found my esteemed boss Heston delegating more and more to me and being around to assist less and less. Before I knew what was happening, I was frazzled and under-appreciated, with no work–life balance.

I have to admit that my bank balance was pretty healthy, thanks to the generous pay increase I received when I began working at Castle Marrian, but what joy was there in that, when I trudged home each night looking like Freddie Kruger's sister?

No wonder Callum, my ex-boyfriend, had got fed up with my ridiculous hours. Still, the fact he found consolation in the arms of his middle-aged boss at the bank hadn't helped either.

After the messy fiasco with Callum, I doubted whether I would be able to trust my instincts with another man ever again.

I blinked and wrapped my arms around myself, forcing

myself back to the present. I could feel my pale blonde hair slipping out of its chignon in the spring breeze, but I didn't care. All I wanted to do was vanish into a lavender-scented bath and ring Grandma to have a good old moan.

My brain screeched on the brakes. Of course, that was no longer possible. A lump of emotion clogged in my chest. The realisation she had passed away just two weeks ago hit me again like a blunt instrument. My shoulders slumped under my suit jacket. When I was occupied, I could compartmentalise, but now I was standing here in the hotel grounds, weary and resentful…

Burning tears clustered in my eyes, but I did what I could to blink them back. From behind me, the chime of clinking glasses and scraping chairs travelled out into the gardens.

I could still smell the pungent white lilies and see Mum's lost expression at the funeral. Dad had embraced both of us, murmuring a string of comforting words.

Grandma Helena had been eighty years old when she died; she'd always been one of those people who gave the impression they were invincible.

It was from her I inherited my love of all things porcelain. Grandma had taught me from an early age about the delicate beauty of crockery, its often fascinating history and the sheer delight of indulging in a cup of tea from a dainty cup and saucer.

We would sit for hours, fantasising about discovering a rare Meissen or Spode.

She'd collected them, and her little cottage sitting room was dotted with glass cabinets, proudly displaying her well-chosen array of tea sets.

She had also possessed a great sense of humour. I could feel myself smiling as I recalled Grandma often referring to her nosey and unpleasant neighbours as Statler and Waldorf, and humming the Muppet theme tune whenever she spotted them in their garden.

My mum would roll her eyes and say, "Do you have to be so sarcastic, Mother?" and Gran's knowing eyes would twinkle and she would say, "It's called wit, my dear girl."

She had slipped away suddenly in her armchair in her cosy little cottage that Sunday afternoon in March, surrounded by her beloved crockery and knowing that we adored her.

A ball of sorrow rose up in my throat.

I dashed away the tears with the back of my hand and snatched up the folder of wedding notes that rested by my feet.

Thank goodness I had a day off tomorrow, but it wouldn't be a restful or enjoyable experience. I had promised Mum I would help her and Dad begin the painful job of sorting out Grandma's things in the cottage.

We really should have made a start on it before now, but Mum couldn't face it.

I straightened the frilly white collar of my blouse and raised my eyes to the sky. It was contorting into twists of tangerine.

I knew I couldn't continue like this. I wasn't happy. I was like a robot, mechanically going through the motions each day. Losing Gran so suddenly like that had made me think about what was important and what I wanted to do with the rest of my life.

I had to make a change of some sort. And soon. Take my

future by the scruff of the neck and give it a good shake. But by doing what?

"Miss you, Gran," I murmured before disappearing back into the hotel to collect my bag from my office and head home.

Chapter Two

My grandma's detached cottage sat opposite a children's play park, not far from my flat and my parents' house in the picturesque little Scottish town of Briar Glen, which was described as the "Gateway to the Highlands".

As we pulled up outside 94 Ferry Loan, the Sunday-morning church bells let out a languid, rusty peal and the hills beyond the park were studded with lilac heather, carrying wisps of melancholy mist.

Dad killed the ignition and twisted round to examine Mum beside him in the passenger seat. "Marnie."

She was staring out of the window at the neat little house, with its cobalt door, tiny manicured lawn and tea-set planters, frothing with green and ivory tulips, hot pink pansies and buttery daffodils. I remember when Gran had spotted the crockery planters at the local garden centre several years ago. She'd taken to them straightaway and scuttled up to the customer service desk to arrange delivery.

Mum had thought she was obsessed but I smiled to myself

at the recollection. They had always reminded me of something out of *Alice in Wonderland*.

"Come on," sighed Mum, unclipping her seatbelt and squeezing my dad's hand. "Let's get on with it."

Dad offered me a soft smile over his shoulder.

We all clambered out of the car and Dad led the way up the little concrete path. He unlocked Gran's front door and it swung open.

I still expected her to be standing there, ready to bundle me into her arms with that throaty laugh of hers. She always wore delicate wafts of lavender-scented perfume.

Instead, there was a heavy silence. Her claret-carpeted hallway was empty except for her familiar oak bureau, still dotted with pictures of us all.

To the right was her sitting room, with its Paisley tie-back curtains, heavy stone fireplace, her squashy duck-egg-blue sofa and two armchairs.

More photographs sat in gilt frames: Mum and Dad before they were married, their youthful eyes sparkling; a six-year-old me and Gran on the sea front in Ayr, laughing as gulls wheeled overhead, the Scottish summer not dissuading us at all from devouring a mountainous ice-cream cone each.

"I don't know where to start," confessed Mum, looking bewildered.

Dad rested his hand on her shoulder. "Just take the things of Helena's that mean the most to you. The clearance company said they will deal with the rest."

Mum pushed her hands into the pockets of her black jeans and suggested we begin in the sitting room.

I stood for a moment after Mum and Dad drifted past me.

Goodness knew how many times Gran and I had sat hunched at her circular wooden kitchen table, nursing cups of tea out of one of her beloved teapots and putting the world to rights. I would often confide in her about Castle Marrian and my frustrations, the occasional joys and more frequent endless demands from people who had no concept of real life.

Gran would sit, nodding and commiserating with me, as I let out my frustrations, her features handsome and regal.

When I had been younger, I used to try and guess which of her many teapots Gran would choose that day to make our brew. Would it be her Royal Albert Roses, her Wedgwood Butterfly Bloom or the Aynsley Blue Crocus set?

She had a number to choose from, so I invariably got it wrong, but on the odd occasion I did guess correctly, Gran would clap her hands with glee and present me with my "prize" – an extra-large slice of her celebrated chocolate fudge cake.

Even if I was wrong about what tea set she was going to use, the slice of cake always verged on the doorstop size anyway.

A lump of grief grew larger in my throat. Biting back tears, I turned in my glittery trainers and moved towards the kitchen door, so that I could give Mum and Dad a hand. I had to pull myself together. Mum was hurting too and I knew I had to be there for her.

As I was about to leave the kitchen, something made me draw up. An oblong white envelope was stashed behind one of Grandma's teapots. All the other pots, cups and saucers were housed behind glass cabinets in the sitting room, but this teapot sat alone, close to the black and chrome toaster.

I frowned. That was odd. She was very particular about looking after her treasured tea sets. Why was that one sitting there alone and with an envelope propped behind it?

Perhaps it was an urgent bill that had to be paid. I reached for it. I was about to call Mum when I turned the envelope over in my hands. *Sophie* was written on the front in my grandmother's dramatic, looped handwriting.

The surprise of seeing her handwriting dancing across the front of the envelope made my heart jolt.

I opened my mouth to call Mum and Dad, before snapping it shut again. I would open it first and then tell them what was inside. What if it was some dark, dramatic secret from my family's past? Perhaps my mother had run away at sixteen and joined a thrash metal band and my real dad was an ageing rocker? Or maybe my Gran had worked for MI5 in her youth?

I almost laughed out loud. It was likely something far more mundane. There was no doubting Ken was my dad. We had the same generous, lopsided smile and would bite the inside of our mouth when we were worried about something. As for my gran being employed by the secret services, she wouldn't have lasted five minutes. She couldn't have kept that to herself, let alone state secrets.

I slid my finger along the seal and pulled out a folded sheet of crisp writing paper in the palest pink.

I started to read. My eyes were scanning what Gran had written, but my brain was fighting to keep up.

As the meaning of her words sank in, my stomach performed an impressive swooping motion, before diving to my feet and back up again. What had she done?

What was all this about? What had my gran being doing?

Chapter Three

Dearest Sophie,

*Please don't be alarmed by this letter and please try not to be
sad. I remember you would often laugh when I said this, but
I've always had a feeling for things and something is telling
me now that I might not have long left. I have had eighty
wonderful years and I don't regret a thing. Well, that isn't
entirely true. There is one thing I wish I'd done and that is
why I've written this letter.*

I re-read the letter, my thoughts skittering everywhere. I
could hear Mum and Dad moving about in the sitting
room next door, oblivious to the sound of my heart pumping
faster against my ribs. Mum was busy exclaiming about my
gran's Yucca plant, which had grown to the size of a Christmas
tree.

I turned my stunned attention back to Gran's letter, as
spools of watery morning light fell across the linoleum kitchen
floor.

*I know how hard you are working at Castle Marrian, running
to the beck and call of all of those greedy, flash brides. Talk
about over-inflated opinions of themselves!*

Despite my head whirring, I smiled, imagining Gran saying
that to me with her light blue eyes glinting with fury on my
behalf.

And that is what this is all about.
*At the beginning of this letter, I mentioned I had one regret –
and that's true.*
*It isn't a huge or momentous one. It isn't that I wished I had
seen the Great Barrier Reef or met the Queen – although both
of those would have been wonderful.*
*To some people, it may be a rather insignificant regret. But
how can it be when you do something that you love?*

I bit my lip. Nothing about Grandma Helena had been
insignificant.

*I should never have allowed my heart to rule my head and I
will always regret that I did.*
*I would like you to go and look in the cupboard under the
stairs, Sophie. Once you have seen what's in there, things
should become a lot clearer.*

I lowered the letter and stared around myself, as though
temporarily forgetting where I was.

My grandmother always did have a penchant for the
dramatic, but she had excelled herself this time.

What on earth was she talking about?

Next door, Mum and Dad were still working away, unaware of what was going on in my head. I could hear Dad heaving a nest of tables to one side, the ones Gran used to set her meals on by her armchair.

I placed Gran's letter on her kitchen table and moved into the hall.

The cupboard under the stairs was painted white to match the rest of the staircase and was inconspicuous enough. I never used to notice it. I always assumed Gran stored her considerable number of shoes in there, or perhaps the remnants of my late grandfather's fishing tackle and equipment.

I crouched down in front of it, tugged at the handle and pulled.

It creaked open, bringing with it a faint aroma of dust and apple air freshener.

I peered in, but there was no light. I switched on the torch on my mobile and lifted it up, illuminating the walls of the cupboard with the bright whiteness.

At first, I was struck by how deceptively large the space was. It seemed to snake away from me and down off towards the left and under the staircase. I shuffled forward on my knees and craned my head in further, swiping the light from my mobile up, down and around.

Four brown cardboard boxes were nestled deeper inside and on top of one another towards the far wall. They were all sealed with brown tape. *Sophie* was scrawled on each box in black felt-tip pen.

What on earth had my grandmother been doing?

I eased the first box, marked with the number 1, out of its concealed space. Its mysterious contents gave a slight rattle.

Realising it would be easier to open with scissors, I scrambled to my feet and fetched a pair from the kitchen drawer.

I sank back down onto my knees in front of the gaping cupboard space and slit open the tape on the first box. The contents were covered with a couple of layers of bubble wrap, and another envelope was placed on top of it.

I lifted the envelope and gingerly peeled back the bubble wrap.

A loud gasp escaped from the base of my throat.

It was the most gorgeous tea set in the palest sunshine yellow, shot through with an ivy pattern. From the stout matching teapot to the dainty cups, saucers and milk jug, it glinted back up at me. I had never seen this one before. I always assumed she displayed her entire collection in the sitting room, along with the others. I lifted out one of the teacups, to appreciate the flowing ivy detail. It looked like a Burleigh original – hand-engraved with copper rollers.

Had Gran left me this in her will? I had no idea she owned something like this. She'd never said. But what about the rest of the boxes? What was stored in those?

I was so lost in admiring the bright golden-yellow crockery, I almost forgot I was clutching Gran's other letter in my right hand.

I tore open the second envelope.

Dearest Sophie,
Knowing you as I do, I suspect you have already stolen a peek

at the contents of this box. It's beautiful, isn't it? I expect you
will have recognised it as a Burleigh. But it isn't the only one.

My widening eyes darted from her handwriting to the three other boxes secreted in the cupboard.

Contained in the other boxes are other tea sets, just as
valuable as this one. I wasn't able to fulfil my dream of
owning my own little crockery shop, so that's why I'm doing
this for you.

I slumped against the wall in shock, my legs sprawled out in front of me. Oh, Gran. What have you been doing all this time?

As though anticipating my next question, Gran's letter carried on;

As you may know, Mrs Cotter is selling up her floristry
business, Bloom with a View. Well, I should say she was
selling it. When I discovered this, I spoke to her, explained my
intentions, and she was a darling about it all. So, I've
purchased her business for you.

What?! My mind took off into overdrive. My late grandmother had bought me Mrs Cotter's business?

Pictures of the sweet little florist's in Briar Glen's main street, sandwiched between the jeweller's and the chemist, flickered into my head and wouldn't leave.

I sat still for a moment, unable to focus on anything. I felt like time had frozen. I licked my lips and let out a long, slow breath. Then I shot forward, scrabbling for the other boxes in disbelief. I scoured the rest of her letter.

At the bottom of this first box, you will find a list, detailing each of the other tea sets and their approximate value. I took the liberty of having each set valued a couple of months ago. I should like you to sell these tea sets and use the proceeds to launch your own crockery business.

My attention was struggling to comprehend what I was reading,

There is also a list of reputable crockery suppliers and their contacts along with the itinerary for when you are ready to select your own stock.

I dragged a stunned hand over the top of my ponytail. This was surreal. I was crouched in Gran's hall, surrounded by lots of very valuable crockery.

Sophie, this is your chance to do something that you love. I know you haven't been happy in your job for a long time. You don't feel rewarded or appreciated for the work that you do.
So, I decided I would help you.
Take the opportunity for yourself. Take this chance for me and know I will be watching over you with so much joy and pride. You have grown into such a lovely young woman and it is a pleasure to call you my granddaughter.

Love always,
Gran. XX

I didn't know how long I sat there, with the half-opened box in front of me and the gorgeous, ivy-sprigged tea set gazing out of its bubble wrap. My mobile phone lay on the hall carpet and the stair cupboard door gaped open.

All I was aware of was the sound of my own tearful gulps and then Mum and Dad dashing out of the sitting room to find out what was wrong.

Chapter Four

I handed Gran's two letters to my bewildered-looking parents and prised open the remainder of the boxes, sniffing back a succession of tears. The boxes held a vast array of tea sets, from classic Wedgwood to an Edwardian antique silver set from 1903.

Dad couldn't decide which deserved his attention first, the tea sets or my grandmother's mysterious letters. "What on earth is all this lot? What's going on? Sophie?"

I shook my head, still reeling from it all. "Read the letters, Dad."

He flashed a look at Mum and read to himself, until he reached the end of the second letter. "Bloody hell! The crafty old…"

My mum's confusion and impatience were growing. "Kenny. What is it?"

Dad passed the letters to her. She began to read them for herself, while I remained hunched over the crockery littering the hallway.

Mum's hand flew to her throat. "She's bought you a shop?"

I nodded.

"But why... how...?"

Dad gave a helpless shrug. "Helena was a very savvy lady, but where the hell did your mother get this lot from?"

Mum flapped her hands in the air. "You tell me. I never knew she had all this. I mean, I knew about the crockery in her sitting-room cabinets, of course..."

I rubbed at my forehead, struggling to process any of this. "Goodness knows how much all this is worth."

Dad cocked one of his thick, greying brows. "I can tell you that this lot will be worth a pretty penny. There must be thousands of pounds' worth of antique crockery here."

I was still sitting on Gran's hallway carpet, my head cartwheeling from the contents of her letters and from the glistening crockery surrounding me.

Mum raised a disbelieving finger and gestured to the boxes parked around our feet. "Where did she get all this?" Her smoky blue eyes widened. "Oh God, you don't think she stole any of it?"

Dad let out a bark of laughter. "Your mother receiving stolen goods? Don't be silly, Marnie. Your mother once scanned Briar Glen high street, trying to locate the owner of a dropped fifty-pence piece."

Despite my shock at the situation, I still laughed at the memory.

"But she must have got them from somewhere. And what does she mean when she talks here about letting her heart rule her head?" said Mum.

Dad threw his arms up in the air. "God only knows. Well,

wherever Helena got them from, she has made it clear she wants Sophie to have them now."

I swallowed. "Yes, and open up my own crockery shop."

Too stunned to undertake any other sorting of my gran's belongings for today, Dad suggested we pack the car with the four boxes of tea sets. "I'll return and collect the nest of tables and the other bits and bobs, once I've deposited you and your mother back at the house."

———————

I could hear the faint clatter from the boot as Dad drove us home. It was fortunate Mum and Dad only lived ten minutes away from my late grandmother's cottage; I would have been a nervous wreck taking such precious items as these on a longer journey.

She must have been planning this for at least three months, possibly longer. My gran had squirreled away that gorgeous crockery for me and then gone and acquired a shop – and not me, Mum or Dad knew a thing.

We made the journey back in stunned near-silence, only speaking again when Dad eased up the drive.

Through the late morning sunshine, Mum, Dad and I proceeded to carry each box into their biscuit-carpeted hallway and deposit them there.

Dad placed one of the boxes, housing Minton Green Cockatrice in bone china, by the corner of the staircase. He shot up straight as a thought came to him. He turned to Mum. "I wonder if that's what Helena was up to when I dropped by a few weeks back."

"What do you mean?"

Dad thrust his hands into his jeans pockets. "At the time, I didn't think much of it, but on two previous occasions when I'd dropped round to check your mother was okay, she was on the phone to someone. She couldn't end each call fast enough when I showed up."

I asked Dad if she had mentioned who she was talking to.

"No. She changed the subject and started talking about something else. She didn't make any comment about who was on the phone at all." Dad shrugged. "At the time, I did think it was a bit odd, but then I forgot about it."

Mum flicked a look at me. "She must have been in the middle of trying to sort all this out."

After the last of the boxes had been transferred from the car and stacked in a corner of my parents' hallway, Mum rustled up some cheese and pickle sandwiches for lunch, before Dad and I returned to Gran's to empty her sitting-room cabinets of her "official" collection of tea sets.

Mum insisted on making a pot of tea on our return and the three of us sank gratefully down in their sitting room, cradling our cups and each digesting the bombshell my late gran had delivered.

I cast my eyes around the room, with its patio doors leading out onto their manicured garden with its assorted ceramic pots and clipped hedgerows. On the far wall was a smudgy, gorgeous watercolour of Briar Glen's moody landscape of soaring hills. It was an idyllic scene but we were all in turmoil.

"But this is crazy!" I blurted. "I mean, I've already got a job." Not one that I was enthusiastic about, but it was secure employment – or as secure as you could expect nowadays.

I glanced out to the hall, where Gran's secret stash of tea sets and teapots seemed to be winking at me as they peeped out from under the bubble wrap. "I can't just give up my job and start a business."

Mum tutted in agreement. "I don't know what she was thinking. I loved my mother so much, but I do wonder where she got her ideas from sometimes." She twisted round on the sofa. "You don't think she was having some sort of episode, do you? Or that she wasn't sure about what she was doing?"

Dad glanced at Mum and then across at me. "Helena was more with it than the three of us combined. She was always a free spirit, or at least she tried to be. That father of yours didn't exactly encourage her to be ambitious, did he?"

Mum considered what Dad had just said. "My father was so staid in his ways and because he was too scared to take a risk, he expected Mum to be the same too." She cocked a cynical brow. "They were very different. I often wondered how they got together in the first place." Mum peered down at the rumpled letters from Gran lying in her lap. "And I haven't a clue what she meant about it being different times back then and that she had one regret."

"Helena wanted you to do what she never did," said Dad to me, dragging our attention back. "And whatever that might have been, it's clear she wants you to take a chance and do something that you love."

I opened my mouth and closed it again.

Mum shook her bobbed red hair. Her voice splintered with emotion. "Well, I think it's selfish." Her confused eyes clouded over with tears.

I shot up from the armchair and towards Mum, pulling her into my outstretched arms. I inhaled her dash of Coco Chanel.

Mum kept her head tilted into the crook of my neck. "I know your grandmother was often frustrated with her life with your grandfather, but she can't foist her lost ambitions on you. It's not fair."

I tightened my grip around her. "Gran thought she was trying to help, Mum. I moaned about all my demanding wedding clients to her often enough."

Mum dashed the back of her hand across her damp eyes. "I know in her own mind she must have thought she was doing what was right but still…" Her voice tailed off as the dappled afternoon sun spilt across their hessian rug.

Dad blinked at me. "So does that mean you aren't even going to consider your gran's idea?"

I rubbed at my forehead, guilt stealing over me. I didn't want to let my gran down. That was the last thing I wanted to do. But what she was asking of me … well, it was ridiculous! I loved beautiful crockery every bit as much as she had, but turning that passion into a successful business – the idea was a ludicrous one! All the reasons why rolled through my mind. I had no retail experience. Briar Glen's smaller businesses were already struggling to survive in the current economic climate. I had no idea how to pull together a business plan. The list of negatives grew larger and darker as I thought about them.

I shook my ponytail, dismissing the punches of guilt

striking me in the chest. It had been a wonderful, loving and very generous idea of my grandmother's and she would never know how much I appreciated what she had attempted to do for me. But it was impossible.

I forced my mouth into a determined, sad smile. "It's a great notion, Dad, but Gran wasn't thinking this through. It's out of the question."

Chapter Five

The next morning swung around too quickly, bringing with it the usual Monday joy of another working week.

I had expected me, Mum and Dad to gather up a few items of Gran's that really meant something to each of us yesterday, not be confronted by a beautiful stash of crockery Harrods would envy and a shop to sell it in.

If I wasn't going to open my own shop, what was I going to do with Grandma's stash?

I had tried to come up with ideas – from selling the business and making a substantial donation to a couple of her favourite charities, to donating the crockery to the Glasgow History Museum.

I sat for a moment in the hotel staff car park, my fingers still clinging to the steering wheel of my rose-gold Skoda Citigo. Castle Marrian reared up in front of me, the April light glancing off its gleaming windows and turrets.

With Briar Glen spread out in all its Scottish, leafy glory, I could understand why it held such an attraction for weddings.

I gathered my bag from the back seat and straightened my knee-length navy skirt.

Guests were milling about in the glass and chrome reception area, resplendent with abstract art installations, and there were polite murmurs of conversation from the chocolate-and-cream flock wallpaper dining room, where a number of leisurely breakfasts were taking place.

I said hello to Una and Derek, the two receptionists on duty this morning, and clipped my way down past the dining room that overlooked the rolling tree- and flower-studded grounds. There was the clink of cups and the rattle of breakfast cutlery.

My office was located past the ice-blue frosted glass of Sensations Spa and further down the corridor.

No sooner had I shrugged off my jacket and fired up my PC to take a look at my diary for the day than Heston barrelled in, with his severe side sweep of ink-black hair and pinched expression. His thin fingers tapered down his claret Castle Marrian tie, with its gold C&M initials stitched into it.

"How was your Sunday?" He bathed me in a crocodile smile.

On high alert, I steepled my hands together on my semi-circular walnut desk, with its couple of photographs of my parents and a lovely shot of my grandma on her seventieth birthday, holding her lilac and pink birthday cake. "Okay, Heston, what favour are you about to ask me?"

He feigned shock. "Can't I just enquire after my favourite wedding planner?"

Before I could reply, he snatched up the chair opposite me and arranged himself in it. "I've decided to take a week's holiday from this afternoon. Pablo wants me to meet his parents in Spain."

I almost shot out of my chair. "But Heston, look at this." I twisted my screen round to face him. My packed calendar glowed out of my PC in lime-green. "This isn't a game of Tetris. This is my calendar of meetings for this week. How can you expect me to juggle all this, as well as your commitments?"

Heston dismissed my clogged diary with a flick of one bony hand. "Don't you go getting your panties in a twist, darling. I'll postpone some of my appointments until I'm back next week."

Well, that would be something, but I was still faced with an avalanche of weddings at various organisational stages to contend with in the meantime.

"But if you could take over the organising of Ulrika Bonnington's nuptials, that would be wonderful. I was supposed to be meeting with her and her mother at eleven this morning, but I've got sooooo much to do before I head off."

Heston's final blow sent me reeling. What!? No way! He couldn't do this to me. He just couldn't.

But judging by the way his wiry frame was now bolting out of my office, he could – and indeed was.

Ulrika Bonnington was the daughter of Chastity and Spence Bonnington, who owned a luxury fleet of cruise liners that gave tourists the ultimate Scottish experience. She was marrying some mealy-mouthed politician's son here at Castle Marrian on 22nd December. When Ulrika had contacted the hotel to say she wanted her nuptials held here, Heston had insisted he handle the arrangements personally as it was such a "sexy and high-profile wedding."

However, according to Casper, our Swedish receptionist, Ms Bonnington was driving even Heston to distraction, with her endless string of ridiculous demands, ranting emails and screechy phone calls.

I darted out from behind my desk in hot pursuit. "Heston. Heston! Hang on a second! You insisted that you wanted this one. You pulled rank on me."

Heston was already making impressive progress back along the floral festooned corridor. Fresh vases of flowers had just been deposited on the plinths, giving off a Columbian rain-forest vibe. "Oh, the experience will do you good," he gushed over his shoulder. "Now must dash. Sorcha said she could squeeze me in for an eyebrow threading at half nine. Ciao!" His suit jacket then disappeared through the spa double doors.

I stomped back towards my office, festering with indignation and temper.

Shit! Shit! Talk about being dropped right in it! But what could I do? A couple of the glossy showbiz magazines would be covering the wedding and the amount of money the Bonnington family were spending here was obscene.

I had no option. I would just have to deal with the Bonningtons in Heston's absence.

My email pinged, irritating me further. It was from Heston. He had fired across notes from his initial meeting with Ulrika Bonnington and her mother. He hadn't wasted any time.

Slumping back down defeated into my chair, I managed to rearrange my intended 11a.m. meeting with a new florist touting for business to later on in the week, so that the Bonningtons could be accommodated.

If I managed to keep my meeting with them to within the hour, I might just have enough time to eat my packed lunch, before my next meeting with a newly engaged couple at twelve-thirty.

I swivelled in my chair to glower out at the throng of trees and rear lawns cascading past my office window.

Heston owed me for this. Big time.

———

Ulrika Bonnington looked around my office, with its petrol-blue carpet and sashed, chequered drapes, as though she were trapped within the bowels of Satan. "I thought Heston Cole was dealing with my arrangements."

So did I.

I hid my annoyance with a professional smile. "Mr Cole is on leave this week and has asked me to step in."

Ulrika Bonnington's snub nose shot upwards.

"So..." I tapped away on my keyboard, pulling up the electronic copy of Heston's notes for the Bonnington-Barclay wedding. "You're getting married here at Castle Marrian on 22nd December."

"Yes, about that," chipped in Chastity Bonnington, the bride's mother, sitting beside her like a nightclub minder. "We've decided we're not happy with the date and would like to change it."

A frisson of concern snaked through me. Don't tell me they were intending to bring it forward. Dates between now and the end of the year had been snapped up. I hoped my voice sounded calm. "May I ask why?"

Ulrika pinned me to my swivel chair. She was looking at me as though I were the village idiot. "22nd December isn't Christmassy enough."

I blinked back at her cascade of bright yellow hair extensions and baby pink fur jacket. "Not Christmassy enough?"

"That's right," she primped. "I've discussed it with Gideon and we would like to move our wedding to Christmas Eve."

Oh, you have to be joking.

A chill wind swirled around my office.

We never accommodated weddings on 24th December – the Marrian family believed that staff were more than entitled to time with their families, especially at Christmas. But a special exception had been made for Sonya and Tony, the son and future daughter-in-law of our longest serving domestic employee, Ivy Dunsmuir. They were such a lovely family. The owners of the Cascada Marrian Hotel Group, Sir Guy Marrian and Lady Josephine Marrian, had insisted they be given special treatment when I'd made a surreptitious call to Head Office and extolled the virtues of the festive heart-warming PR this would generate. Head Office had even insisted on paying fifty per cent of the final bill, knowing the publicity this would draw was priceless.

"I'm afraid we don't accommodate weddings on 24th December. It's company policy."

I smiled pleasantly, aware of the two women training their unimpressed attention on me.

"Let me see if I can find an alternative." I scrolled to

December. The bright red of reservations shone back at me. All that was left was a cancellation for the afternoon of 18th December.

Ulrika Bonnington erupted. "The 18th? That's even less Christmassy than the 22nd!"

I jumped back with alarm as Ulrika Bonnington bolted around to my side of the desk and directed an accusing, ruby talon at my computer screen. "You don't accept wedding bookings for Christmas Eve? Well, what's that then? What's that at 11a.m. on 24th December?"

I scrambled to click away from the wedding diary but it was too late. She had already seen it. I should have been more careful, but I didn't expect her to move so fast in those Perspex wedges. I tried to bluff my way out of it. "What booking?"

Ulrika Bonnington wobbled back round to the other side of my desk and stood beside her still seated mother, her hands planted on her bony hips. "That booking which said Sonya and Tony – Dunsmuir and Lovegood wedding."

My widening eyes darted across to the bride's mother, who was now aiming suspicious daggers at me, every bit as chilling as her daughter.

Ulrika Bonnington thumped herself back down in her chair, eager to hear my explanation.

Now it was my turn to look grim-faced. I folded my arms. I could guess what their reaction would be. "I do apologise. That event can't be moved. It has been in the diary for months." There was no way I was about to sacrifice such a special day for Ivy and her family, just to accommodate the fluctuating whims of Ulrika Bonnington.

Ulrika's cat-like green eyes narrowed. "Yes. Well, I'm sure these people will understand when you tell them about us."

I made a tiny noise of indignation. Did she really just say that? The audacity of this woman was staggering. They would understand that a spoilt, demanding heiress had suddenly decided she wanted their wedding slot?

I shook my head, my vanilla blonde plait waggling down my back. "I'm very sorry, Ms Bonnington, but that's impossible." I delivered a cool smile. "As I've just explained, we can accommodate you on the 18th or you can keep your reservation for the 22nd. Either way, I would be more than happy to lay on – on a complimentary basis, of course – our Christmas horse-drawn carriage around the grounds for you and your guests to enjoy."

I ignored Ulrika's grunt of disapproval. "Castle Marrian would also ensure that your snow and ice magical kingdom theme is second to none."

Ulrika Bonnington's complexion grew puce under her make-up. "I don't want a carriage with some knackered old donkey pulling it! I want Christmas Eve for my wedding."

I fought to maintain an aura of calm, while inside, I was beginning to rage at the blatant privilege. Beside Ulrika, her mother reached out one ringed hand in an attempt to calm her. It wasn't working.

"Ms Bonnington, I understand your disappointment," I lied through my teeth, "but I can assure you that your wedding on 22nd December will be the perfect festive experience for you and your guests."

Ulrika's twiglet-brown arms peeped out from under the fluffy sleeves of her jacket. "This is ridiculous. Where's

Heston? I want to speak to him." Her cold eyes flashed. "What's that saying about the organ grinder and not the monkey?"

I could feel my fists balling under my desk. "Ms Bonnington, I have just told you that Mr Cole is preparing to go on leave."

"Ah. So, he isn't away on holiday yet then."

Ulrika Bonnington sat back, arms folded, like a glowering blonde Medusa.

Bugger! I didn't mean to let that slip.

I looked across at her mother. She averted her attention to my office carpet. So, whatever her daughter wanted, she got. Well, not this time. Not at the expense of dear, sweet Ivy and her family.

I snatched up my phone and put a call through to the hotel spa. Heston was unimpressed. "I'm mid-eyebrow!" There was a scuffling sound as he propelled himself upwards. "I can't go to Spain looking like I'm half surprised!"

He let out an agonised moan as I gave him a potted version of events, under the gimlet eye of Ulrika. "Oh, for pity's sake! We can't afford to lose their cash! Give me five minutes and I'll come along to your office."

I placed down the receiver with a quiver of concern. No, Heston wouldn't side with Ulrika Bonnington. He was my boss and would support me. We were representing Castle Marrian as a united front. Cash or no cash, I wasn't prepared to ruin Ivy's family wedding and despite Heston having as much depth as a teaspoon, I reassured myself he would agree.

Heston burst through my office door five minutes later, with a pink plucked-turkey look to his forehead area.

After effusive greetings to the Bonningtons, he pulled up a spare chair from the hallway.

"So, Heston, I've already explained to Ms Bonnington that 24th December isn't possible."

I widened my eyes at him for added emphasis, but watched with a growing sense of anger and disbelief, as Heston fidgeted. "Can't we swap them over?" he muttered after a few moments.

I drew myself up, blinking with hot fury. He was prepared to capitulate to this horrible woman?! I pretended not to understand.

"I'm sure if we explain to Ivy and her son, we can move their wedding to 22nd December and allow Ms Bonnington to have her Christmas Eve ceremony."

Ulrika Bonnington's sugar-pink lips broke into a self-satisfied smirk.

My professional façade crumbled. Sod it with the diplomatic effort. "But that's not fair," I blurted, my indignation burning on behalf of Ivy and her family. "We promised them months ago, that Sonya and Tony could get married on Christmas Eve. Ivy and her late husband got married on that date and it means the world to her."

Heston fluttered one pale hand around and indulged Ulrika Bonnington with one of his stomach-curdling grins. "Ivy won't mind, I'm sure. She's a very understanding lady and so easy-going. I'll have a chat with her."

My head snapped from Heston to Ulrika and her mother. This was ridiculous – and so heartless!

I set my shoulders under my suit jacket. "I'm sorry, but this is unacceptable. I don't agree with it at all. All our brides deserve the wedding day of their dreams, not just a select few."

Ulrika Bonnington jutted her pointy chin at me.

Heston rolled his watery, light eyes up to his waxy smooth forehead. "Of course, I agree with you, Sophie." It was evident that he didn't. "We pride ourselves on providing every bride with the wedding day that they deserve. But Castle Marrian thrives on its high-profile clientele."

Ulrika and her mother exchanged self-satisfied glances at being described as "high-profile." I drummed my nails on my desk. "Well, we wouldn't have high-profile clientele if it wasn't for hard-working, dedicated employees like Ivy Dunsmuir. In fact, we wouldn't have a hotel like this at all, if it wasn't for people like Ivy. They are the heart and soul of this place."

Heston's irritation was growing. Before I knew what was going on, he'd jumped round to my side of the desk and steered me by the elbow out into the corridor. He closed my office door behind me.

"Yes, yes! I appreciate that," he hissed. "But you have to see this from a purely business point of view."

I didn't have to see anything. It was staring me straight in the face. Realising I was taking a huge risk, I swallowed and leant in a little closer to him. I wouldn't be able to look Ivy in the eyes again if I agreed to this. I couldn't. "Can you imagine the negative publicity this would attract if the press found out we had moved a long-standing member of staff's family wedding to accommodate the nuptials of a cruise liner magnate's daughter?"

Heston let out a dismissive snort. "Well, that's not liable to happen, is it?"

My heart was thudding in my ears, but I couldn't square any of this. It was heartless. I raised one eyebrow. "Isn't it?"

Heston let out a horrified gasp at what I was implying. He clutched at the occasional table next to him, as though he were being tortured. His startled, hooded eyes grew. "That sounds like blackmail!"

I trained my best intense stare on him, as my heart pounded in my ears. "It isn't blackmail. It's the truth."

Heston whipped his permanently surprised eyebrows (or what there was left of them) towards my office door and then to me again.

He let out a grinding noise and sprung my office door back open. Like someone flicking a light switch, he was again sporting a shark-like grin for the Bonnington ladies' benefit.

Chastity Bonnington offered us both a pensive look. She reached out to her daughter's pink, fluffy arm. "Darling, please think very carefully about this. If you were to insist on 24th December and it meant another couple having to move their wedding to accommodate you…" Her voice was charged with meaning. "Imagine how that would look for your father and me. It could have an adverse effect on the business."

Either the woman had overheard our conversation or she had weighed up the situation for herself. Either way, Ulrika Bonnington's eyes were brimming with resentment. The prospect of her inheritance becoming somewhat depleted made her have a re-think. Her Adam's apple throbbed up and down like an out-of-control lift. "Fine," she ground out after an agonising few moments. "Fine! We'll stick with our original date of the 22nd."

She lurched to her feet, wobbling precariously in her Perspex hooves.

Heston trailed after her. "Are you sure that's acceptable, Madam? Is that all right?"

When Ulrika grunted a brief yes, Heston picked up his pace. "Are you leaving already? I thought you came to discuss the reindeer and white Christmas trees you wanted for decorating the aisle."

Ulrika Bonnington faltered to a halt in her wedges. She shot me a glower over her furry shoulder. "Sorry, Heston, but I would really rather deal with you."

I plastered on a polite and relieved smile. "That's your prerogative, Ms Bonnington."

Heston looked like he had swallowed something foul. He began escorting mother and daughter away from my office and up the hallway, but not before delivering me a look at would have frozen Antarctica. "I will be back at work next Tuesday. I'll contact you straightaway, Ms Bonnington, and we can arrange another meeting to further discuss your arrangements."

He was almost bent double with subservience.

Ulrika Bonnington thrust her cream and gold Marc Jacobs handbag further up her shoulder. She speared me with another white-hot glare. "Thank you. At least I know I will be dealing with a professional."

I cocked one eyebrow at her. Someone standing up to her clearly wasn't a common occurrence.

Heston oozed after them. I watched the three of them disappear around the corner in a flurry of expensive scent and growls, then prepared myself for his verbal onslaught.

When he returned a few minutes later, he banged my office door shut behind him. My tie-back curtains gave a shudder of protest. "What the hell was all that about?"

"It's about having morals, Heston. I wasn't only thinking about Ivy and her family, I was also thinking about the reputation of Castle Marrian."

Heston sucked in his cheekbones as I continued.

"I don't have to tell you Castle Marrian's reputation is second to none. If we had caved in to Ulrika Bonnington's demands and given her the Christmas Eve slot, we would have been committing a PR disaster."

Heston opened his thin lips to speak, but clamped them shut again as he digested what I said.

I flicked him a look. "Something tells me the Marrian family wouldn't have approved either."

I could see Heston's hooded eyes registering this. They had been more than happy to bend the rules for Ivy's son and prospective daughter-in-law to have their wedding here on Christmas Eve. They were only too aware of the years of dedicated service Ivy had given.

In fact, when I had mooted the suggestion to them, Head Office had come back almost immediately, saying that Mr and Mrs Marrian had insisted on it.

"Yes. Well." Heston adjusted the cuffs of his starched, white shirt.

I tapped my keyboard, casting an eye over my emails, which seemed to have multiplied within the last half an hour. "I'm sure Ulrika Bonnington will get over it."

Heston didn't look convinced.

Chapter Six

The rest of the week was a blur of juggling my work commitments, as well as keeping on top of Heston's calendar.

Every time I thought of him sunning himself in Spain with Pablo, and downing sangria under a tangerine sunset, my resentment fired up again.

I didn't object to my boss taking a holiday, but he couldn't have picked a worse time. April saw the start of wedding madness and I found myself screeching from one meeting to the next. From finalising details with anxious brides to meeting with new suppliers who were keen to have their wedding décor/floristry/bands recommended and recruited by Castle Marrian, the days melted into one.

The faces of loved-up couples, in the majority of cases from privileged and monied backgrounds, soon became a blur. They exclaimed and sighed at the rambling, romantic grounds, before admiring the hotel's understated yet sumptuous artwork.

All were keen to lock in their preferred weekend, in some cases twelve to eighteen months in advance, to avoid disappointment.

At least none of them were as vile as Ulrika Bonnington.

I drove home to my flat each evening, my eyes scorched with weariness. If I had to look at one more eight-tier cake encrusted with diamonds or another swathe of French silk tulle, I was in danger of experiencing a meltdown.

Mum was concerned about me "not eating properly" when I arrived home, and insisted on delivering fish pie one evening and lasagne with salad and crusty garlic bread another night.

Despite me only living ten minutes up the road from them in Briar Glen, Mum was so laden down with provisions, she would stumble out of her car outside my block of flats, as though she had struggled through a hostile jungle to get here.

Both my parents did mention Gran's letter and her valuable crockery stash on several more occasions, but I brushed it off. The thought of running my own business triggered flurries of panic and pessimism. It just wasn't realistic to think that someone with my lack of experience could run a business of their own.

Friday arrived in a fanfare of phone calls, emails waiting for replies and plenty of preparation ahead of Saturday's Bollywood-inspired wedding which I was looking forward to.

The couple whose wedding it was, Nina and Dev, had been a delight to work with over the past twelve months and it was such a joy to see the fruits of my organisational labours when they were appreciated. Then I had Sunday off again.

I had planned to do very little, except sleep, eat and catch up with *Money Heist* on Netflix, although I did mention to Mum and Dad that I would be available for giving them a hand with more sorting of Gran's house. There was no way I was prepared to let Mum deal with the emotional fall-out from that and not be around.

Mum had insisted I relax. "Me and your dad can deal with things. You need a break, lovey. Recharge your batteries."

But I had already decided that if they needed me, I would be there, despite Mum's protestations.

On Friday morning, I parked up in the humble employee car park at Castle Marrian, with the usual array of Lamborghinis, Porsches and Aston Martins, glossy and glinting in the lemon sunlight from the guest car parking area.

I had only got as far as the theatrical display of spring flowers of creamy roses, lemon-sorbet tulips and indigo irises inside the grand entrance, when Carrie, one of the receptionists on duty, came hurrying towards me.

"Morning, Carrie. How's things and how is that gorgeous little boy of yours?"

Her pretty, elfin face was carrying concern. She hesitated, failing to make eye contact. "Morning, Sophie. Carter is great, thanks. He's obsessed with tigers at the moment." She shifted from foot to foot. "Look, you should know Taylor McKendrick is here to see you."

I was aware of a couple of smartly dressed guests meandering past, morning newspapers thrust under their arms.

This was a surprise. Taylor McKendrick was head of HR at The Marrian Hotel Group.

She was feared and admired in equal measure. She also didn't conduct courtesy calls. If she ever did show up unannounced, it was never a positive sign. A squiggle of nerves invaded my stomach. Had I done something to upset management? I wasn't aware that I'd done anything illegal, immoral or underhand. I searched my mind for a clue but couldn't think of anything. "Oh. Right. Did she say what it's about?"

Carrie shook her halo of brunette curls, but I could read the unsaid apprehension in her hazel eyes. She dropped her voice. "She's waiting in your office. I took her a coffee five minutes ago."

"Hopefully with lots of sugar in it," I remarked, trying to play down my growing concern with a smile. "She could do with sweetening up."

I thanked Carrie for the heads-up and for supplying Taylor with a coffee, and clipped over the polished toffee-and-white tiled floor of reception and down towards my office. The sound of mesmerising harp music emerged from the spa, together with the scent of lime candles and essential oil.

What did Taylor McKendrick want? And why turn up unexpectedly to see me, first thing on a Friday morning?

My kernel of concern grew. I wasn't aware of committing any heinous crime, but ...

Oh, stop it, Sophie! You're catastrophising!

I reached my office door, making out the long, angular shape of Taylor McKendrick through the frosted panel of glass.

I raised my hand and then felt an utter idiot. Hang on! It was my office. I didn't need to knock!

This was the effect this woman had on most people. One look and you folded in on yourself and became a gibbering wreck.

I straightened my back and smoothed my swish of ponytail. I arranged my mouth into what I hoped was a warm but professional smile.

I pushed open my office door to see Taylor sitting poised and clasping the cup of freshly brewed coffee Carrie had made for her. She was all glossy red pointed heels and severe peroxide bob. She coiled upwards out of her chair. "Sophie. You're looking well."

I knew this was a lie. I had craters under my eyes from the long hours I'd been working and a washed-out tinge to my complexion. "Thanks, Taylor. As are you."

Feeling her studious gaze on me, I was about to slip off my tailored jacket and then thought better of it, deciding I looked more professional with it on.

I slid behind my desk, feeling like an awkward teenager who was too long for her limbs.

"So how are things at Head Office in Glasgow?" I asked her.

There was a measured look. "All is well, thanks."

Then why are you here to see me?

I fired on my PC. I realised I was fidgeting with the mouse and stilled my fingers. "So, to what do I owe the pleasure, Taylor?"

Oh God. Why am I talking like someone out of a 1950s Ealing comedy?

She took a considered sip of her coffee and rested the cup and saucer on my desk with a decisive rattle. "I'm afraid this isn't a social call, Sophie."

I'd guessed as much. Taylor didn't do those. I felt my throat narrow.

She sat back in her chair, elegantly draping one toned leg over the other. My stomach leapt with tension. What the hell was going on?

Her cool, azure eyes raked me from head to toe. "I'm sorry to say there has been a complaint made."

I blinked back at Taylor across my desk, hoping I could ignore the twisting sensation in my chest. "Sorry? A complaint? By who? What about?"

Taylor laced her manicured fingers together in her lap. "I'm afraid the complaint is about you."

I could feel my mouth opening and closing and clamped it shut. A strange noise echoed around my office. For a brief moment, I wondered where it had come from, before realising it was me.

"About me?" I croaked, with a forced half-laugh. "I don't understand. What am I supposed to have done?"

The dappled Friday morning light glanced against Taylor's coiffed tresses. I could see she was couching her words with care. "It's not about your work, Sophie. It's widely known your wedding planning skills are exemplary."

I could hear my voice becoming more tense. "Well, what is the complaint about? I'm very confused."

Taylor shifted forward in her sleek silk charcoal suit. "I'm sorry to say a complaint has been made about your attitude."

My eyebrows zinged up to my hairline. "My attitude? Sorry. I'm lost."

Taylor read my bewildered expression. "A complaint has been lodged by a Ms Ulrika Bonnington."

It took a few seconds for this revelation to sink in. My initial shock gave way to a bark of laughter. "You have got to be kidding me."

Taylor lifted her hands in a helpless gesture. The light caught the elaborate amber dress ring on her right hand. "She claims you were intransigent, rude and unhelpful when she and her mother had a meeting with you on Monday."

"That's rubbish," I blustered, catching images in my head of her medusa like extensions. "She was demanding we move her wedding from 22nd December to Christmas Eve. I apologised and explained to her that would be impossible—"

Taylor cut me off. Her plucked brows arched. ""And why would that be impossible?"

I prickled at the inference. "The problem is that 24th December is the date of the wedding of Ivy Dunsmuir's son. You know Ivy, one of our cleaners here who for twenty-five years has shown excellent dedication and service to this hotel." My voice was heavy with sarcasm, but I didn't care.

One of Taylor's brows arched further.

"You must know that it's traditional that the Marrian hotels don't stage any weddings or huge events on Christmas Eve. Sir and Lady Marrian have always made it clear this is a time for families. But when I explained to them about Ivy's son and his fiancée, they were only too happy to bend the rules on this occasion."

Taylor nodded. "I am aware of that policy, Sophie. I've worked for this organisation for twelve years."

I straightened my shoulders, determined to defend my record. "I've never had a complaint about my work before. Not a single one. All my appraisals have been exceptional. You know that." I reached down to my desk drawer. "And I've got a pile of thank-you letters from happy couples, delighted with my organisational skills." (Describing six thank-you notes as a pile was somewhat of an exaggeration, but it was a reference in itself. I don't think the majority of Castle Marrian brides ever gave my strenuous efforts a second thought after their nuptials. Hey-ho.)

Taylor adopted a more conciliatory tone. "Look, I sympathise. I really do." She dropped her husky voice another octave. "But you have to realise the financial and social profiles of Ulrika Bonnington and her family."

I rolled my eyes, my temper at the injustice of this situation growing. "But as they were leaving, the bride-to-be agreed, albeit grudgingly, to stick with their original date of 22nd December. What's changed?"

Taylor waggled her brows. She was siding with them.

She sucked in her red lips as I tutted under my breath. "Ms Bonnington reflected on the situation and decided that an actual Christmas Eve wedding would afford them and us far more publicity in the long-run. She also said that as her parents got married on Christmas Eve, the date carried a great deal of sentimentality for them. She has therefore said she will let her complaint drop, if Castle Marrian are able to rectify the situation."

Seething resentment took over. Why didn't Ulrika

Bonnington mention before about her parents supposedly marrying on Christmas Eve? I knew why. The conniving madam had no doubt made it up to try and manipulate the situation to her own advantage. I folded my arms. Taylor's implication was clear. She wanted me to capitulate. She was expecting me to perform one unholy U-turn, just so that spiteful woman could have Ivy's family wedding moved, to allow her to sashay down the aisle on Christmas Eve instead. I sucked in a mouthful of air. I was fighting to maintain an element of calm. "But we have already explained to Ulrika Bonnington that 24th December isn't available for her. I did however assure her that her Ice Palace themed wedding on the 22nd would be spectacular—"

Taylor cut me off with a sudden raise of her jewelled hand. "They are spending a great deal of money here, Sophie. I don't have to tell you that. Plus, what with all the glossy magazine coverage and the importance of that date to them..."

I rubbed a furious hand across my forehead. "Well, I don't believe what she says about her parents marrying on the 24th. It wasn't mentioned by either the daughter or the mother when they spoke to me." I tried to steady my voice. "So, you're prepared to shunt Ivy's son's wedding, just to accommodate that spiteful Barbie doll?"

Taylor's lips pursed with disapproval. A chilly silence ensued. All that could be heard was the chiming of music from the Spa along the hallway.

"Sophie, I'm sure that once you explain to Ivy the ramifications of all this, she will be more than happy to have her son's wedding moved to the 22nd." She flicked me a charged look. "And once you have apologised to Ms

Bonnington, we can put this unfortunate mess behind us and move on."

I shot forward in my swivel chair, my head whirling with the injustice of it all. It wasn't even that I was being ordered to apologise to that horrid woman, it was more the accepted fact that Ivy should be inconvenienced. She was a hard-working, gentle lady who was worth a million of the likes of Ulrika Bonnington. The injustice was fanning my anger far more than having to bite my tongue and apologise. "This just gets better and better," I ground out, sinking back in my chair and folding my arms. "So you want me to switch Ivy's wedding to make way for Ulrika Bonnington's – and I have to apologise to her as well?"

Taylor jutted out her powdered chin. "Sometimes in business, Sophie, you just have to suck it up."

Suck it up?

My heart was pounding in my ears like an out-of-control bass drum. As I sat there, listening to this drivel, I could feel the blood bubbling in my veins.

"So can I trust you to sort out this rather unfortunate situation straightaway, please, Sophie, and we will say no more about it?" Taylor rose from her chair, smoothing down her skirt with an air of smug satisfaction.

I didn't answer. I couldn't. I just stared around at my office, with its walnut desk, tie-back curtains and the acid-green views of the sumptuous gardens.

Taylor stalked towards my office door in her killer heels. "Thank you for your co-operation, Sophie. I'll head back to the office now and tell Ms Bonnington you have everything in hand and that she can expect a call from you today." She adjusted the strap of her bucket bag. "And I'm sure you will be able to smooth things over with Nancy."

As though my legs didn't belong to me, I rose in slow motion and pressed the heels of my hands against the edge of my desk. They dug into the wood. Decisions and conflicting thoughts jostled in my head. "It's Ivy," I managed to growl out. "The name of our devoted cleaner is Ivy."

Taylor stood framed in the doorway, a look of self-satisfied relief in her features "Silly me. Not great with names. Of course. Ivy."

I watched her prepare to slink out of my office.

"Taylor." Her name came out of my mouth in a snarl, but she didn't seem to notice.

She spun round on her heel, a smile tweaking the corners of her mouth. "Yes? Was there something else you wanted to raise with me?" She gave a little tinkle of self-indulgent laughter. "Probably a good idea while I'm in the vicinity."

The endless hours of work – scrolling through reams of emails; waking up in the night with visions of bridal bouquets, chocolate cupcake wedding cakes and ice sculptures – twirled in front of me; the way Heston would "delegate" so that I was struggling to keep my head above water.

I was good at what I did. But now the injustice of this situation with Ivy – I couldn't square that with my own conscience.

I wouldn't do it. I couldn't. Maybe they didn't think it was unacceptable for them to ask me to do it, to *expect* me to. But it was morally wrong. It wasn't the apology. That would have stuck in my throat and choked me, but for the sake of the hotel and its reputation, I would have done it.

It was the way they were treating a loyal, long-standing employee. I would not be party to that.

And with that thought, I informed a stunned Taylor of my decision – and changed my future.

"I quit."

Chapter Seven

"**Y**ou've done what?!" gulped Mum. "But you can't have!"

The three of us were standing in my parents' hallway.

I'd just told them I had quit my job two hours previously. To be honest, I was struggling to comprehend it myself.

I lifted my chin, hoping I looked and sounded more convincing and resolute than I felt. Doubts and rising panic were clawing at me, despite my conscience slapping me on the back. "I couldn't do what they were asking, Mum. What they were expecting me to do was wrong."

Dad gestured for us to go through to the sitting room, where I sank down on their squashy leather sofa.

"So, what happened?" probed Mum, flashing my dad in the chair beside her a concerned glance.

They listened as I described the situation with Ulrika Bonnington. "And to cap it all, she also put in a complaint about my attitude and demanded I apologise."

I was having difficulty gauging their thoughts as I

explained the whole messy and needless situation. Well, my mum looked far more anguished than Dad did.

"All the PR and HR bods at the hotel were concerned about was the Bonningtons taking their money elsewhere and us losing out on the glossy mag publicity."

"So, what is happening about the wedding of Ivy's son?" asked Dad after a few moments.

I took a long, steadying breath, hoping to calm myself. "My parting shot to Taylor McKendrick – she's head of HR – was that if they made even so much as a murmur about moving Ivy's son's wedding from Christmas Eve, I wouldn't hesitate to go straight to the press."

"Oh, Sophie," groaned Mum, wringing her hands together. "That's blackmail."

"Yes, I know, Mum, but what was I supposed to do? I wouldn't have been able to look Ivy straight in the eye again."

Dad gave an understanding nod. "And this HR woman agreed?"

"She promised me that Ivy's family wedding on Christmas Eve will go ahead as planned and that she will ensure Ulrika Bonnington's takes place on the 22nd. She knows I will go straight to the papers if they don't."

"I bet the spoilt little madam won't like that," Dad grunted.

My mouth curved into an angry snarl. "Oh, she has accepted it, by all accounts. Once she heard that I'd resigned and that Castle Marrian was offering her a twenty-five per cent discount on their reception bill, she grudgingly agreed to stick with their original date of the 22nd. Something tells me she was far more delighted about me being out of a job than the discount." I shook my head.

"At least now, Ivy's wedding won't be impacted and I won't have to witness Ulrika Bonnington's Ice Palace circus."

I could feel a small, inner flicker of satisfaction. About an hour after I'd cleared my desk in a mental haze and marched out of Castle Marrian, trying to ignore the frightened, wobbly sensation in my legs, Carrie from reception had called me.

She had overheard Taylor speaking to Ulrika Bonnington in what was no longer my office, as she had headed for her coffee break. Carrie had lurked near the spa and had heard their heated exchanges. From what Carrie relayed back, Ulrika Bonnington was still not happy about not getting her own way. However, she'd eventually agreed, knowing she was out of options, but that a generous discount was being dangled in front of her snub nose.

"I think she got a fleeting kick when she heard I had resigned, but then finding out she was having to play second fiddle to a cleaner's son took the gloss from it."

"So you walked away from your job out of principle?" asked Dad.

I glanced around at their vanilla walls and ornate fireplace, studded with photographs of the three of us, plus other pictures of my gran, through the years. "Yes, well, partly. There's also all the hours I have been working and Heston taking me for granted..."

I pinned a pleading look upon Mum, hoping she would be able to understand. "This has just been the catalyst."

Mum looked worried. "Sweetheart, I love how principled you are. I really do. But having a sense of duty won't pay the bills."

I pushed out a smile. "I know that. I'll start looking for something else."

"You make it sound so easy, Sophie." Dad made a face. "I think you are forgetting the length of the employment queues at the moment."

It was true. Oh God. I was unemployed. I hoped I was concealing my rising worry from my parents. "I've got a degree in event management," I rushed. "I'm sure I'll get something else."

Mum's expression was grim. "Goodness knows when."

"Thanks for the support, Mum. If Gran had been here…" I let my unfinished sentence hang there.

"You mean she would have understood, unlike me," supplied Mum.

"I never said that."

Dad intervened. "Come on, you two. What's done is done."

Another period of awkward silence ensued, before Dad raised a finger. A small smile broke out over his craggy features. "Your gran! Of course! Bloody hell! We're sitting here with grim faces and yet the answer is obvious."

I blinked across at him. "What about Gran, Dad? What do you mean?"

"Don't tell me you haven't given it any more thought – her crockery shop suggestion?" Dad glanced at Mum. "I've moved all her haul up into the spare bedroom."

The truth was, I hadn't forgotten about Gran's letters and crockery at all. Ever since I'd discovered what she'd done, it had been lurking at the fringes of my mind. But the very idea of me running my own business was crazy! What retail experience did I have? None. I knew my grandmother had arranged it all with the very best of intentions and I loved her even more for it, but it was a non-starter … wasn't it?

"Kenny, that was a pipe-dream of my mother's. She didn't really expect Sophie to do anything about it."

"Then why all the cloak-and-dagger? More importantly, why did your mother go to the lengths of buying that shop for Sophie?" said Dad.

Mum made a dismissive noise, but Dad ignored her. "Why don't you at least look into it, lovey? Have a chat with Mrs Cotter. You have got nothing to lose."

I felt like common sense had taken hold of my left arm and passion was tugging at my right. I was being pulled and pushed in each direction. Dad was right. If Gran hadn't been serious about me following the dream, why go to all that effort of hoarding those tea sets and buying the business from Mrs Cotter in the first place?

I pressed my lips together. This delaying wasn't like me; I was a doer. The prospect of sitting wallowing in self-pity and torturing myself as to whether I had in fact made the right decision about leaving Castle Marrian after all was horrific, not to mention the dire thought of subjecting myself to endless hours of excruciating daytime TV.

So many people faced with my predicament would think they had been presented with a gift. It was a bloody big and daunting one though.

Could I at least have a go at being my own boss? Did I stand a chance of making it work and honouring my Gran's faith in me? I couldn't not do anything about it. Perhaps it was meant to be, me leaving Castle Marrian behind?

Callum used to sneer and make sarcastic comments

whenever I mentioned crockery or enthused about a lovely tea set I had seen. "What bloody use is all your knowledge about crockery?" he would crow. "It's not as if it's going to benefit you in any way, is it?"

A flicker of wanting to prove him wrong took hold.

I'd spent all week refusing to engage with the notion and dismissing it as a whim, but now... I got to my feet. "I'll give Mrs Cotter a ring this afternoon and ask if I can drop by A Bloom with a View tomorrow. It won't hurt to have a word with her."

Mum still wasn't convinced. She aimed a disapproving look at Dad, but he chose to ignore her. He rose up from his armchair and clapped his hands together. "Right. That's a plan then. Anybody for a cuppa?"

Chapter Eight

I woke up the next morning with what felt like a weight pressing down on my chest.

It was Saturday, the day of Nina and Dev's wedding at Castle Marrian. They were such a sweet couple and it had been a pleasure and an honour to organise their special day for them.

I let out a guilty groan and pushed my head back under the pillows. All the ramifications of me quitting were gradually seeping into my conscience and swimming around.

I should have been working today but Taylor had insisted she put me on gardening leave straightaway, so that was that. I was done with Castle Marrian.

Through my lavender cotton bedroom curtains, fingers of sunshine were pushing their way in and feeling their way over my white duvet. It looked as if the weather would be kind to them and provide a backdrop for what I knew would be their stunning wedding photographs. Good. They deserved it.

I snaked my hand out from under the covers and reached for my mobile on the bedside table.

As soon as I switched it on, it made incessant pinging noises. I had purposefully switched it off after clearing my desk yesterday. I decided it would be best not to speak to anyone straightaway, especially anyone connected to work.

I had to get all this straight in my own head first.

Now, I was paying the price.

A series of voicemail messages ruptured my eardrum. First there was Ivy, who had been told by reception staff about the short, sharp email circulated by Taylor, to say I was no longer employed with The Marrian Hotel Group "with immediate effect" but that I was thanked "for all my excellent work over the past three years and I'm sure I speak for everyone when we wish Sophie well in her future endeavours."

"Please ring me back, pet," insisted a concerned Ivy down the line. "There are all sorts of rumours flying around. Derek on reception even said that you leaving was connected to some row with management over Tony's wedding. Is that true?"

I chewed my lip. I would return Ivy's call later. She sounded so upset and as I was feeling fragile from the events of the last twenty-four hours, the last thing I wanted to do was make her feel worse. The decision had been mine and mine alone and from a moral perspective I knew I had made the correct one – even if I did end up eating baked beans every night and becoming paranoid about my central heating use.

Then there was a frosty call from one of Taylor's minions at HR, wishing to clarify how much leave I had owing to me, as they would be content to pay me for that (as far as I was concerned, that was the least they could do) followed by a panicked Heston from Spain. "What the hell is going on, Sophie?! Tell me this is a joke! I've just had the Ice Queen on the phone, telling me you've quit!"

I could hear Spanish accents in the background and the whispered hush of the Mediterranean Sea. "Ring me, Sophie. You should know you are ruining this shitting holiday for Pablo and me. This better not be true!"

I gave my phone a bored look and moved onto the next message. Heston was just terrified his workhorse had finally bolted.

The following message pulled at my heart, just as Ivy's had. It was Nina. She had only just called me. She sounded distraught. "I stayed the night here at Castle Marrian," she sniffed, "and was so looking forward to catching up with you before the ceremony." There was a pause. "Dev and me got you a little something, just to say thank you for all your hard work and for putting up with my demands."

I gave a sad smile as I clutched my mobile to my ear. Nina didn't know the meaning of the word "demanding". I swallowed a ball of emotion.

She added, "Ring me when you can," before ending her message.

I pushed myself upright in bed and caught sight of myself in my long, bleached-wood mirror. I looked like a demonic ragdoll. My hair was a blonde dandelion.

I pushed it this way and that, before admitting defeat and returning Nina's call.

I ploughed on with an emotional apology as soon as she picked up. I didn't dare stop speaking, otherwise I knew that in my frazzled state, I was liable to succumb to tears. "I will be thinking about you and Dev at two o' clock today. I wish I could have been there. I'm so sorry."

"Well, you obviously had your reasons for leaving, but it was still a shock when one of the beauticians at the spa told me last night. We couldn't have made this day possible without you." I could sense Nina smiling down the phone. "Dev and I had wanted to present you with a bouquet of flowers and another little something, to say thank you for everything you've done, but we'll arrange for them to be delivered to your flat now instead."

I bit my lip, feeling wretched. "That is so kind of you, but it's really not necessary."

Nina refused to take no for an answer. "Nonsense. Now are you going to give me your address or will I have to get a private investigator on the case?"

I capitulated and gave her my address. "I'm so sorry, Nina. I had no option but to leave Castle Marrian. It was a decision of conscience."

"So we understand," she muttered darkly down the phone. "I had to all but torture a Swedish guy on reception this morning to get the truth out of him about why you quit."

Despite the ball of emotion in my throat, I laughed. Poor Casper.

"Sometimes you just have to follow your heart and do what feels right for you. It might not be much consolation, Sophie, but you did the right thing. Nothing worse than not liking who you are."

I felt flat and confused when the call ended with me batting away questions from Nina about what I intended to do about looking for another job.

I decided I couldn't look back. It wouldn't make me feel any better. Castle Marrian was part of my past now.

I glanced over at my alarm clock, with its vivid, glowing numbers. *Bugger!* I had better get up and get ready. I was due to see Mrs Cotter in just over an hour.

I felt as though I were inhabiting somebody else's body.

Having showered and dressed, I threw on my best jeans and my rose-pink pussy-bow blouse with a matching cardigan. It was so weird, not reaching for one of my work suits.

I didn't regret it, I assured myself for the thirteenth time that morning as I pushed my bran flakes around my bowl. What is done is done, as Gran would often lament.

I would have a chat with Mrs Cotter. I had to find out about business footfall in Briar Glen, not to mention find a contact at the local Briar Glen Business Association for any advice about preparing a business plan and financial management … what advertising I should undertake for the business… Oh bugger! There was just so much to think about. Deep down, my apprehension squirmed, but I did my best to ignore it.

Once I had brushed my teeth and given my ponytail a final titivate, I prepared to set off from my flat to the florist's, but my plans were interrupted by an insistent knock on my front door.

There was the sight of a familiar short and curvy shape through the frosted pane of my door. "Ivy?"

I pulled open my front door and she rushed towards me, just visible behind an extravagant bouquet of yellow roses, multi-coloured germini and pale pink tulips. Still clinging onto the flowers, she managed to somehow contort her body, clad in a long, swingy, red raincoat, so that I found myself pressed into her ample bosom. Her dyed chestnut hair had been washed and set. I got a whiff of hairspray.

I ushered her into my sitting room and she thrust the flowers at me. "What are these for? They're beautiful."

Ivy flicked out her raincoat and took up residence on my sofa. "What are these for, she says?" She regarded me, her jowly face kind. "I can't let you do this, Sophie. It's not right." She gave her shampoo and set a shake of disbelief. "I can't believe you did what you did."

"Ivy, it's fine. Really." I gazed down at the flowers. "These are beautiful. Thank you." I darted into the kitchen and popped the huge bouquet into one of my vases, which I filled with water. I hurried back into the sitting room and sat down in one of my armchairs opposite her.

Ivy's tone was imploring. "Why don't you call Ms McKendrick first thing on Monday morning? You can tell her our Tony and Sonya don't mind moving their wedding to another date."

I shook my head so hard, I thought I was going to dislodge it from my neck. "No. It's a matter of principle, Ivy. You have had that slot booked for your son for months. I was not prepared to pander to the whim of some spoilt little rich girl."

Ivy reached out one hand and took mine in hers. I could feel the cool gold band of her wedding ring.

"I told Taylor McKendrick that if they made any attempt to shunt your family wedding from 24th December, I would go straight to the press." A dark thought occurred to me. "Oh no!

They haven't, have they? I mean, they haven't tried to persuade you to move your ceremony?"

"No, of course not," soothed Ivy, her expression melting with appreciation. "You know what management are like at that place. They are obsessed with publicity." She lowered her voice to more of a conspiratorial whisper, even though there were only the two of us in the room. "After you left, Ms McKendrick sought me out. When I got the call to go and see her in your office, I thought I'd left my cleaning mop in reception again."

Ivy pursed her lips in a disapproving way. "She was all sugar, saying that Castle Marrian would ensure that Sonya and Tony's wedding was a day to remember. But she never mentioned you. I had to hear that from the Swedish lad working on reception." Frustration darkened her face. "But your job!"

I could feel my chest pounding at the cold realisation that I was now unemployed. But then I remembered Gran and my meeting with Mrs Cotter. "Don't worry about that," I assured her after a pause. "I'm sure I'll get myself sorted soon."

Ivy's steel-grey eyes widened with optimism. "Have you got something else lined up then? Someone of your calibre should have no problem getting another job."

I shuffled in my armchair. "Yes ... no ... well ... possibly..."

"Oh, stop teasing me, young lady. What is it?"

I started to say the words, but it sounded like they were being voiced by someone else. "I am considering starting my own business. A crockery shop."

Ivy's lined mouth, daubed in heather-coloured lipstick,

flapped open. "Well! I never expected you to say something like that."

"Neither did I," I confessed with a nervous laugh.

Ivy allowed this revelation to sink in. "I didn't think you were into crockery."

"I am, actually. It's always been an obsession of mine. I've got my grandmother to thank for that. She could tell a Royal Doulton from a Royal Albert from three miles away."

"That's the lady who passed away recently?"

I nodded with a sad smile. "It all came as a bit of a shock."

"I bet it did I don't think anyone is ever prepared for losing a loved one."

"It wasn't just losing her that came as a shock." I heaved a sigh. "It turns out my gran left me a few sets of expensive crockery to auction off."

"Oh, bless her!"

"And not just crockery," I admitted, still surprising myself as I said it out loud. "I found out that she has also purchased me a shop."

Ivy's face was priceless. "Go on! Are you serious?"

"I've never been more serious." I let out a stunned half-laugh. "It turns out she bought me Mrs Cotter's business in the village."

Ivy's jaw dropped. "Hang on. Is that the little florist's?"

I shot her an apprehensive look. "That's the one."

"And how do you feel about it all? Did you have any idea what she was planning?"

I glanced across and out of the sitting room window.

Before I knew what I was saying, all my tied-up feelings of anticipation and apprehension unravelled. "I've no idea where

66

that valuable crockery came from or how she was able to afford that shop." I shook my head. She had never failed to surprise me all her life. "What I do know is that I'm worried that if I do try to make a go of the shop, I'll end up letting her down."

Ivy listened, nodding, murmuring and every so often, giving my hand another squeeze. When I finished talking, I felt drained. "So that's it."

Ivy's apple-cheeked expression was a study in shock. She recovered herself. "Well, if you're adamant about not going back to Castle Marrian, I think you know what you have to do." She leant forward, her buckled, brown leather shoes emitting a squeak. "Your grandma thought you could do it and so do I."

I tilted one brow at her.

"If you don't, you will spend the rest of your life wondering what if." She let out a little laugh. "And believe me, you don't want to be doing that."

She rose from the sofa and I got up from my armchair. She scooped me into her arms again and held me for a few moments. "Thank you, Sophie, for what you did."

Then she took a couple of steps backwards in her solid, wedge-heeled brogues and held me at arm's length. "I shall be one of your first customers. It's about time me and Len treated ourselves to a new teapot."

Once Ivy departed, making me promise to keep in touch, I decided not to take the car, but to walk it instead to Briar

Glen's main street. The fresh air would do me good, help me to clear my head.

My mobile trilled from the depths of my shoulder bag. It was Heston again. Oh for pity's sake! Ringing me on a Saturday, when he was still supposed to be on holiday? That was a bit much, even for him. Pity he hadn't been as attentive when I'd worked for him. I knew I would have to speak to him at some point, but right now, the prospect of listening to his selfish moans about me "dropping him right in it" wasn't at all appealing. I decided not to answer it.

There was the languid burr of a wood pigeon, as the morning sunshine pushed its way through the trees on the other side of the road. Dusty trumpets of daffodils waggled their heads as my trainers tapped past the manicured gardens of thatched cottages.

At least Nina and Dev had a lovely day for their wedding – though it didn't assuage my pangs of guilt about missing their big day. Still, they were such a lovely couple and Nina had been so understanding.

I had three years' experience as a wedding planner at one of Scotland's most exclusive hotels, not to mention my university degree in events management. That should help bolster my chances of securing another job, should this crockery shop venture not work out.

I nodded as I walked along, as if convincing myself.

Carved into the brickwork of a few of the cottages was the recognisable emblem of Briar Glen: the blue rose, said to symbolise achieving the impossible. Hopefully, I could achieve the impossible and make a go of this.

The main street of Briar Glen, with its hotch-potch of shops and carriage streetlamps, hove into view. Snaking up the centre of the pedestrianised walkway was a series of rectangular planters, bulging with tulips and crocuses in bursts of white, mauve and buttercup-yellow.

The local and enthusiastic volunteers who made up "The Friends of Briar Glen" had been busy, sprucing up the place for the expected influx of spring visitors.

A Bloom with A View was halfway up the street, nestled in between the chemist and the jewellers. It possessed mullioned windows and a four-panel, half-moon frosted-glass door in varnished beechwood.

The shop exterior was painted bright white, with claret windowsills and a sign swinging from a silver pole, "A Bloom with A View" scrolled on it in wine-coloured paint. Delicate burgundy roses were inscribed either side of the shop name.

Mrs Cotter's window display featured an assortment of yellow blooms in a variety of shapes and sizes, presumably to signify the arrival of spring.

A "Closing Down Sale Due to Retirement" sign sat in each of the two windows.

I entered, the clattering bell above the door heralding my arrival.

I was greeted by plumes of flowers and plants in an assortment of pretty, flute-like vases and ornate tubs, placed on a series of white wooden benches. It was like stepping inside an extravagant perfume bottle. The air was rich and warm with the aroma of pollen and roses. Next to the benches was an old-fashioned shop counter, with a flip hatch to get in and out.

The walls were decorated with the odd sketch and painting of flower arrangements. Towards the rear of the shop was what appeared to be a workroom, where a young woman in a candy-striped apron was busy attaching a sash of tartan ribbon to a bouquet of stargazer lilies. She gave me a small smile, before returning to what she was doing.

Mrs Cotter beamed at me from behind the counter and raised the wooden flap to beckon me through. "Lovely to see you, Sophie. I'm so sorry about Helena. How are you all?"

Once we'd exchanged pleasantries, Mrs Cotter led me through past the workroom. I could see trails of assorted ribbons in rainbow colours and textures draping from a stand on top of a Formica table and sheets of tissue paper in pastel colours stacked next to it. There were also sheaths of dried reeds and artificial flowers labelled up and housed in two cabinets.

Mrs Cotter took me into her little side office located next to the workroom, which was crammed with glossy brochures from suppliers, all stacked up on one side of her cluttered desk, alongside her computer and phone.

Mrs Cotter closed the door behind her and urged me to sit down opposite her in a highbacked chair that had seen better days. There was a sash window and through it the morning sunshine was spilling and pooling onto the russet carpet.

Mrs Cotter flapped her loose denim shirt out behind her as she sat down. She was dressed casually but with style, in a lemon top and comfortable jeans.

She nodded her well-cut puff of silvery gamine hair at me. "Your grandmother was a wonderful woman. They broke the mould when they made that one!"

I smiled. "You can say that again."

Mrs Cotter clasped her hands together on top of her desk.

"So, you're here about your new business then," she twinkled out of carefully made-up hazel eyes.

"Well," I laughed with apprehension, "I suppose I am."

I cleared my throat. "I wanted to ask about potential customer numbers and footfall first of all, please? And if you were able to provide me with a contact at the Briar Glen Business Association, that would be really helpful." I offered a shy smile. "And I wanted to make a start on looking at a business plan and marketing opportunities." I explained I had quit my job and that it was a conscious decision on my part, but didn't go into deeper detail. "If things don't work out as I hope, I'll going to have to start looking around for something else straightaway. I'm sorry if that sounds defeatist, but I suppose I'm just trying to be realistic. It doesn't have to be in wedding planning, although I do love event management…"

I was aware I was rambling and clamped my mouth shut.

Mrs Cotter let out an indulgent chuckle. "I have to tell you, Sophie, that when I started A Bloom with a View, I had no retail experience either."

I blinked at her. "Really?"

"Yes. But what I did have was enthusiasm, determination and a knowledge of what customers wanted, because I was one!"

She offered a kind smile. "Something tells me that if you are anything like your dear, late grandmother, you will throw everything you have at this business and make it work."

I blinked at her immaculate appearance across the desk. "Thank you. I do hope so."

She gestured with one hand around herself. "Welcome to

your little kingdom, Sophie. I know you'll do this place proud."

I shifted forward in my chair. It was a cosy, quaint little shop space in a good location.

Mrs Cotter shot her hand across the desk and let it sit in mid-air. Her tiny stud earrings flashed in the light.

I was out of work, I had nothing else lined up and my grandmother had gone to so much trouble. It was as if I had one foot dangling over the edge of a cliff. I remembered my gran's enthusiasm and love of crockery and how she had instilled it in me. Perhaps it was time I took a chance, like Ivy said. I owed my gran that much.

For fear of driving myself demented with over-thinking, I took her hand in mine and we exchanged a business-like handshake.

Mrs Cotter's fine cheek bones lifted in a triumphant smile. "Excellent! Now, let me put the kettle on and then we can chat properly about the boring paperwork stuff."

I watched her disappear in a flap of denim shirt out of her office door. My stomach performed an impressive cartwheel. There was no going back now. This was really happening.

Chapter Nine

15th June 1970, 12 Cadder Grove, Briar Glen

"**S** ay that again. You want to do what?"

Helena's pink cheeks ripened. She didn't want Donald to raise his voice. She had just collected Marnie from school, who wasn't impressed that in addition to numbers homework, she had to read over two pages of Janet and John.

From their avocado-coloured fitted kitchen, Helena could see Marnie seated at the dining table at the rear of the sitting room, swinging her spindl, six-year-old legs. She looked like Pippi Longstocking, with her severe dark blonde plaits either side of her face. Every so often, she would award her reading book a cross stare. It made Helena smile.

"Are you listening to me?"

Helena turned back to her husband. "Of course I am. Are you listening to me?"

Donald's weary eyes, a washed-out grey, glinted with annoyance. "I do nothing else."

Helena's spine prickled. That was a ridiculous comment. He was never here. Donald would go off to his work as office manager at the local glass factory just as dawn was breaking over the rooftops of Briar Glen. Helena would ensure Donald's breakfast things were set out for him the night before, together with his packed lunch prepared and sitting in the fridge in a Tupperware box. He was never home before six o'clock at the earliest.

She and Marnie were lucky if they were able to spend a couple of hours in his company, before it was time for Marnie to go to bed, and Donald would call it a night not long after his daughter. Then the whole circus would begin again the next morning.

Helena played with the ends of her long, centre-parted, brunette hair. She had tried to emulate the actress of the moment, Ali McGraw, from Love Story. Someone in the corner shop had remarked to her the other week that she bore a resemblance to Ali McGraw and she'd blushed with delight. God, she loved that film!

"But what about Marnie?"

Helena blinked out of her kohl-lined eyes. "What about her?"

"She'll end up turning into one of those latch-key kids."

"Oh, don't be ridiculous! That's the whole point, Don. She wouldn't." Helena observed Donald's body language. He was all folded arms and grim mouth under his Peter Wingard-influenced moustache. "It would be perfect. That new gift shop in the village has only been going a few weeks and they are desperate for part-time staff."

Donald's fine brows twitched. They always did that when he disapproved of something.

"They're opening up a crockery section and when I mentioned to Mrs Auld that I was very interested in tea sets…"

Donald shifted his position against the sink.

"I haven't forgotten about Marnie at all, Don. She's at school from 9a.m. till three. That's why a job like this would be perfect. Mrs Auld said I can work 9.30a.m. till 2.30p.m. three days a week to begin with and then I can increase it to five days if I want to."

Annoyance swept through her like a giant wave. "Do you really think I would have even considered it, if it had been inconvenient?" Her attention swung back again to her daughter, who was now slurping her orange juice through a straw and swinging her legs in a wilder, more uninhibited fashion than before under the table.

"Of course not," snapped Donald. This was one of those rare occasions when he was home at a reasonable time, thanks to an optician's appointment. He was still dressed in his suit and had now loosened his paisley kipper tie. "I just think that a woman ... wel l... a wife and a mum ...should be running the house."

Helena stared at him, her jaw slackening. She felt as if she was trapped in one of those dire American sitcoms. "It might have escaped your notice but there are some women who do go back to work after having children. Look at Connie at number three. She works three days a week in the hair salon."

At the mention of their glamorous neighbour, Donald's moustache twisted. "That's a case in point. Look at her. That poor sod of a husband of hers has to do some of the shopping and take Louise and Paul to school."

"Only every so often and that's because she's been made a senior stylist now."

So that was what all this was about. Donald was worried he was going to be asked to help out with Marnie. Heaven forbid, he might even have to undertake the odd school drop-off or pop to the corner shop if they ran out of bread and milk.

Was that his issue? Was it because he was concerned that Helena working a few hours a week might emasculate his role as breadwinner?

Helena viewed her husband with resentment across the linoleum-floored kitchen, with its grass-green-and-white tiled backsplash and woven blind. She wondered what the likes of Germaine Greer would make of this conversation. Ms Greer would want to put Donald's testicles in a vice. The way she was feeling right now, Helena knew she would happily volunteer to turn the screw.

Signalling that, as far as he was concerned, the discussion was closed, Donald pushed himself away from the sink and took a stiff Helena in his arms. He smelled of Old Spice and factory machinery. "Don't you worry your little head about anything, Hels. I'm earning more than enough for the family."

It isn't about money, Helena screamed to herself. Can't you see that? I'd just like to do something for me.

He indulged her with a condescending smile. "You continue to do what you do best. That's taking care of Marnie and me. We are very grateful for it, you know."

Her eyes scorched into his back as he strode off towards the sitting room to see his daughter. Helena could hear Marnie giggling at some corny joke Donald was telling her.

Helena snatched up a tea towel. How often had she tried to have this conversation with him? How many times had he dismissed it, as though she were experiencing some sort of episode, and if she gave it time she would recover and come through the other side?

She gripped the edge of the pine kitchen table. Enough was enough.

She was thirty years old and didn't need the approval of Donald Hamilton. She had believed she was doing the right thing in raising the subject with him again. Couples were supposed to talk about things. Wasn't marriage supposed to be a partnership? At least that was what she had read in a copy of Cosmopolitan.

She had made an effort to talk about it rationally and yet Donald had just responded with his usual platitudes.

Marnie let out a bored sigh. "Mummy. Can you come and test me on my words please?"

Helena crossed her arms. "Of course, sweetheart. I'm just coming."

She studied her surroundings. There was more to life than doing the weekly shop and housework. More images of confident, glossy women in the magazines that she'd been reading when Donald wasn't around fluttered in her head like tropical, exotic birds. She didn't just want to be known as a wife and mum.

She knew her genuine love of crockery would be such an asset to the little gift shop and how rewarding would it be? She would be out of the house, meeting people, indulging her passion and earning a bit of money for herself – and still be here to be the mother to Marnie that her gorgeous little girl deserved.

Helena's heart pumped with adrenalin. Her mind was made up. The possible consequences and prolonged arguments that would no doubt ensue when she had to tell Donald she was working flapped in her chest. She dismissed them. She would call in to see Mrs Auld tomorrow morning, straight after taking Marnie to school, and tell her she could start straightaway.

"Gran bought this shop," I murmured, a mug of tea in one hand as I gazed wide-eyed at my surroundings. "It still doesn't seem real."

Mrs Cotter's dark eyes shone. "She did indeed. I have all the paperwork to prove it."

I twisted in my chair, now that we had returned to the office. "Mrs Cotter, when did my gran first speak to you? About buying the shop, I mean?"

Mrs Cotter grew thoughtful. "Now let me think. It was a while ago." She screwed up her eyes. "Ah. Yes, now I remember. It was just before my husband's seventieth birthday weekend, so that was fourteen months ago now."

I almost slopped my tea everywhere in shock. "My grandmother had been planning this for that long? Are you sure, Mrs Cotter?"

"Absolutely. I remember it well. Your grandmother dropped by for a chat the Friday afternoon, just as I was getting ready to close earlier to whisk Martin to the shores of Loch Lomond for a surprise birthday dinner with the family."

My mouth shot open. So, Gran had been planning this all that time and never said a word to me or to Mum and Dad.

As though reading my stunned thoughts, Mrs Cotter interrupted them. "She swore me to secrecy, Sophie."

I gave my head a disbelieving shake. "I'm sure she did."

Mrs Cotter rolled her eyes good-naturedly. "It's typical of Helena Hamilton. Always springing a surprise."

I searched Mrs Cotter's amused expression. "But … but why not tell me before?"

She sank back into her chair. "Perhaps she thought you would change your mind once you had thought about it and say no. This way, she hasn't given you much time. Perhaps that's the best way. Carpe diem and all that."

I rubbed at my face. Dear God. Talk about a life-changing

decision. My emotions were travelling between being grateful, worried sick at what I was taking on and then excited about the future. One minute I'm organising high-end weddings, and the next, I find out I own a shop and boxes of tea sets.

Mrs Cotter took a sip from her mug of tea, watching me closely. She allowed me to digest it all for a few moments before she spoke again. "I know it must have come as rather a shock—"

I let out an incredulous bark of laughter.

"But your gran would never have done this if she thought you weren't capable of making a go of it."

I blew out a cloud of air, still struggling to speak. "That's what people keep telling me." I took another gulp of tea. "It's just the reality of running a business here in Briar Glen." I paused. "I don't suppose you could recommend a good accountant?"

"Of course," beamed Mrs Cotter. "I'll give you the details of the local chap I used. His name is Craig Adler and he's very professional, but very approachable too. He has been my accountant for this place ever since I started."

"Thank you," I smiled, a kernel of relief and – dare I say it – optimism promising to bud. "That would be great."

" See?" cajoled Mrs Cotter. "Things are slowly starting to fall into place already. Once we finish our tea, I'll take you on a little guided tour. This place is as big as a minute, but it's like a Tardis at the back, so plenty of storage facility."

Her plucked brows gathered. "Your gran was adamant she wanted this shop. I told her the old barber's was going to go up for sale as well, but she wasn't interested." She tutted in sympathy. "Poor Keith McLeod and his arthritis. He and his partner have decided to sell up and move to Spain for the warmer climate, so they will be putting The Steadings on the market as well."

I snapped my attention back to Mrs Cotter. "Sorry. The Steadings?"

She looked at me as though I had grown two heads. "Where Keith and Andrew live."

"Oh yes. Of course." My jumbled-up thoughts managed to pull up pictures of Keith's modern detached villa, with its sweeping vista of the Briar Glen hills.

I refocused. "So, you say my grandmother wasn't interested in the barber's?"

"Not at all." Mrs Cotter savoured another mouthful of tea. "I mean, Hair Apparent is situated closer to the train station and sees a bit more passing footfall, but she insisted it must be A Bloom with A View."

I gazed around me. I wondered why Gran was so insistent it had to be this shop. "Do you know what this place used to be before you took it over?"

"Oh, it has changed hands a few times, but I do know it was a very successful bicycle shop back in the day."

Mrs Cotter leant forward in her chair, nursing her mug in her freckly hands. "I'm officially closing in two weeks, on 1st May." She paused for dramatic effect, her chocolate eyes shining. "Then she's all yours."

"I still think this whole thing is utter madness!" muttered Mum, dumping her tea towel on the kitchen table. "Where did Mum get the money to purchase a shop?!"

"I know she used to dabble in stocks and shares." Dad gave a shrug. "She was a canny woman, your mother."

Despite Mum's clear frustration, she agreed with a fleeting smile. "That's one way of describing her."

Dad turned back to me. "So, you've decided to go for it then, sweetheart?"

I gave a fierce nod. "I have. Gran has bought me the shop and left me those tea sets, and I'm going to make a go of it."

I could hear myself saying it, but it was as though my body had been inhabited by someone else. "And I've already started thinking about possible names for the business, how I want the layout of the shop to look and what social media and marketing it will need to get it off the ground."

"But selling teapots," said Mum, her concern for me evident.

"Well, why not?" replied Dad. "You know how much the lass has loved all that since she was little and it's not like she doesn't know what she's talking about. Helena had our Sophie talking about Royal Doulton before she learnt the alphabet!"

He gave me an encouraging wink. "You know that this might have happened for a reason – you quitting your job, I mean."

Mum snatched up her tea towel again. "Oh, he's off on one of his philosophical rambles!"

Dad grinned at her and squeezed her waist. She made a show of protesting, by batting him away.

As I watched them, I mulled over where my future was

about to take me. Could I do this? Could I not only do it for me, but also for my grandmother? She had put so much faith in me and was giving me the opportunity she never had.

I straightened my back.

Oh God.

It was about to happen. I was going to start my own business.

Chapter Ten

The next couple of weeks were a blur of phone calls and emails and I had no time to really miss Castle Marrian.

The first of May saw the closure of A Bloom with a View and the transfer of the shop keys to me.

I wasted no time in contacting the auctioneer Gran had recommended, Howard Thrall, who couldn't have been more helpful. He was very sorry to hear of my grandmother's passing, but was very enthusiastic about the tea sets she had instructed me to sell – especially when I emailed him pictures of them that I took on my phone.

In fact, he was on the verge of salivating. "I knew Helena had some interesting pieces, but I had no idea she possessed the likes of a Theodore Wende and a Roy Lichtenstein," he gushed into my ear. "I know of several buyers who will be falling over themselves to bid for such acquisitions for their collections."

I frowned into my mobile. "And you have no idea how my grandmother came to be in possession of them?"

"None at all. All she did say was that she was given them as a present many years ago, but by whom and why, I don't know."

Though my heart lifted at the prospect of some additional, much welcome capital to fall back on for launching the business, I couldn't help but puzzle over who had given Gran those very valuable tea sets and why. It was one thing to give a friend perfume or a treasured photograph, but crockery that could sell for thousands of pounds?

Howard spoke again, breaking though my thoughts. "I will arrange for the crockery to be collected by a couple of my people."

Fortunately, Mrs Cotter had taken great care of the shop premises and it didn't require any major refurbishment. All I intended to do was have it redecorated and put my own stamp on the place. The front of the shop would benefit from a fresh lick of white paint and I'd opted for lilac windowsills and decided to paint the door in the same shade. I wanted to have the shop display an eclectic mix of crockery, from the antique and traditional to retro and more funky, modern sets. I also had ideas charging about my head, about regularly changing the window displays to follow certain themes and ideas, not just reflecting Christmas and the seasons. Maybe I could have a display dedicated to *Alice in Wonderland*, with my own take on the Mad Hatter's tea party? Or do a homage to Mrs Potts and Chip from *Beauty and the Beast*, with a Disney-themed display?

I had also conducted a little bit of detective work around the other businesses, dropping in and asking the owners and customers what they thought of Briar Glen having its own crockery shop. The feedback I received was very positive.

Comments ranged from "That will attract the tourists" and "There's a definite gap in the market round here" to "Oh God! My wife would never be out of the place!" Hearing the enthusiasm for my new business was heart-warming, but I knew I was only starting out and I was therefore keen to take things steadily by not recruiting too many staff to begin with.

Coming up with a catchy and memorable name for my business was on my ever-expanding to-do list lot as well! I had made a list of four or five possibles and continued to mull them over.

As Dad was a plumber, albeit on the brink of retirement, he knew many of the local tradespeople. "You let me know when you've decided on the décor you want and I'll speak to a couple of the decorator lads I'm friendly with."

Mrs Cotter too, had been so kind, offering her assistance. "No doubt I'll be bored to tears during my retirement, so you don't hesitate to give me a call when you want," and she had pressed one of her old business cards into my hand.

It was fortunate in so many ways that in my previous life I had been a wedding planner. Like my mother, I had always been a ferocious to-do-list maker, keen to be organised, and being able to put those organisational skills into practice with the shop at least gave me a shred of confidence – and was now vital!

I brainstormed what I thought I needed to do: everything from redecorating the shop to accessing a till and credit-card machine; setting up a website and social media accounts for the business; making contact with the crockery suppliers Gran had recommended in her letter, and thinking about what I should do with regard to taking on staff, as well as factoring in the costs of local and regional press advertising.

Craig Adler, Mrs Cotter's accountant, was now on board, which was a huge weight off my mind. I had trawled through online crockery businesses, to get a feel for prices. Although much of my stock would be at the higher end of the tea set world, I would also be selling more modest but just as pretty and eye-catching designs. I wanted to bring the joy of crockery to the masses and I wouldn't be doing that if I was solely selling expensive sets.

My aim was to establish a cosy haven, where my customers could browse, admire, appreciate – and then buy!

After ploughing through a ridiculous number of glossy interior design brochures and coloured paint charts, I decided upon lilac (my favourite colour) for the shop walls and Scottish Mist, a soft white with a tinge of grey, for the shelves and counter.

The rich, dark wooden floor was, to my relief, still in good condition, so Dad suggested another coat of varnish just to freshen it up.

Mrs Cotter's old workroom, once the place that housed all her blooms, ribbons, tissue paper and extra stock, would also have the same lilac walls and off-white shelving and would be the ideal space to contain my new arrivals of crockery and hold all the stock in their boxes.

Mrs Cotter had left behind her old desk in the office. It was a rather forlorn-looking, scratched affair in morose mahogany, but possessed a lot of character. I imagined it all glossy and injected with new life, so I decided to undertake this task myself and research the best technique for restoring mahogany.

From the advice I located online, the consensus was to buff it up with some petroleum-based lighter fluid and fine-grain sandpaper and then paint it with an oil-based varnish.

Dad helped me transport the desk home and I proceeded to spend the next few evenings in old denims and my hair pulled up into a severe topknot, lost in buffing, sanding and then sweeping a topcoat on. I found the whole process rewarding and relaxing, watching the tired wood ease back to life. It was a pleasant escape from the frantic days.

As I slicked on the topcoat, watching the bristles of the brush glide and sweep, I wondered what Gran would have thought if she could see me now.

I was working flat out, my mind careering from stock one minute to debating and searching for shop name ideas the next. I was even thinking of checking out the cost of having a special Briar Glen teapot commissioned to sell. Something with an image of the Briar Glen blue rose on it would look lovely.

I was determined to give this venture everything I had. But that didn't stop echoes of apprehension stealing over me at regular intervals.

What did help calm my nerves somewhat was a welcome phone call from Howard Thrall.

I assumed it would be several months until there was any hope of him being able to sell Grandma's acquisitions. Instead, it took us two weeks.

"I have good news for you," he said down the phone with an almost audible grin, as I pored over my lists of outgoings and things still requiring action. "I had no problem at all selling the lot."

I sat up straighter on my silver and grey hessian sofa. There had been a mid-May downpour that afternoon and the fields out of my sitting-room window dazzled under a blanket of raindrops.

It took a moment for my brain to catch up. "Wow! Thank you so much," I breathed with surprised relief.

"The pleasure is all mine," he insisted.

I could hear an efficient tapping of his computer keyboard in the background.

"The Lichtenstein, Paragon and Josiah Spode were much sought after, especially by buyers in the States and Italy." There was a dramatic pause. "So would you like me to tell you the total earned from our private auction?"

"Yes, please."

I snatched up my notebook and pen and began writing. My pen froze on the page. That couldn't be right. There seemed to be rather a lot of zeros. I took a sharp intake of breath. "Er … sorry. I don't mean to sound rude, but are you sure that's correct?"

I could sense Howard Thrall smiling down the line. "I can assure you that is correct. Those tea sets are a collector's dream, Sophie. They're rare and in excellent condition and, in the world of antiques, such items attract genuinely serious bidders. There was quite a squabble between two individuals in the end to secure them."

I gazed down at the considerable amount I'd just scrawled in black ink. I fought to keep my voice level. "I only wish I knew where on earth my grandmother got them from. I always knew she had a collection, but nothing like this!"

I wouldn't need anything like that amount of money to pump into the crockery shop. "I'll give donations to at least a couple of Gran's favourite charities," I blurted out to a bemused Howard. "And then I'll give some to my parents. The rest I will save for now, in case this shop idea turns out to be an unmitigated disaster."

I could feel my cheeks stinging with red, as I remembered Howard's role in all of this. "And of course, I'm not forgetting your commission."

"I should hope not!" he said in faux indignation.

Howard confirmed he would arrange payment straight into the business bank account I had set up for the shop within the next five to seven working days and deduct his commission from that. "And don't forget I'm on hand, should you have any queries about the value of any other tea sets that might come your way."

"Thank you," I sighed with relief. "That's very comforting to know."

We were about to hang up when he said, "Oh, and Sophie – about this new business of yours failing… It won't happen."

I unfurled my legs from underneath me. "I wish I had your confidence. What makes you say that?"

He laughed. "Because I sense you have too much of your grandmother in you."

Chapter Eleven

The end of May passed in a hive of activity and the start of June saw the redecorating of the shop about to commence. Mum and I pushed up our sleeves, donned old clothes and wiped down the shelves and dusted and hoovered in preparation for Dad's painter friends, Ally and Finn, to come in the following day and begin painting.

Finn had recommended his student artist son, who would be able to make me a new shop sign, and I gratefully accepted his offer.

I just couldn't come up with a suitable name for the business! I had narrowed my preferred list of names down to four, but was still struggling to decide.

I had been browsing online and racking my brains, but without success so far.

Dad had joined Mum and me that morning. I'd noticed one of the sink taps in the staff toilet was leaking, so he set to work with his toolkit.

The sun was doing her best to struggle through a gauze of

cloud and the main street saw a few quizzical faces wavering behind the bottle glass of the shop window, as they strolled past and had a peer in.

I emptied the hoover into one of the bin bags and stretched.

I was sure I could still detect the faint fragrance of tea roses from when my shop was in its previous guise as a florist.

My shop.

I was still struggling to process this a lot of the time.

"So, Mum, you don't know why Gran was so insistent on this shop, rather than Hair Apparent?"

"You've asked me that already. I have no idea." She rolled her eyes. "Your grandmother was a law unto herself."

I wondered whether this place brought back happy memories for her or had a connection in some way to the family. But sadly, I would never know for sure.

"Right," I exclaimed, planting my hands on my hips. "It's almost lunchtime. How about I pop up to the baker's and get us a sandwich?"

At the mention of food, my overall-clad father appeared from the back, a spanner glinting in his hand. "Sounds good to me, sweetheart."

I scrambled around in my bag under the counter for my purse.

"Oh no you don't," said Mum. "You need to take care of your cash for this place."

Dad laughed. "Sophie is hardly scraping by, love. After that auction guy did so well selling those tea sets of Helena's, she has a good bit of money to fall back on now."

Mum was still struggling to get her head round how valuable those sets of crockery had been. Over the last couple of weeks, I'd suggested the two of them book themselves on a luxury cruise and use the money I gave them from the sales proceeds, but my mum had been so used to budgeting and being careful with their finances over the years, I guessed it was a hard mindset for her to escape from.

I brushed away Mum's protests. "You and Dad are doing me a big favour helping me like this. I'm buying lunch. End of."

Once Mum requested a brie, grape and salad sandwich and Dad put in his order for his favourite – a bacon, lettuce and tomato – I snatched my sunglasses in hopeful anticipation.

I'd already decided to also treat the three of us to one of the baker's infamous Briar Glen Danish Pastries with a blueberry topping. We could enjoy one of those each with our afternoon cuppa. Mum had brought with her a few flasks of tea and some fruit to keep us going.

I was all messy ponytail, an old baggy T-shirt and denims, but felt like I was accomplishing something again.

What I'd experienced with Castle Marrian still stung, but I found I was now able to push the feelings of resentment and anger more and more to one side. And I still didn't regret leaving. I knew that – despite my initial fear that I'd jumped in head-first and done the wrong thing – with each day that passed, I was becoming more certain that I had made the right decision.

I stepped out of the shop and inhaled, dispelling the smell of fairy liquid and polish.

"Excuse me?"

There was an apprehensive-looking woman loitering outside.

There was something about her slight smile and conker-brown, shoulder-skimming hair that was vaguely familiar. She pushed both her hands into her cardigan pockets. "I'm so sorry to bother you. You're Sophie Harkness, right? The new owner?"

As if to emphasise the point, she raised a finger and pointed over my shoulder at the shop.

"Yes, that's right. Sorry, do I know you from somewhere?"

A rosy tinge spread across her freckled cheeks. "You might not remember me. I'm Cass Dunlop. I worked for Daphne Cotter when this was A Bloom with a View."

My memory fixed on pictures of her in the florist's workroom, deftly arranging a bouquet and sliding me a brief smile when I came to speak to Mrs Cotter. "Oh yes. Sorry. Hi! How are you?"

"Oh, you know," she managed, focusing her dark eyes on the pavement for a few seconds. "I'm actually looking for another job now that A Bloom with a View has closed down. I used to help out Daphne when she was busy and needing an extra pair of hands."

She gulped a mouthful of air and fiddled with the strap of her shoulder bag. "I hope you don't think I'm being forward, but I wondered if you were looking for any staff?" Her almond-shaped eyes were eager, searching my face.

"I will be," I replied. "It will be for a couple of part-time posts to begin with, just until I see how things go."

Her tight shoulders relaxed under the crocheted cardigan. "I am a trained florist, as you might have worked out, but there isn't much call at the moment round here for my skills." She scooped a hunk of loose, shiny straight hair back behind one ear. "I'm hard-working and trustworthy, Ms Harkness, and Mrs Cotter said she would be more than happy to supply a reference."

Warming to her theme, she continued, "I've got a little boy called Hudson. He's five and starts school in August."

As shoppers weaved around us, Cass carried on with her informal job interview. "We live locally in one of the houses up by St Jacob's Church."

I began to speak, but enthusiastic Cass was on a roll. "A local, part-time job like this would be ideal for me, especially with Hudson." She explained about her husband Jamie having his own building business. "He works such ridiculous hours and is away a lot, so…" Her voice dried up as she continued to stare at me out of desperate, dark eyes. "I'm talking too much, aren't I? I'm so sorry. I always do that when I'm nervous."

"It's fine," I assured her with a smile. She seemed so eager and there was something gentle yet capable about her demeanour. Having a trained florist working in the shop could be very handy too. My ideas accelerated, with visions of crockery displays in the window accompanied by seasonal flowers. "I'm not yet at the stage where I'm ready to open, as you can see." I gestured behind me to the open shop door. Mum could be seen wiping down its glass panels from the inside and Dad was tightening up one of the shelf screws.

"I reckon I should be in a position to open in about four to six weeks at the latest, though."

Cass was nodding fiercely at everything I was saying.

"Tell you what, why don't you ping over your CV and reference from Mrs Cotter?"

I darted back into the shop and located one of my old

Castle Marrian business cards lurking at the bottom of my bag. I took a pen and underlined my private email address and mobile number on it, before scoring through my old contact details at the hotel and where it said "Wedding Planner" under my name.

I stepped back outside and handed it to her. "Here. Email me at that address and feel free to ring me if you have any questions."

A spark of hope flashed across her face. "Thank you so much, Ms Harkness. I really appreciate it. I'll go straight home and do that now."

"It's Sophie," I insisted. "And there's no immediate rush." But Cass Dunlop was already striding away from the shop, with an optimistic bounce in her step. She drew to a sudden halt and spun round in her silver trainers. "Oh, and I hope you come up with a name for your shop soon. We all need a cup of cheer now and again!"

I watched her march off again with renewed purpose, her red leather bag swinging off her shoulders. The emerging sun was glancing against shafts of burgundy in her hair.

Her parting words lodged themselves in my head. *"We all need a cup of cheer now and again."* A cup of cheer... No, hang on... How about The Cup That Cheers? I conjured up an image of a lilac and white painted sign swinging in the breeze above the shop from a silver pole. The words "The Cup That Cheers" were dancing across it.

It was catchy, heart-lifting and memorable.

An excited smile broke out across my face. I liked it. I really liked it.

The decision was made. That was it. That would be the name of the shop.

I glanced down at my watch. Bloody hell! It was well after midday.

I picked up speed as I headed towards the bakers up on the corner to bring back lunch for me, Mum and Dad.

I had better not return empty-handed to The Cup That Cheers, I thought to myself with a lurch of excitement. The workers would require fuel!

Chapter Twelve

No sooner had I arrived back at The Cup That Cheers (each time I repeated the name in my head, I liked it more) with our sandwiches, than my phone let out its familiar ping.

It was an email from Cass Dunlop, not only attaching her CV and a reference from Mrs Cotter, but also another from a florist she worked with for two years on Glasgow's south side.

I set the sandwiches down on the counter and smiled to myself. She was certainly keen.

As we sat in a semi-circle on folding chairs that Mum had insisted we bring with us, I relayed the name I'd decided on for the shop and explained it was inadvertently suggested by Cass Dunlop.

Mum dished out three takeaway cups of her tea from her chrome flask. "Oh, was that the young woman I saw you talking to? That's such a cute name for this place."

Dad took a passionate bite of his bacon, lettuce and tomato

sandwich. "It's very memorable as well. So do you think you might take this Cass on?"

I savoured the ripe Wensleydale cheese in my salad sandwich. "I haven't had a chance to read her CV yet, but from first impressions she seems suitable and she has solid retail experience."

"See?" beamed Dad with a dollop of satisfaction. "Things are starting to come together already."

He shot Mum beside him a knowing look. "And now you've decided on a name for the shop, I'll speak to Finn and he can have a word with that artist son of his about designing a sign for you."

"Thanks, Dad. That would be great."

He thrust one finger in the air. "Oh, and that mahogany desk you were refurbishing, love. I can collect it from your flat in the next day or two and bring it down here for you. That will be one less thing for you to worry about."

"If you could, I'd really appreciate it. Thank you. "I took another bite of my lunch and chewed, as I surveyed the bare, clean surroundings of my new business. Maybe Dad's philosophy about things happening for a reason had some substance after all.

I spent the rest of Monday making sure the interior of The Cup That Cheers was spotless for Ally and Finn to begin the decorating tomorrow morning.

And even though they already had strict instructions from me on what shade of paint to use and where, I had typed up a brief note, clarifying Lilac Heather for the walls and Scottish Mist for the ceiling, shelves and counter, with the colour scheme extending into the store room and what would be my office.

I folded it up and slid it into an envelope, marked for Ally and Finn's attention. Dad watched me place it on top of the counter. "You are your mother's daughter all right!"

I managed to contain myself until the next afternoon, before dropping by The Cup That Cheers to take a look at Ally and Finn's progress.

I'd spent part of the morning reading Cass's very impressive CV and the sparkling references supplied by Mrs Cotter and Flower Power, the other florist's that had employed her for a couple of years. When I rang Mrs Cotter and the owner of Flower Power, a lady by the name of Flora Graham, they both enthused about Cass, extolling her reliability and her conscientious attitude.

That was good enough for me. I made up my mind to ring her and offer her a part-time position before the end of the day.

Then I would riffle through more catalogues, selecting what I considered suitable teapots and crockery sets to sell in the shop. I felt like a child on Christmas Eve waiting for Santa, once I'd ordered them online!

As soon as I stepped inside The Cup That Cheers that afternoon, I started to smile.

Ally and Finn were making good progress. One wall was already finished, boasting the gorgeous shade of lilac I'd chosen, and Ally was busy attending to the counter with his paintbrush, delivering a coat of the off-white Scottish Mist.

The shop was going to look gorgeous when it was all finished.

Finn put down his lilac-loaded paintbrush and strode over to me. A digital radio was cranking out energetic music in the background.

"Checking up on the workers, eh?"

"Not at all," I smiled. "Just came to admire your handiwork."

Finn gave a gap-toothed grin. "I think you're going to be pleased, once it's all done."

"I'm sure I will."

"Once the interior is finished, we'll get cracking on the outside of the shop."

He tapped his forehead, as though to illustrate the point that he had thought of something else. "Can you hang on for a few minutes here? Ewan, my son, was going to pop into the art shop to stock up on a few supplies. I could ask him to drop by and have a chat with you."

"Oh, of course. That would be great. Thanks."

Finn retrieved his mobile from his dungaree pocket with paint-smeared hands and dialled Ewan. A minute later, he turned to me and said, "He'll be here in a few minutes."

"Wonderful. Thanks, Finn. Can I get either of you guys anything?"

Ally shook his shaggy head of blond hair. "No, you're okay, thanks, Sophie. If I see another cup of Finn's anaemic tea, it will be too soon."

Moments later, a young lad of about nineteen loped into the shop, all legs, a thatch of messy brown hair and a shy smile.

"Ah! Here he is. The prodigal son!" joked Finn from halfway up his ladder.

Ewan blushed and rolled a set of light eyes at his dad. "Sophie?"

"That's me."

He was clutching a brown paper bag, out of which thrust several artist's brushes in varying sizes. "Dad just told me you would like a new shop sign for this place."

"That's right. Well, I will need two, if that's okay. One large one and a smaller design to suspend from the pole that's already there." I led Ewan outside, so he could get a clear view of the shop's exterior.

Ewan tugged a small notebook from the back pocket of his black jeans, together with a short, stubby pencil. "I'm on summer holidays from art college at the moment. I'm just going into second year."

He squinted up in the vanilla sunshine. "So do you have a rough idea of what you're looking for?"

I told Ewan the name I'd chosen for the business. "I take it your dad told you I will be selling crockery, teapots, tea sets…?"

Ewan's wavy, toffee-coloured hair lifted a little in the breeze. "He mentioned that the other night. I'm sure you will do well with the locals, but especially the daytrippers."

"I do hope so."

Ewan began to pull together a rough sketch of the front of the shop. His pencil skittered across the page of his notebook, effortlessly producing an uncanny resemblance of the shop.

"What I could do is provide you with a few suggested designs and then you can decide which one you prefer?"

"That would be great. Thank you."

We headed back into The Cup That Cheers, where Finn and Ally were discussing last night's football results over the top of the radio. Finn gestured to the lilac wall his dad had painted. "And you want to keep the same colour scheme for the signage?"

"Yes, please."

Ewan nodded and pushed his notebook back into his pocket. "Thanks for this, Sophie," he said with a blush, looking down. Finn and Ally had smothered the wooden floor in squares of cloth to protect it from dripping paint. "I'm working as a part-time waiter in that new fish restaurant on the outskirts of town just to earn a few quid during the holidays, but any extra income is more than welcome."

"Not at all," I insisted. "Believe me, you're the one doing me the favour."

I gave him a note of my email address and, as Ewan moved to leave, he promised to get a few sketches to me by the end of the week.

He gave his dad a mock salute on the way out, almost colliding with an older woman coming in.

Cradling a sealed cardboard box in her arms, she was wearing an expensive-looking tailored burgundy belted coat and possessed a head of wavy, short, silver hair.

"Is this the place?" she asked Ewan with a hint of desperation. "Is this the new crockery shop?"

Ewan blinked at her. "Er … yes … well, it will be."

She barged past Ewan, who pulled a face at her as he

wandered off. She appraised me from head to toe with an odd look. "Are you the owner of this shop?"

"Yes, but…"

Before I knew what was happening, the woman thrust the box towards me. It gave an indignant rattle. "Here, I don't want this. Please. I'm sure someone will take it, though."

I stared down at the sealed cardboard box as I took it from her. "Sorry, Madam, but what is in here?"

"Well, it's not a luxury cruise liner!"

From behind me, Ally and Finn paused mid-decorating, to witness more of our exchange.

I placed the heavy box on a nearby fold-out camping table which Mum had left for me to use while the counter and shelves were out of action.

As I began to open the box, the older woman's tight features seized up further. Then, with a flap of her coat, she wrapped her arms around herself and made for the door.

"Excuse me?" I called, abandoning the box. "Hang on a second. Who are you? I don't know your name."

Whoever she was, she wasn't prepared to hang around and make polite conversation. She shot out of the shop.

With the sound of Ally and Finn's radio pumping out behind me, I hurried into the sun-streaked main street after her. "Excuse me? Wait. Please stop!"

I whipped my head left and right, but the woman had vanished.

I retreated into the shop, frustrated.

"Where did she go?" asked Ally from under his shaggy fringe.

"No idea. She didn't even leave her name. She just dumped this box and vanished."

Finn loaded up his brush again with paint. "Maybe whatever is in that box has fallen off the back of a lorry."

Ally frowned over at him. "Did she look like someone who would handle stolen goods?"

Finn tapped the side of his regal nose. "You never can tell, mate. You never can tell."

I turned my attention back to the partially open box. Whatever it was, the woman had been very keen to offload it.

I peeled away the Sellotape and unfurled the flaps of the box. The action reminded me of when I was at Gran's and discovered her haul of beautiful crockery in the cupboard under the stairs.

I slid one hand into the depths of the box and eased apart sheets of yellowing old newspaper. They crinkled and rustled against my fingers. Underneath the layers of newspaper was a battered old case in cream leather, with a gold clasp fastening. It smelt of mothballs and lavender.

What on earth was in here? Well, seeing as the fleeing woman had asked if this was the new crockery shop, I could hazard a guess. But why had she been so keen to rid herself of whatever was in this leather case? And why wasn't she interested in selling it or leaving contact details? I pictured her again, flapping out of the shop in her expensive-looking coat. She couldn't get away fast enough. Whatever it was, she had been keen to put as much distance between her and this as she could.

Conscious of the delicate condition the contents inside

might be in, I slid both my arms underneath the case to ease it out of where it was nestled in the box.

"Here," insisted Ally, marching over the canvas floor sheets in his work boots. "Let me give you a hand."

"Thanks. It's bloody heavy!"

Ally transferred the box onto the floor, so that it was out of the way and then laid the leather case on the table. Finn sauntered over for a closer inspection.

I touched the gold clasp and it released itself with a classy rasp.

I pushed at the lid and it glided backwards to reveal its mysterious contents.

My eyes almost fell out of my face.

I had never seen anything like it before.

Chapter Thirteen

The interior of the leather case was plush black velvet.
Nestling inside its various compartments was a tea set, consisting of four cups, saucers, a milk jug and a teapot.

The porcelain crockery was composed of rich greens and golds, with an intricate peacock motif. On the teapot, the peacock's swathe of impressive tail feathers fanned out to reach up into the spout.

It was a little too fussy for my taste, but the detail and rich colours were gorgeous: olive, petrol-blue and racing green, all pulled together by the deep gold running around the handles of the cups and the teapot.

"I wonder how old that lot is?" asked Ally, peering over my shoulder.

I traced one puzzled finger around the edge of one of the saucers. "I reckon it's pretty old. The gold edging around the teacup handles is very worn in places, so it looks like it has been well used."

Finn jerked his dark, cropped head at the contents. "It's certainly unusual. I bet my missus would like it, though."

I couldn't get over the bizarre situation. A woman depositing an old tea set on me and then vanishing. "I wish my gran was here. I bet she would have some sort of idea about it."

It was true I didn't have my grandmother here to bounce this off, but I did have Howard Thrall.

Ally and Finn returned to their painting and I took a couple of photos of the tea set with my phone. I forwarded Howard the photographs of the crockery, together with a picture of the closed leather case, and put my phone away, to get on with wiping down the shop windows.

Less than fifteen minutes later, Howard's number flashed up on my screen.

"Well!" he exclaimed down the line. "You certainly threw me a curve ball with this one."

I headed back out into the main street to take the call. The other shop windows were now bathed in gilded June light and there was a light clatter of cutlery from the café around the corner. My stomach performed a pirouette of disappointment. "You don't recognise it?"

Howard confessed that he didn't. "It's rather enchanting in a busy sort of way, isn't it?"

I gave a short laugh. "That's the perfect way to describe it." I peered through the bottle-glass windows of the shop to study the open leather case and its contents again. The tea set glistened out. "So, you have no idea who the artist might be or how old it is?"

"Well ... yes and no."

I frowned down the line. What did he mean?

"I don't recognise the artist or that pattern," he confessed, "but what I can tell you is that there have been a couple of similar tea sets to that one that were discovered last year, which were traced back to the 1800s."

I swallowed. Bloody hell! If that was how old this one was, why would someone be so keen to get rid of something so valuable? Perhaps the lady who brought it here had no idea that she was in possession of an antique?

"Would you be able to do some investigative work please, Howard?" I glanced through the shop window again to where the tea set was on the foldout table. "I'm at a loss as to why that woman was in such a hurry to deposit it on me and then leave like she did."

Instead of the enthusiastic agreement from Howard that I'd hoped for, there came a sincere apology. "I would if I could, Sophie, but I'm afraid I've been called away on business tomorrow to Venice. I will be abroad for the next few weeks."

My heart deflated, but I tried to make light of it. "Oh, never mind. I don't blame you going to Venice for a few weeks."

There was a thoughtful pause at the end of the line. "But I've just had an idea. For something as alluring as this, I suggest we call in the big guns." He dropped his voice a little, implying a degree of reverence. "Have you heard of a chap by the name of Xander North?"

I admitted I hadn't.

"Xander is a respected art critic. I've known him for a number of years and worked alongside him on researching background to more elusive pieces of artwork. In my opinion, he would be the go-to guy when it comes to unravelling something like this."

Howard then mentioned a couple of high-profile auctions within the last couple of years, which Xander North was involved with. "He was instrumental in a Tiffany & Co. silver tea and coffee set from 1873 being sold for four times its original estimated worth in Boston."

I let out an appreciative, stunned gasp. I recalled the newspaper coverage of the highly publicised auction at the time.

"And he helped to secure the sale of a Theodore Wende tea set at Sotheby's for a six-figure sum. It was in the same vein as the Wende your late grandmother owned."

Now I remembered. There had been a glossy Sunday-supplement feature on it months ago and I remembered discussing it with Gran at the time. "Wasn't that the set that had a silver and ivory teapot and was stamped with German hallmarks?"

"The very same," said Howard, sounding impressed. "It was from 1927 and was considered very avant-garde at the time."

I heard Howard bustling around at his desk. "I'm not making any promises, but I can contact Xander now and try to pique his interest?"

I could feel my anticipation growing. "That would be wonderful, Howard. Thank you."

"No problem at all. Sorry I won't be around to help, but I will get back to you, once I've spoken to Xander and forwarded the photographs to him."

"You enjoy your jolly to Venice and please tell Mr North I look forward to working with him."

Howard made a snorting sound. "I can assure you I won't have much free time to ride on a gondola. I'm going over to price some art acquisitions for a number of private collectors." There was a pregnant pause. "Sophie, I should warn you that Xander North doesn't tend to do teamwork. Not even with me, although you must find that very difficult to believe. He's what you might call a lone wolf."

I laughed and dismissed Howard's hidden warning. I was used to organising weddings for the most demanding clients.

How hard could getting along with a renowned art critic be?

Chapter Fourteen

Howard texted me back that same Tuesday afternoon, to say he had managed to speak to Xander North, who was intrigued by the tea set and had agreed to meet with me.

It all sounded rather grand and cloak-and-dagger, but I was just so pleased that I might have a chance of finding out more about this tea set, where it had come from and why that well-dressed lady had been so keen to get rid of it. Perhaps I could even locate her and find out the reason for myself.

At ten the next morning, a mysterious number appeared on my mobile phone screen, while I waited in The Cup That Cheers for the delivery of a new telephone for the shop. Mrs Cotter's one had been rather unreliable and a boring shade of grey, so I'd opted for a retro style in pale pink to complement the shop interior.

A deep, well-spoken voice greeted me. Well, when I say greeted, it was more like an instruction.

Through in the main part of the shop, Finn was lapping

Scottish Mist onto the ceiling with a long roller brush and Ally was making good progress on the shelves.

I opened my mouth to speak, but the man carried on.

"Sophie Harkness? Xander North here."

I straightened my shoulders and hoped my tone sounded professional. "Good morning, Mr North. How are you?"

"Fine, thank you," he clipped. "About this mysterious tea set – Howard sent me the pictures."

There was a long pause. I wasn't sure if he was expecting me to fill it. "Yes," I said, just to break the silence.

"I can drop by in about an hour. I have a business lunch straight after in Glasgow."

I told him I didn't have the tea set with me, but that it would only take me ten minutes to drive home to collect it.

"Good," he barked into my ear.

I blinked. Something told me he wasn't much for polite conversation.

I gave him the address for the shop.

"See you shortly."

And then he was gone, leaving me standing clutching my phone and in a bit of a tailspin.

I gave my outfit an appraisal. Suddenly, my black jeans and electric-blue vest top didn't seem appropriate for coming face to face with an officious art critic.

When I explained to Ally and Finn, who were now undertaking a final touch-up of the skirting boards, they ushered me out of the shop. "We will keep an eye out for your new phone arriving," Ally assured me. "You pop off and do what you need to do."

So, with grateful thanks, I jumped into my car and drove

back to my flat. I retrieved the peacock-embossed tea set from where I had stored it at the bottom of my wardrobe. I settled the off-cream leather case onto my bedspread, before rattling my array of coat hangers, trying to locate something smart to change into.

It wasn't until I came across a pair of slim-fitting pinstriped trousers and my high-necked, frilly ruby blouse that I was satisfied.

I threw my jeans and vest top on top of the bed in a rumpled heap and changed, all the while making a tutting noise of disapproval at my out-of-control ponytail.

With very little time to spare, I grabbed a handful of hairgrips from my bathroom cupboard and fired my hair up into a hurried French roll. Not exactly perfect but it would have to do.

Once I'd slipped on my red ballet pumps in place of my trainers, I locked up my flat again and made my way back to the car, carrying the case with its rattling crockery as though it was my first newborn.

The thought of greeting Xander North with a mish-mash of smashed crockery was making my cheeks flush with horror.

I wrapped the tea set case in a couple of blankets I kept in the boot of my car and secured it on the back seat.

I drove slowly back to The Cup That Cheers, grateful to locate a now empty parking space at the rear of the shop. Finn greeted me at the shop door. "You look very smart. Just like one of those contestants on *The Apprentice*."

"I don't know how to take that," I joked.

Ally dashed a smudge of paint from his freckled cheek. "Oh, your new phone arrived right after you'd gone. We told the guy to install it where the old one used to be. I hope that was okay."

"Great. Thanks."

"And we've finished painting the windowsill in your office," beamed Finn. "You might want to go and take a look."

I stashed the case containing the tea set under the counter and hurried through to the back of the shop before the arrival of Xander North.

I pushed open the office door, which was now gleaming in strokes of Scottish Mist. My refurbished mahogany desk nestled there, complete with my new black leather chair with its chrome arm rests, which had arrived a couple of days ago.

I let out a thrilled gasp and sat down, running my fingers along the edge of the desk. Like a little girl presented with a new doll's house, I slid the freshly varnished drawers open and closed several times. They made a satisfying gliding motion.

I swished this way and that in my new plush chair, feeling a faint rush of air beneath my ballet pumps as I lifted my feet up from the new petrol-blue carpet Dad had fitted for me. I experienced a rush of excitement. I felt like a Bond villain.

I swivelled around, giddy with growing excitement and put on a Sir Sean Connery accent. "You eshpect me to talk?" I then transformed my voice into the sinister Blofeld. "No, Mr Bond. I expect you to die."

I let out a giggle, spinning gaily around and around, before the chair slowed and stopped to face the doorway.

A pair of hard, unimpressed eyes the shade of the Mediterranean was appraising me. "Ms Harkness, I take it?"

My bottom felt stuck to the leather of the chair. I sprang

upwards, my face illuminated hot pink. "Sorry … er … I was … er … checking the ergonomics…"

Stop talking, Sophie, for goodness' sake!

The startling blue-green gaze flicked over me. "I don't have a great deal of time," he remarked, unable to conceal his boredom.

My stomach pirouetted to my feet. Oh no. Don't tell me this was him.

I glanced down at my watch. It was 11a.m. My shoulders sank under my blouse in horror.

Resignation took hold, as the owner of the striking yet unimpressed eyes let them drift over me again. "I'm Xander North."

Chapter Fifteen

He wasn't what I was expecting.

I had envisaged Xander North as a crumbly older man, carrying a stick and wearing a cravat – perhaps a stately, mature gentleman with a handlebar moustache and a polka-dot handkerchief sticking out of his suit pocket. In reality, he was a towering, intense man in his late thirties, with a sweep of thick, dark hair and a scowl. The arch of his black brows was intimidating. There was no cravat either. Instead, he was dressed in an open-necked white shirt and a well-cut navy suit.

I stood there, lacing and unlacing my fingers. Oh God. He must have heard my dire James Bond impersonation. My cheeks flared with embarrassment. I was struggling to look him in the face.

I cleared my throat and extended one hand. "Sophie Harkness. It's good to meet you."

He took my hand in his and gave it a brief, but professional shake. Sarcasm dripped from his words. "I hope I'm not disturbing you."

My skin cringed. *No. Not at all. You were just watching me make an utter tit of myself.*

"No," I insisted. I pushed my mouth into what I hoped was an easy smile. "Would you like a tea or coffee…?"

He glanced down at his chunky watch with an air of impatience. "No, thank you. I am rather pressed for time. If I could see the tea set for myself, please."

I blinked at his crisp attitude. "Yes. Of course."

I indicated for Xander North to follow me through the shop towards the counter. My skin still crawling with embarrassment, I closed my eyes for a few seconds as I stalked ahead of him to retrieve the tea set. He must have thought I was a right muppet!

Ally and Finn took this as their cue to disappear up to the bakers for more fresh coffee and brunch.

I bent down and eased the case from the shelf and set it out on the counter. I flicked the lock and it opened up, to reveal the crockery set, all blues, greens and golds, glowing out of their respective compartments.

I risked a brief look at Xander North beside me. He made an appreciative murmur and examined the different shades, as they winked under the June sunshine pinpricking its way through the shop windows. He took one long, tapered finger and gestured to one of the teacups. "May I?"

"Of course."

He eased it out of its setting in the black velvet surround and turned it this way and that. His arched brows rose and fell as he examined it. He turned it upside down. I noticed him studying the bottom of the cup. "And Howard tells me this set was just handed over to you?"

"Yes. A smartly dressed older woman came in here, thrust it at me and then left. She didn't leave any contact details."

I glanced up at him again. His profile was all sharp angles, a hawkish nose and powerful jaw.

The silence was palpable. Did he know who might have crafted it? If so, he wasn't giving much away.

Xander North twisted the cup around again in his hand, before up righting it. "It's strange," he murmured, his anglified accent infused with faint traces of Scottish. "Usually, there's some sort of mark or indentation on it from the artist, but there's nothing here."

He set the teacup back into its cushioned setting. "How much do you know about crockery, Ms Harkness?"

I raised my chin. "I have some knowledge. My grandmother was a very keen collector of antique crockery. That's why I'm starting this business."

Xander North's stern blue gaze swivelled around, incredulous. "You're going to sell crockery? But this is in the middle of nowhere. Don't the locals round here already have a teapot each?"

I pinned on a tight smile, irked by his suggestion that The Cup That Cheers was the shopping equivalent of Satan's armpit. "Briar Glen attracts many tourists and the locals have been very enthusiastic and supportive about a crockery shop. It's going to be an eclectic mix of modern and traditional. The Cup That Cheers—"

He hitched a judgemental brow at me and I could feel my teeth grinding with indignation. He seemed to think he was the sole authority on all things tea sets.

"Howard said he would have assisted me with tracking

down more information about it, but he's in Venice on business – more's the pity." I let the implication hang in the air. It was such a shame Howard hadn't been around to help. I would much rather have liaised with him than with this Xander North, with his flinty stare and brusque attitude.

Xander North appraised me. "You might not be aware, but I am an expert on antique crockery."

I pressed my lips together. "I thought Howard said you were an art critic."

"That's right. I am. But I also buy and sell antique tea sets. Very successfully."

I inwardly rolled my eyes. Nothing like blowing your own trumpet.

His attention fell on the peacock tea set again. "They are a particular passion of mine."

I was having difficulty imagining this man getting passionate about anything.

Xander North slid both hands either side of the worn leather case and lifted it up from the counter. The muscles tensed under his shirt as his attention swept the top of the case, before he carefully turned it upside down to inspect the bottom of it. "I have to confess I've never seen anything like this before."

"Do you have any idea what era it might have come from or who the artist might be?"

His eyes raked the peacock motif. "The use of the gold fleck detail became very popular in the late 1800s."

"Yes, so Howard has already told me." He flashed me a look from under his sooty lashed eyes, as if to say, *So why waste my precious time by asking me then?*

I watched him gaze dismissively around the painted shop walls in their pretty lavender and misty white. "If I'm correct and this set is this old, I really don't think these surroundings are conducive."

My irritation rose. Was he implying that the tea set was in unsafe hands with me? The bloody cheek of him! "Mr North, I have been keeping the tea set in a secure place at home. I have been very vigilant looking after it and that won't change."

He arched another brow. Good grief! Anyone would think I was selling top shelf magazines to men in dirty raincoats. That was it. He was supposed to be here to give advice, not judge me or my new business.

I reached out and seized the crockery case. "Excuse me, Mr North."

His jaw dropped. "What do you think you are doing?"

"I'm looking after it," I bit back. "I will speak to Howard on his return. There's no great hurry."

Irked, Xander North motioned to me to return the case now held in my arms. It was bloody heavy, but I wasn't about to admit that to Mr Starchy here. I gritted my teeth for a moment longer under its weight, hoping the strain wasn't showing in my expression, and set it down again on Mum's spare table.

I was about to click the leather case shut, when something slid sideways out of what appeared to be a pocket secreted in the lid. It was a piece of paper.

As though it were in slow motion, it rocked like a feather in front of us and slid down to rest on the canvas sheets protecting the wooden floor.

I crouched down to retrieve it. It looked like a letter, in black, loopy handwriting.

"What is that?" asked Xander North.

He moved to read it over my shoulder but I snatched it away from his view. "I'm sure it's nothing."

He frowned at me with disapproval. "It looks like a letter."

"Yes. Well. I'm sure it's nothing for us to concern ourselves with."

I folded the letter carefully and slid it from view under the counter. I would have a read of whatever it was, once Laughing Boy here had left.

He had irked me with his preconceptions about Briar Glen and the dismissive way he had viewed my business.

I shot him another cold look. Pity Howard hadn't been around to help me instead!

Chapter Sixteen

31st March 1900

Jonathan,

Why are you and your family treating me this way?
The lies and the fabrications are cruel. You cannot hide away
forever from your guilty conscience. You must realise your
behaviour, and that of your family towards me, has been
abominable.

Though this is undeniably beautiful, I would never have done
what you implied. Nor do I want or expect any treasures. All
I want is for the truth to be known and acknowledged and for
justice to be served.

You must realise it is inevitable that one day, the truth will
prevail? You cannot escape from what has occurred and the
implications for all concerned. Would you not consider my

request for justice is therefore treated as a priority? Do you not understand what I have suffered?

I ask that you reconsider my plea and admit that I am not guilty of what I am accused of. You are only too aware of the guilty party and what I have been forced to confront.

Sincerely,
Briar Forsyth

Xander North offered his watch a pained look. "Apologies, but I really must go, otherwise I'm going to be late for my business lunch."

I was too preoccupied thinking about the flimsy, yellowing letter now under the counter that I had just read to take any notice of what he was saying.

"Ms Harkness," began Xander North again with irritation.

I snapped my head up. "Yes? Sorry."

He gave a discernible tut under his breath. "If you will allow me to take the tea set with me, I'll make contact with a celebrated pottery friend of mine. I can run it past them."

I shook my French roll. "If you don't have any objections, Mr North, I'd rather hang onto it for now."

He folded his arms across his chest. "I thought you wanted to have the set valued."

"I do," I insisted, nodding at Ally and Finn as they strolled past us into the shop, clutching their brewed coffee and a bacon roll each, which emanated a delicious smell from greasy brown bags. "But now that this letter has turned up, well, I don't mind doing a bit of digging myself."

Xander North's hawkish silhouette remained impassive. "I thought you were trying to launch your new business."

"I am," I replied.

"Multi-tasking," he murmured with a tinge of amusement.

My indignation prickled. "If you like."

He straightened the cuffs of his snow-white shirt. "So, you're not prepared to let me take the tea set?"

I could feel my cheeks ping with awkward colour under his gaze. "I would prefer to hold onto it for now."

Xander North didn't try to conceal a frustrated eye-roll. "It seems I don't have much say in the matter. Well, if you have no objections, I'll do some research into my antique crockery archives, see if there is anything of a similar design documented there."

"Thank you."

I watched him reach into his suit jacket pocket, revealing a flash of blueberry satin lining. He plucked out a black business card, embossed with gold lettering. *Xander North, Art Critic & Fine Arts Auctioneer*, followed by his email and mobile number. "I'll be in touch."

And then he strode out of the shop.

I bristled at his tone and as soon as he had disappeared, I reached under the counter for the letter and began to read its contents again.

My eyes widened at the sense of pain and anger flowing from Briar Forsyth's pen as she wrote it. Who was she? And had she been named after this town? It seemed so. It was an unusual first name to give someone, and if she was named after the town, there was a good chance she must have been local. And who was this Jonathan the letter was addressed to?

I pulled my attention away from the intriguing letter and glanced over at the tea set, its bold, marine colours and peacock motif now carrying a deeper significance. Was there some sort of connection between this Briar Forsyth, the tea set and this Jonathan? And if so, what could it be?

It was the oddest sensation. Having just read this impassioned and frustrated-sounding letter from this woman, I felt as though part of her had reached out to me; as though there were many things left unsaid in this letter, and many others that should be answered.

Chapter Seventeen

20th June 1970, Briar Glen

Helena had only worked for Mrs Auld for a couple of mornings, but she was enjoying herself.

Mondays, Wednesdays and Fridays from 9.30a.m. until 2.30p.m. had been designated her regular shift pattern at Sparkling Gifts.

The gift shop occupied the old haberdashery on the corner of the village square. Mrs Auld had worked her magic on the place, turning it from a staid little effort with basic wood and glass counters, tailored, headless dummies and dark panelled walls, into a colourful haven, laden with everything from Briar Glen embossed pens, coasters and tumblers, to notebooks, greetings cards and even tea towels that boasted of the town's immaculate gardens.

Mrs Auld had been keen to expand on her stock and had ordered in some flower-themed crockery to fill the middle, shelved section of the shop. That would be Helena's domain.

Despite the interior of the shop carrying something of a mish-mash of tartan and Scottish-inspired pictures of misty lochs and crumbling Highland castles, Helena loved it.

The couple of mornings she had worked so far, Helena would walk Marnie to school, before heading off to the shop. She would bury the festering worry about Donald discovering her little secret.

As she approached Sparkling Gifts, with its shiny windows and its sign painted duck-egg blue and silver, she allowed herself a little glow of satisfaction. The June morning was nondescript, but the other businesses were waking up from their slumber.

Helena felt part of something. She flicked her dark, shiny hair back over her shoulder and hurried in.

There had been the first delivery of crockery, and Mrs Auld, an ample-bosomed woman with a permed ball of coppery hair and warm smile, hovered over the sealed boxes that the delivery driver had deposited on the counter. "Ah. Just in time, Helena. I think these are for you."

While Mrs Auld fussed around, rearranging some ornamental picture frames, Helena tugged off her fitted white jacket and hung it in the cloakroom.

She thought back to when she was hesitating at the welcoming gift-shop door that morning after noticing the job advert, tiny pinpricks of light beaming out, like a shy, inviting smile. The opportunity had presented itself right there in front of her.

Before she married Donald, Helena had worked in a couple of different department stores in Glasgow. It was there that her passion for crockery had manifested itself.

She would read up about the latest fads and fashions for crockery, learn about Bisque pottery being the most popular type of firing, transforming the object into a porous state for glazing and allowing the potter to do much more decorative work with stains, underglazes, and glazes, with a greatly reduced risk of the pot being damaged. She learnt that many potters preferred pulled handles to strap handles, with pulled handles possessing a more organic quality and a more fluid line. So, unlike the other young women who worked beside her, Helena could enthuse with genuine knowledge about the various crockery styles and fashions, rather than just spout empty facts about how pretty that particular teacup was, or what a competitive price that teapot was going for.

Originally, Helena had been employed in the perfume department of the prestigious Glasgow store Drury's. She enjoyed being surrounded by the incessant exotic scents and the sumptuous engraved bottles, but it was the crockery department that drew her attention, with its displays of gingham tablecloths, glossy cups and ornate teapots, set amongst plumes of flowers.

So Helena, once she felt confident enough in her knowledge, braced herself and approached Mr Hannigan, the crockery department manager.

He had been puzzled at first as to why this doe-eyed young woman with the hair and the curves had wanted to switch from perfumery to his domain.

But when Helena drifted around the various displays, appreciating what she saw and talking with such enthusiasm and conviction about a teapot lid not fitting properly if it was separated during the drying process, Edgar Hannigan knew she would be an asset to his team.

Helena continued to build upon her knowledge, and after gaining further experience at Drury's for the next two years, she was headhunted by the store manager of the rival department store

Carter's. Promised an increase in salary and the role of crockery department manager, Helena was unable to resist.

Carter's was not the usual type of store Donald frequented, but he was running out of ideas for presents for his mum and hoped the crockery department might provide the answer. But, as it turned out, it wasn't the Spode or the Royal Albert that drew his attention. He'd admitted afterwards that it was the lovely sales manager, with the sparkling light blue eyes and her tumble of dark hair, that he had been far more interested in.

Her life had changed so much since meeting and marrying Donald. Now, Helena saw this job as the chance to retrieve some of her old self that she felt had become lost.

Donald had no idea his wife still longed to own her own little crockery shop; to indulge her deep love while possessing more of her own independence. He also didn't know Helena had held onto her prized tea set acquisitions.

They were all secreted away in boxes, stashed behind her assortment of shoes at the back of her wardrobe. She couldn't be parted from them. That would have been like confessing that her ambition would never come true, and she couldn't bear to think that.

Helena set her shoulders now as she occupied herself with the delivery. She was already mentally planning how she would arrange the first of these new arrivals on the empty shelves.

She had entered the door of Sparkling Gifts that day a couple of weeks ago and put it to Mrs Auld that she could boost her sales if she stocked some crockery, saying she would love to help her get her fledgling business off the ground.

At first, Mrs Auld's reluctance had been visible. But there was indeed, as Helena pointed out, a generous section of space in the centre of the shop, which needed to be filled, and after some nail-biting suspense Helena had managed to persuade her.

So here she was now, two weeks later, ready to begin another shift and another new day.

Helena's happy fingers reached for the pair of scissors on the counter and proceeded to dismiss the brown tape. She knew that it was a question of when, not if, Donald discovered what she was doing. There would be angry recriminations and accusations that she had been sly and deceitful.

But right now she refused to engage with the nagging worry lurking at the back of her mind. She was enjoying herself too much.

The next few days vanished before my eyes, as I confirmed stock orders and the delivery dates for my shiny new till and credit-card machine and looked over the designs that Ewan had come up with for signage for The Cup That Cheers.

He'd conjured up three different suggestions, which were all lovely. In the end, however, I opted for his second design. It jumped out at me from my laptop screen and there was just something so traditional and old-shoppe about it, which would complement the atmosphere I was aiming for. It composed of the words The Cup That Cheers in elaborate white looping letters on a deep lilac background.

Sat to the left, beside the word The, was a lilac and white teapot, with a matching teacup to the right of Cheers. Ewan had also designed a smaller version of the signage, which would be suspended from the silver pole above the shop door.

All the strands seemed to be coming together at the moment, which was a relief, although I wasn't prepared to take this for granted. From my previous life, I knew only too well how things could go wrong, however much organisation and forward planning went into something.

Still, if arrangements continued to progress as I hoped they would, I planned to open on 30th June.

As Ewan's email sat on my laptop screen in front of me, I curled my feet up and underneath me on the sofa.

Ewan had rung to clarify a couple of minor details and was delighted by my enthusiastic response to his artwork. He confirmed he would send an electronic invoice within the next couple of days. "Oh, any luck with the tea set that woman dumped on you the other day?"

"Not really," I admitted. "The auctioneer my late grandmother knew put me in touch with a guy called Xander North and…"

There was an impressed gasp at the other end of the line. "Did you just say Xander North? Seriously?"

"Yes. Why?"

Ewan's voice was brimming with reverence. "He delivered a lecture at my college several months ago on the topic of whether graffiti was in fact fine art. Most of the girls in the class couldn't take their eyes off him."

I gave an indignant sniff. "Well, he wasn't able to shed much light on the tea set. It even threw him. He did say he would do some research through his antique crockery archives, to see if they threw up any clues."

Ewan still sounded starstruck. "From what I have read

about him and from what he said to us, antique crockery is a labour of love for him. I don't know if he was being modest, but he told us he struck it lucky with those mega auction sales. "

My eyebrows flexed upwards. "Modest" wasn't a word I would have associated with Xander North. I was only in his company for a short time, but he gave the distinct impression he was the sort of man who winked at his own reflection every morning before heading out the door.

I made myself concentrate again on what Ewan was saying. "But he does know so many people in the art world, so I'm sure he will be able to get you a lead from somewhere."

Remembering Ewan's passion for anything arty, my eyes shot across my sitting room to the closed leather case. I'd tucked the letter back in its original place in the pouch, for fear of losing it. I thought of the desperate tone in the letter and the woman's appeals for understanding. "As it turns out, there wasn't just a tea set in that case," I admitted after a considered pause.

"Oh?" Clearly, Ewan's curiosity was fired up.

I told him about the letter, with its mysterious impassioned plea to "Jonathan". "Wow!" he exclaimed. "And you said the woman's first name was Briar? That's cool. Do you think she's a local then, with an unusual name like that?"

I picked up my half-drunk mug of tea from the glass coffee table, took a sip and grimaced. It was cold. "I wondered the same thing. It's too much of a coincidence. She must come from here and be named after the town."

Ewan murmured in agreement. "Did you ask Xander North's advice?"

I rolled my eyes. The way Ewan insisted on talking about Xander North, anyone would think he was Captain America, Spiderman and Black Panther rolled into one. "I don't think he would be anywhere near as interested in the letter as he was in the tea set."

"I bet he would be, if there is some definite connection between the crockery and the writer of that letter. Do you think there might be?"

"It's possible, but I'm not sure. This Briar Forsyth does mention something valuable in the letter, but I'm not sure whether she is referring to the tea set or not." I fiddled with the ends of my ponytail as I sat cross-legged on my sofa.

"Well, I've still got a few months on my hands yet till I go back to college," said Ewan. "Any digging about you want me to do, just say the word."

That was welcome, especially as I was intending to open The Cup That Cheers in a little over three weeks and my list of final things to check over and follow up on was growing.

"Thanks, Ewan. I appreciate that. I'll see if I can come up with anything on her too. In the meantime, I'm going to check online for any tea-set-related art to put up on the shop walls, play up the theme of what I'm selling."

"I can recommend someone, if you like. He's one of my new lecturers. His name is Jake Caldwell and his still life work in amazing. He has a website if you want to go and take a look at his work."

"Oh, that would be great," I enthused. "Thanks."

I scribbled down Jake Caldwell's name. "I'll look him up."

Once our call had finished. I entered Jake Caldwell's name into the search engine and located his website.

It was a classy black and cream affair, with some examples of his work fading in and out for effect, beside a professional, moody-looking photograph of him. He was attractive, with Slavic dark blond cropped hair and twinkly amber eyes.

I decided I should be focusing my attention more on his artistic capabilities, rather than what he looked like. And his artwork didn't disappoint either. In a section labelled "Gallery," there were gorgeous, smudgy watercolours of tables groaning with Mediterranean-style breakfasts and vases of tropical flowers, portraits of pouty, pensive women at rain-lashed windows, and a chalk drawing of an elderly man asleep in his armchair.

Then one in particular leapt out at me. It wasn't as showy as some of the other pictures, but was of a huge beige farmhouse teapot on an old wooden table.

There were two teacups, decked out with pink and yellow flowers around the saucers and brim, as well as a plate of sumptuous, flour-dusted scones. The mismatched colours and shadowy effect leapt out of the screen. It looked so real, so lifelike – my fingertips were itching to trail over the shiny, hot ceramic surface of the teapot. I was already imagining it on one of the walls in the shop.

There were no prices listed on the website, which made me wonder how expensively Jake Caldwell valued his work. The extensive bio beside his photo, listing his various commissions for minor royalty (an ex-UK Prime Minister and two, well-known Scottish actors) testified to that.

"Jake studied under the auspices of the much-lauded modern artist Dickens Muirfield in France, before making a name for himself

in the London art scene with his thought-provoking, rich and considered interpretations of the human condition," raved the bio. *"He then moved back to Scotland ten years ago, to lecture at the City School of Art and continue with his passion for producing work that not only informs, but also reaches out and ensnares the senses."*

I could feel my eyebrows twitching as I read on. If he wrote this himself, he wasn't lacking in the self-confidence department. No doubt this would be reflected in the cost of his paintings.

Still, thanks to my grandmother, I could afford to splash out a bit.

I scribbled down Jake Caldwell's mobile number from his website and decided to ring him the next day.

———————

Saturday was not a typical June day, with a stiff wind bullying the trees across from my flat.

My electronic cash register and credit-card machine were due to be delivered at 10a.m., so I decided to arrive at the shop a little before that with my laptop, so I could ring Jake Caldwell and do a bit more work on the Twitter, Instagram and Facebook accounts for the business.

I'd scribbled down ideas for having promotional offers, including one where I'd choose a unique historical "Tea Set of the Week" for the website, with a picture and a brief piece about its interesting background. I could also stage the occasional competition, asking customers to post on Twitter who they would most like to have afternoon tea with and why.

The winner could receive a teapot of their choice from my stock and a discounted voucher to pass on to a friend.

I wasn't as confident about setting up the website and resolved to have another word with Ewan, in the hope one of his art-college friends might be able to help. Thank goodness Finn had recommended his teenage son to me. The young man's expertise was proving to be invaluable.

I rang Jake Caldwell's mobile first, but his silky accent, a mish-mash of Scots and American, turned out to be his voicemail message, so I left a brief description of my new business and asked him to call me to discuss the price of his teapot painting.

The Cup That Cheers carried an air of expectation and newness, as I took a grateful sip from my flask of tea and then set up my laptop on the shop counter. As I glanced at my wristwatch, I realised that we didn't have a clock for the shop. An unusual wall clock would complement the old-world atmosphere I wanted to create.

I turned away from the counter and looked down towards the far wall. Something eye-catching would look good there.

I'd only just pulled up a website, boasting the most gorgeous and unusual assortment of wall clocks, when a movement outside the bottle-glass windows drew my attention. It couldn't be the delivery of my cash register and credit-card machine, at least not yet. They weren't due for another half an hour.

I picked up the shop keys, which were resting on the counter, and tapped over the wooden floor in my trainers. I could see through the frosted glass of the shop door that someone was hovering outside, looking in.

They moved towards the shop windows and it took a moment for my brain to catch up, before realising with a surge of excitement who it was.

It was the well-dressed silver-haired lady who had abandoned the peacock tea set.

Chapter Eighteen

My hopeful fingers fumbled and jabbed the gold key into the lock. Did she know that letter was in there? Whether she did or not, I had to talk to her about that – and the tea set.

But I was allowing my optimism to run away with me. The woman realised with a start that I'd spotted her through the window. She paled under her makeup.

Shit.

She jerked up the collar of her floaty, loose peach shirt and whirled away from the window.

"Wait!" I called in desperation, struggling to unlock the door. "Madam, please. I need to talk to you!"

I tugged open the shop door and bolted out, but she was no longer there. Not again.

I stared up and down the main thoroughfare. There were a couple of elderly gentlemen with fat weekend newspapers tucked under their arms and a little girl in a checked dress playing hopscotch on the steps of the gold and white town clock. But there was no sign of the silver-haired lady.

I closed the door behind me with a deep sense of frustration. If she wasn't bothered by the tea set, why was she still hovering around outside the shop? Perhaps she was experiencing some kind of crisis of conscience about leaving it with me? And did she even know about that letter tucked into the pouch of the crockery case? It was likely she didn't. Surely if you found something like that in a family move or clear-out, you would want to keep it and discover more about it.

Unless she did know about it and was now wondering whether she had done the right thing by handing it and the tea set over to me? Maybe she had had the tea set independently valued and now wanted it back. But if that was the case, why did she shoot off like that, rather than speak to me about it? Had she been peering through the window wondering if I was still in possession of it or whether I had already sold it on?

My rambling thoughts were interrupted by a cheery knock on the door

I unlocked the latch.

"Good morning, Miss," beamed a rotund man in dark overalls. The Saturday-morning light was sifting through his wisps of sparse, greying hair. He held up a laminated card dangling around his neck. " "Cash register and credit-card machine?"

I reached for the bunch of lilies and assorted roses I'd bought Mum and was going to take round. She had insisted on rustling up one of her delicious Sunday roasts for lunch and who was I to argue?

I removed them from the vase in the kitchen and began drying the wet stems with a square of kitchen towel, when my mobile phone let out its indignant rings in the hall.

I abandoned the flowers and hurried to answer it. A strange number glowed on the screen.

Jake Caldwell introduced himself, his voice light, with strange overtures of the States and Edinburgh.

"Thank you for calling me back, Mr Caldwell."

"It's Jake and please accept my apologies for not ringing you back yesterday. I had an urgent commission to finish."

As he spoke, I pictured the gorgeous, earthy painting he produced of the farmhouse teapot.

"So, you were interested in my farmhouse table piece?"

"That's right. I'm opening up a crockery business and I thought your painting would be perfect up on the wall."

He sounded genuinely interested. "That's great. I can see why it piqued your interest then."

I steeled myself for Jake Caldwell to reveal its price, and, as if anticipating my question, he named a figure which, although expensive, was more reasonable than I had expected. "That's fine by me," I said with a smile.

"Excellent. Well, if you give me your address, I can deliver it in person to you tomorrow."

"Are you sure that isn't an inconvenience for you?" I asked, a little surprised.

Jake Caldwell insisted it wasn't. "My studio is based to the north of the city, so it isn't an inconvenience at all."

I relayed the address of The Cup That Cheers. "Do you have a rough idea what time you will be able to drop it off?"

I heard a couple of taps on a computer keyboard in the background. "Would bringing it round to you around eleven tomorrow morning suit?"

"That would be perfect, thank you." I beamed. "I'm expecting another delivery around 10a.m."

As soon as the call ended, I plopped my mobile back into my bag and started towards the kitchen to retrieve Mum's flowers from the sink.

My phone had other ideas.

I had only got as far as my butterscotch linoleum floor when it rang again.

I whirled on my heel and darted back to answer it, not paying any attention to the screen. "Did you forget something?"

There was a puzzled pause. Then a different male voice – huskier and formal – travelled into my ear. "This is Xander North speaking."

My cheeks flipped pink with embarrassment. "Oh, I'm so sorry. I thought you were someone else."

I straightened my back.

"Is this an inconvenient time, Ms Harkness?"

I glanced down at my watch. I had a few minutes to spare before I would have to set off to Mum and Dad's. If I was really pushed for time, I could take my car, but I wanted to walk. The rain had cleared and everything outside looked rinsed and fresh.

"No, it's fine," I assured him.

"All right. Well, I managed to take a look at my crockery archives and that has given me an idea."

There was a trace of anticipation in his tone, which put me on alert. "Yes?"

"Now it may just be a coincidence, though I very much doubt it, but can you look at the underside of the teapot handle? I seem to recall there was a motif there and if there is and it's the one I think it is…" His rich voice tailed off.

I glanced up the hall towards the kitchen, where Mum's bouquet was thrusting out of the sink in a sea of ruby, vanilla and apricot blooms. My anticipation was rising. "What am I looking for?"

"A rose emblem," explained Xander North. "It will be very small."

I digested what he was telling me. "And if this rose emblem is there? What might that mean?"

Xander North sounded animated for him. "According to my research, it could mean that this tea set was crafted in the late 1800s by someone called Ernest Telfer."

It took me a moment or two to process this. "Ernest Telfer?" I repeated for assurance. "*The* Ernest Telfer?"

I could almost hear Xander North raising his arched, dark brows. "So, you have heard of him then?

"Of course I have," I answered, not able to conceal the prickle in my voice. I could recall Gran describing the delicacy of his flowers and his penchant for using nature and animals in his work. "He was by all accounts an underrated local artist, but I never would have dreamed that this tea set might be one of his."

I could feel my enthusiasm building. "Come to think of it,

when you look at the peacock tea set, it does have some characteristics of that other ceramics artist, Thomas Brogue. I think it's all the gold and the sweeping details…" I realised I was beginning to ramble on and checked myself. "My grandmother really admired Ernest Telfer's work."

Xander North had fallen so quiet down the line, I wondered for a moment if he had passed out. "Mr North? Hello? Are you still there?"

"Yes. I'm still here," he faltered. There was another brief silence. "So, you're aware of Thomas Brogue's work as well?"

"I am." Now it was my turn to go quiet. "Why do you ask that?"

Before he could reply, a thought came to me. "Ah. Is it because I own a shop, but not a degree in fine art from Cambridge?"

"Not at all," he replied. "It's just both artists are rather niche and I have to admit I was rather surprised you had heard of them."

I could hear my voice turning starchy. "Well, I might not have formally studied crockery, but you're not the only one who knows what they're talking about."

He hesitated, processing what I had just said. "It would seem so."

Then he morphed back into businesslike mode. "Now, about this possibly being an Ernest Telfer. I should warn you that it could well be an excellent copy. However, very few people knew about his secret insignia, which is a rose etching that he always put on the underside of his teapot handle."

I swallowed, my excitement gathering momentum. "Right. I see."

"Do you have the tea set to hand, Ms Harkness?"

I rubbed my hand across my brow. "Yes. Yes, I do. It's in the bottom of my wardrobe."

"Then would you like to go and take a look at the teapot handle? I will hold on here while you do."

I made a rather unattractive gulping noise. "Er … oh, yes … of course… I won't be a moment."

I set my phone down on the hall table and with jelly-like legs, made my way up to my bedroom. My anxious fingers fumbled at the closed door of the mirrored wardrobe, pushing it back to reveal the discoloured leather case, stationed beside a few of my handbags.

I eased it out and set it on top of the duvet. My heart was jumping in my chest.

I swiped my sweaty palms down the front of my jeans and reached for the clasp. It made its clicking noise and triggered the lid to glide backwards, revealing the tea set with its rich pattern and peacock motif.

I reached for the teapot and lifted it out of its cushioned setting. Part of me was fearful about looking at the handle, in case this rose emblem wasn't there after all. If it wasn't, it would feel like taking a giant step backwards.

Steeling myself, I raised the teapot mid-way into the air and removed the lid, setting it down back in the open case. The last thing I wanted to do was drop that.

I angled the teapot to one side.

My fingers travelled along the gilded gold detail, before slowly working their way around its elegant curved handle.

At first, I couldn't find anything at all. Disappointment sank in, as the tips of my fingers made their way under the handle. Then a gasp of excitement shot out of my throat, as I located the finest groove of something. I angled the teapot more to the right, eager to see what I might have discovered there.

My fingertips drew to a stop. Just under the stem of the handle was a tiny engraving.

Chapter Nineteen

It looked like it had been etched into the ceramic with a small, sharp implement and consisted of a tiny, unpainted representation of a four-petalled rose.

I sat the teapot back into the case and ran back to my phone, snatching it up. "It's there!" I breathed. "Just under the stem of the handle. A four-petalled rose."

If Xander North was excited, I wish someone had informed his voice. "Then it sounds like there is every chance it is a genuine Ernest Telfer."

"Oh, God," I gasped to myself. "Oh, God."

There was a surprised pause on his behalf. "I have to say again that I was rather taken aback that you had heard of him."

My mouth flipped into an Elvis curl of indignation. "Yes. You indicated that a moment ago. And why is that, Mr North? Is it because you assumed my knowledge of crockery only stretched as far as a Breville sandwich maker?"

An irritated sigh travelled down the line. "Don't be ridiculous. Of course not."

I stuck my tongue out, even though he couldn't see me. It made me feel a lot better.

Xander North continued, "We will have to have the set independently verified of course, but that should just be a formality. Then it can go to auction."

I held the phone tighter to my ear. A concerned thought lodged itself. "But what about the letter?"

Xander North's confusion was evident. "Sorry?"

Reluctantly, I explained about the contents of the letter concealed in the case. "Whoever this Briar Forsyth is or was, she sounded like she was in some sort of trouble." I pushed a hand into the pocket of my jeans. "Maybe the woman who left it with me did know about the letter, or at least she had some knowledge of the tea set's background. Perhaps that is one of the reasons why that lady wanted rid of it in the first place."

Xander North made a dismissive noise. "I think you are rather romanticising all this, Ms Harkness. However, a letter from that era could potentially add value to the set."

I jutted out my chin. Nice to see he was more bothered about the possible added financial value the letter could bring than about finding out its background. "It's good to know what your priorities are, Mr North," I bit back, "but I'm not letting the tea set out of my sight, until I have at least tried to find out more about that letter."

"Right. Fine. Have it your own way." There was a considered pause. "I suppose it is relevant to the provenance, so…" He paused as if trying out an alien concept. "I'll help you look into it."

I blinked in surprise. I hadn't been expecting that. "Oh. Right. Okay. Thank you." Xander North's connections would no doubt prove very useful. "That would be much appreciated."

"Yes. Well. Don't get too optimistic about it all. It might have nothing to do with the provenance at all."

The idle thought that Xander North was offering his assistance out of the goodness of his heart died like a flickering candle in a gust of wind. "Of course," I ground out under my breath. "Silly me for thinking that beneath the frosty exterior existed an element of compassion."

"Pardon?"

The glinting face of my wristwatch caught my attention before I could repeat myself. "Bugger! My mother's Yorkshire puddings will be ruined!"

_____

The Monday-morning light was spilling through the bottle-glass shop windows, as I let myself into The Cup That Cheers.

The smell of fresh paint had dissipated, the newly decorated pebbledash exterior of the shop glowed snow white, and the windowsills and door shone with their new gloss of deep lilac. Now the shelves were waiting for the delivery in a few days of the crockery and teapots.

Mum had offered to help set everything up, as had Cass, my new member of staff, who had already emailed me a few times, insisting I was to let her know straightaway if there was anything else she could help with, prior to opening.

Outside in the main street, the other shops were sleepily opening their doors and the plumes of trees over by the pedestrianised walkway, were stirring their leaf-heavy heads.

I had just removed my leather jacket and draped it over my chair in the office, when there was a polite knock on the shop door. Through the frosted glass, I could make out a tall, willowy figure, clutching something large and rectangular under their arm.

I took a closer look through the side of the nearest window. It was Jake Caldwell. He was prompt.

I straightened my sparkly T-shirt and opened the door.

"Sophie Harkness?" He had a wide smile and his amber eyes twinkled.

"Yes. Jake?" I asked, with a hint of blush.

"Guilty."

I laughed and invited him in, noting he had concealed his painting in sheets of brown paper and tied it with string. He set it down on the counter. "One painting delivered as promised."

I moved towards the counter and gestured to the wrapped painting. "May I?"

"Of course. You're buying it."

I blushed again and untied the string. The paper fell away to reveal the sweeps of watercolour. I marvelled at the way he had captured the light and shadows smudging across the teapot and teacups. There was even the odd chip and dent in the shabby wooden farmhouse table. "It's even more gorgeous, seeing it in person," I breathed.

Jake Caldwell's gaze lingered on my face. "It's always lovely to have your work appreciated. Thank you."

There was a charged silence.

"So," I said brightly, clapping my hands together. Why had I just done that? I must have looked like an idiot! The sound echoed around the empty shop like a gun going off. I cleared my throat. "What payment method would you prefer?"

Jake dashed a hand over his cropped dark blond hair. "Is a bank transfer okay?"

"Absolutely."

Once he had presented me with his bank account details, I insisted on transferring the money from my account to his straightaway.

Jake protested there was no immediate rush, but I shook my head. "No. I really would rather pay you now, and then I know where I am with my finances."

He gave a slight smile. "That's appreciated. Thank you." He took in the shop surroundings. "So not long till you open then?"

"No. We officially open on 30th June, so less than three weeks. I'm really looking forward to it."

He flashed a winning smile. "I'm sure it will be a success."

"I hope so."

"What business were you in before?"

It felt almost as though I were talking about someone else. "I was a wedding planner up at Castle Marrian. I decided to do something different," I added.

His attention lingered on my face for a few more seconds. "I'm sure you'll make a success of whatever you turn your hand to." Then he delivered a million-dollar smile, still appraising me. I gazed at his Slavic features, all sharp cheekbones and golden hair. Was I imagining it, or was Jake Caldwell flirting with me? Bloody hell! I was so out of practice with this sort of thing, it was embarrassing.

Now it was Jake Caldwell's turn to clap his hands for no discernible reason. It must be catching, like 'flu.

"Right. Well, I'll head off now." He strode towards the door, then paused. He looked over his shoulder at me, his gaze warm. "I think I may have to drop by when you open. I could do with a new teapot."

The mischievous spark in his eyes made me grin. "Please do. It won't be anything fancy, but I'm marking the opening with warm scones and tea."

Jake's eyes locked with mine. "How can I refuse an invitation like that? Count me in."

He dipped one hand inside his leather jacket, took out a business card and slid it across the white-painted counter.

"I've already got your number."

Jake's smile was teasing. "This is a back-up. I would hate for you to lose it." His eyes danced. "And you will need to find out what flavour scones I like."

Then he walked out with a confident swagger.

Chapter Twenty

3rd July 1970, Briar Glen

The last couple of weeks had vanished for Helena.

She carried on as normal, getting Marnie ready for and taking her to school, before hurrying off down the road, leaving the chattering playground noise behind her to go to work.

On Tuesdays and Thursdays, when she wasn't at work, she found herself looking forward to the following day. In her head, she would come up with promotional sales gimmicks to suggest to Mrs Auld or conjure up ideas for the crockery displays.

A couple of times, Marnie would appraise her mother with questioning blue eyes. "You look pretty, Mummy. Where are you going?"

Helena would smooth down her floral shift dress or wing-collared shirt and murmur something about going to the shops.

She felt a stab of guilt about not telling her little girl the truth, but she knew it would only take one excitable slip of the tongue from Marnie to Donald and her secret would be revealed.

There had been a summer shower, which had decorated the trees and the pavements, and gilded sunlight was now brushing its way over everything, like a delicate paintbrush.

Mrs Auld (whose first name, Helena discovered from one of the submitted invoices, was Catherine) had popped to the bank to pay a couple of bills.

Helena wasn't sure she looked like a Catherine – she seemed more of an Alexandra or Victoria – but even if Mrs Auld had insisted on Helena calling her by her first name, she would have found it difficult. Although friendly towards Helena and the customers, Mrs Auld carried a perpetual air of authority and Helena considered it was only right to continue to address her with her official moniker.

While her boss was no doubt trapped in a queue at the bank, Helena buzzed around Sparkling Gifts, titivating the tea sets and serving an elderly lady and her daughter, who were visiting the area. "We were hoping to see the blue briar rose," admitted the older lady, fishing around in her handbag for her purse.

Helena's soft smile was sympathetic. "As far as I know, Madam, the rose hasn't been seen blooming here for years, but you never know your luck."

Helena wrapped up their purchase of a jar of Briar Glen honey and a couple of postcards of the village and waved them a cheery goodbye.

Being in the snug, welcoming surroundings of Sparkling Gifts sent her imagination into a spiral. She pretended the shop belonged to her and that it was her name gliding across the sign above the door.

Mrs Auld's brown and chrome transistor radio was delivering a fuzzy rendition of "Love Grows (Where My Rosemary Goes)" by Edison Lighthouse. Helena felt herself swaying along in time to the music.

If she owned Sparkling Gifts, she would run regular competitions in the local newspaper to promote the new business. Should she suggest that to Mrs Auld? She didn't want to seem as if she were trying to tell the woman what she should do, or come across as a busybody. Briar Glen had its quota of people like that and they didn't need any more. She just wanted the shop to reach its full potential, that was all.

The sharp rattle of the doorbell made Helena swing round from behind the heavy wooden counter. That must be Mrs Auld. Oh dear! She had been away for a good twenty minutes now and would no doubt be gasping for a cuppa. Helena grinned, ready to tell her bustling boss that she was on her way to put the kettle on.

But it wasn't Mrs Auld. It was a pair of tawny eyes that belonged to a man who made her draw up.

The man, who she estimated was about thirty-five, had sweeping, collar-length dark blond hair. He gave her a wide smile.

Helena found herself flicking her hair and she didn't know why. "Can I help you?"

"I wondered if Catherine was about?"

It took a few moments for Helena to realise he was referring to Mrs Auld. The way he said her boss's first name with such confident ease threw her.

"Mrs Auld," she began, "is out at the moment. Can I take a message?"

The man's grin grew. "No, that's all right, thanks. I'll just wait for her. That's if you don't mind."

Helena noticed she had become more self-conscious under his gaze. Good grief. Was he just intending to clutter up the place until Mrs Auld returned?

Helena thought of the usual frustrated queues at their local bank.

The tellers there tended not to be known for their speed or customer service. "She could be a while." She watched him swagger backwards and forwards between their new acquisitions of boxes of Briar Glen clotted cream fudge and tartan pin-cushions.

Well, he wasn't lacking in confidence. He was making her straighten the winged collar of her top. Helena scolded herself and dropped her hands. She cleared her throat, pleased that the shop radio was now churning out Mungo Jerry.

The man was tall and clad in bellbottom jeans and a denim shirt, which seemed to enhance his louche persona. He also possessed a full mouth and a cleft in his chin, like Kirk Douglas. Helena realised she was staring and averted her eyes. He didn't appear to have a briefcase with him and the casual clothes he was wearing weren't the usual smart suit and tie that the other sales representatives wore.

Was he here looking for a job? He didn't give the impression he was keen to work in a gift shop, but then you never could tell.

The way he was strolling around the shop though, lifting and examining things, was unsettling her. Yes. That's what it was. It had nothing to do with the fact that he was very attractive. "There's no need for you to hang around," stated Helena with a greater degree of firmness. "If you leave your name and details, I'll tell Mrs Auld that you called."

To emphasise the point, Helena reached for a notepad and pencil on the counter.

The man picked up one of the tiny crystal figures in the shape of a West Highland terrier and peered at it, before placing it back on top of its gift box. He turned to Helena and said nothing for moment. His rich light brown eyes twinkled at her. "Thank you for the offer, but I'm suddenly in no great hurry."

Helena swallowed and fiddled with some change in the cash register.

Relief enveloped her when the shop doorbell announced the arrival of a couple of tourists. She waited until the new customers were distracted by the swirling plastic rack of postcards. "Look. Please don't think I'm being rude, but if you are a salesman, could you leave your details? Mrs Auld isn't very keen on cold callers."

The man's smile was teasing, which infuriated her. "Oh, I know that. The old dear is a traditionalist."

Helena's spine stiffened with loyalty. "I don't think you should be referring to Mrs Auld like that. It's not very professional."

She moved out from behind the counter. She wanted him to leave. He was making her uneasy and she didn't appreciate the way he was talking about Mrs Auld. "I think you should give me your name and the reason why you're here, please, and I'll pass it on to her."

A shocked gasp from the shop doorway made Helena jump.

"Christopher! I don't believe it! What on earth are you doing here?"

Helena watched Mrs Auld almost fall through the door when she saw the blond man. One hand flew to her mouth. She paused for a moment before picking up speed again and engulfing the stranger in a prolonged and fierce hug. She was holding onto him as if she were struggling to convince herself that he was there in the flesh. "Why didn't you let me know you were coming?"

"I wanted to surprise you."

"Well, you've certainly managed that! Come here." She planted a series of frantic kisses on his cheek. "Have you lost weight? You look a bit thinner since the last time I saw you." Her fingers reached round and ruffled the ends of his hair snaking over his collar. "And I was going to say you need a haircut, but…"

The man rolled his eyes and smiled. "But?"

She gazed up at him. "But it suits you like that."

Mrs Auld switched her attention back to Helena, like she had just remembered her employee was observing everything. She was flushed with happiness. "I see you two have already met."

A creeping embarrassment crawled over Helena. Oh no... She knew him ... and he knew her, very well, by the looks of things.

Helena noticed he had slid his arm around Mrs Auld's ample waist. Dread pooled in her stomach.

"This is Christopher," she beamed.

The man gave Helena a wink, which made her flush a deeper shade of pink. "It's Chris, but Mum always insists on giving me my Sunday name."

Mum?

Reading Helena's shocked expression, Mrs Auld let out a tinkle of mischievous laughter. "Helena, I'd like you to meet my son."

My new Cunningham Clan purple tartan curtains were delivered not long after Jake Caldwell's departure.

I proceeded to hang them on the white curtain poles that Dad had installed for me, scooping them back in their purple ribbon tie-backs and allowing them to frame the window, like a gilded frame would enhance a painting. They complemented the white shelves and lilac walls and would add a touch of pizazz to the many window display themes I would have to come up with.

I had rung Dad, asking if he could drop by to help me put Jake Caldwell's new painting up on the far wall. He said he could be there in about ten minutes. There was also a dodgy light fitting I wanted to ask Dad about. It had come loose and was dangling down like a jungle vine into the centre of the shop.

Moments later, there was a knock on the shop door.

I stepped back from admiring my new painting acquisition, which I'd propped up against the skirting board of the wall I wanted to put it up on. "Blimey, Dad. You were quick."

I yanked open the door, to be confronted not by my silver-haired, craggy-faced father, but by Xander North.

"I know I might have had a bit of a rough night, Ms Harkness, but I hope I don't look like your father." His dark, intense looks remained impassive.

I invited him into the shop. "No. No, of course not," I blustered, wrong-footed. "I'm expecting my father to arrive soon to help me put up that piece of art over there."

Xander stepped further into the shop space, looking at me and unaware of the dangling light from the ceiling. "Xander! Look out!"

But it was too late. He turned his head and gave his forehead a swift bang against the silver and white light fitting. "Sod it! Ouch!"

"Oh, God! Are you all right?"

Xander had one hand on his forehead. "Yes, I'm great. Terrific, even. I've just walloped my forehead on this sodding thing!"

I guided him to behind the counter and ordered him to sit down on one of the two stools. "Now, where does it hurt?" As soon as I asked him that, I could have bitten off my own tongue.

"My left knee," he growled, glowering out of one turquoise eye. "Where the hell do you think it hurts?"

I bit back a laugh. "I've got a first-aid kit in the store room."

I gestured to him to remain seated and went to fetch the first-aid kit. I hurried back with it towards Xander, who remained seated and grumbling to himself. His right hand was still placed on his forehead.

I put the red plastic box – a gift from Mum – on the counter and unfastened it. I let out a snort of laughter. Was Mum expecting me to undertake open-heart surgery? There was everything inside it, from waterproof plasters and bandages to safety pins, disinfectant, insect repellent and arnica cream.

"Once you've quite finished perusing the contents, Ms Harkness, I wouldn't mind some attention here?"

I felt my cheeks redden. I reached for a pack of the cold compresses Mum had bought from the chemists and wrapped one in one of the small hand towels she had also placed in the bottom tray. Did she think I was going to deliver someone's baby? "Here," I said, guiding Xander's hand away from his forehead. "Place this on it."

"Thanks."

As the cold hit his skin, he winced.

I moved in a little closer and received a wave of his aftershave, which reminded me of salty, crashing waves. His lashes were long and furling. I focused on his forehead. "I think you might have a bit of a bump there later."

"No! Really? Whatever makes you think that?"

"There's no need to be sarcastic. I'm trying to help."

"What would have helped is if you hadn't left that death trap hanging there."

"And if you had been more careful where you were going, you wouldn't have done that!"

Xander opened his mouth to say something else, but decided against it and clamped it into a flat line.

"Here," I murmured, picking out the tube of arnica cream. "Put some of this on it."

"What is it?"

"It's cyanide," I ground out. "What do you think it is?"

His eyes blazed. "That's why I'm asking."

Oh, good grief! "It's arnica cream. It's very good for bumps and bruises." I eyed him. "How are you feeling right now?"

"Like an utter dick. Now, do you have that cream there, please?"

So, concussion looks unlikely then, I thought to myself.

I took the tube and squeezed the end of it. "Give me your other hand and I'll put some arnica cream on your finger."

Xander removed the cold compress for a second. His handsome but stony face examined mine. "It might have escaped your notice, but I'm not a cyclops. I'm struggling to see what I'm doing." He flicked his eyes away from me for a second. "Would you mind putting some of that on my massive, melon-sized lump, please?"

I planted one hand on my hip. "I can assure you that there is no melon there – well, apart from the one sitting on the stool."

Xander pulled a sarcastic face. "Very droll."

I asked him to lower the bright blue compress from his forehead. If there was a bump there, it was tiny. The area was red and beginning to morph into fetching shades of claret and purple. "Here. Sit still, please."

Xander angled his chin upwards and I tried not to stare at his square-jawed profile and the way his crisp, dark waves fell over each other. I cleared my throat and smoothed some of the cream over the bruising.

My fingers shifted over Xander's skin, rubbing in the arnica cream in small, deliberate circles. He gave a tiny flinch. "If you're a good boy, you might get a sticker."

Xander raised his eyes to me.

An odd sensation shifted through me, making me snap my fingers away, as though I'd been plugged into a set of jump leads.

I turned away, snatched up the tube of arnica and fiddled for a few seconds with the lid. *For goodness' sake, Sophie! What is the matter with you?*

I managed to screw the lid back on and shoved it back into the first-aid box. "There," I exclaimed far too loudly. "All done."

I turned back around to see Xander was studying me. "Thank you."

"You're welcome."

I picked up the first-aid box, eager to put some space between us. "So why crockery for you? Why did you become so interested in it?"

Xander stared up at me. "My late father was always fascinated by antiques and often brought weird and wonderful objects home. It drove my mother mad." There was a ghost of a smile. "Then, one day, he returned from an auction with this stash of crockery. One set in particular – it was a Royal Porzellan design, set in pearl porcelain – well, that was it. I was captivated by it." He flicked me another look as he continued talking. "It depicted three mysterious girls on it. They looked like wood nymphs. I must have only been about eight at the time, but the craftsmanship and beauty of it stole my imagination."

There was another faint twitch of his mouth, hinting at a smile. "Then I started wondering who had owned it and where it had come from. According to me, everybody from pirates to princes had used it." ·

Xander explained that he and his parents lived in Jedburgh, a pretty market town in the Scottish Borders, and that his mum still resided there. "She is a keen landscape painter, so she gets plenty of inspiration with the scenery. I make sure I drive down there to see her as often as I can." He gave a shrug." I was surrounded by art from an early age. I think my future in the arts was preordained."

"So, you studied art at university?" I asked.

"Fine art at Oxford and then I went on to study ceramics and glass for another three years in Glasgow. The pottery and ceramics side was always my first love." He looked more relaxed. "That's what I love about living in this part of the world. There are so many museums and art galleries close to town, which you can lose yourself in."

Xander's fingers reached for his forehead. "I think you missed your calling," he teased to my retreating back. "That feels better already."

I returned the first-aid box to the store room and loitered in there for a few moments, in order to compose myself.

I smoothed my hair before lifting my chin and striding back towards Xander, who was still seated behind the counter. His attention was locked onto the painting behind me. It was as though the air in the shop had frozen around him. His square jaw clenched as he examined it. "Is that a Jake Caldwell?"

"Yes, it is. Are you a fan of his work?"

Xander's grim expression drew darker. "No." He continued to stare at the painting with such ferocity, I half expected it to burst into flames at any moment. He swung back to me. "Where did you get it?"

It took me a few seconds to reconcile the almost flirtatious man of two minutes ago with the one now glowering at Jake's picture. "From his website. I happened to notice the painting—"

"Do you know him?"

I blinked back, noting the rough edge that had crept into his voice. "No. But I did meet him earlier. He insisted on bringing the painting round himself."

He allowed himself another scowl at the painting. Why had he flipped like that, from charming to morose? I glanced over my shoulder at the moody watercolour painting. It was something to do with Jake Caldwell. That was clear. But whatever the issue was, he wasn't prepared to discuss it with me.

"So, I have some news, which I was going to tell you before my little accident."

He rose from the stool and stuffed his hands into the pockets of his navy jeans.

"You don't have the tea set with you at the moment, do you?" Xander had reverted to his regular stand-offish persona.

I shook my blonde plait. "Sorry, I don't. I've left it for safe keeping in my flat." A thought came to me and I moved towards the counter to retrieve my phone. "But I did take a couple of new photos of it. I concentrated on close-ups of the rose emblem."

I pulled up the two photographs I took and passed my phone to him.

Xander's long, spiked lashes fluttered as he studied the pictures of the just visible rose etching on the underside of the teapot handle. "It's just as I expected."

My heart quickened. "So, you think it is an Ernest Telfer original?"

Xander nodded his dark head. "Everything is pointing that way."

My hand flew to my chest. "Bloody hell. I wish my late grandmother was here right now. She would love all this." I swallowed and gathered myself together.

Xander flicked me an unreadable look. "So, this news I have," he announced after a pause. "It's to do more with that letter, rather than the tea set itself."

I could feel my eyes widening in my face.

"Now, please don't get all excited," he cautioned. "It could all come to nothing."

Before Xander could finish what he was saying, I hurried to my office and retrieved the two deckchairs Mum had left behind for me to use. I gestured for him to sit down.

Xander eyed his lime-green, black and daffodil-yellow striped affair as though it were about to take a sizeable chunk out of his leg. I concealed a smile as I sat down in mine. If I hadn't known any better, I might have thought he had never sat in a deckchair before.

Xander dashed a hand over the top of his dark hair, careful not to aggravate the attractive bruise now popping up above his right brow. Was he that posh that he had never clapped eyes on a folding chair before? He was all legs in it.

"Well, it looks like we may have a positive lead in the hunt for more information about Ernest Telfer, through an arts contact of mine."

I nodded, encouraging him to explain.

"And," he continued, "although Saffy – Saffron Clements – isn't from this area, she knew someone very well who was."

I leant further forward in my daisy-studded, lemon-coloured chair. I attempted to read his expression, but all I received in return was a roll of the eyes.

"Good grief, Ms Harkness. I'd better tell you before you pass out."

He leant forward too now, steepling his hands together. His chair let out an indignant creak. "Saffy's great-grandfather was born and grew up near here, in Darroch. He was a librarian and was fascinated by local history. I assume that's how she was aware of the work of Ernest Telfer."

My optimism was growing. Perhaps we would be able to find out more about the letter, after all. "Well, I'm ashamed to say that although I am local, I don't know much about Briar Glen's history, other than the town was named after the blue briar rose that was said to grow around here."

Xander North's expression was clouded with cynicism. "Ah yes. The elusive blue flower. Saffron mentioned that."

I frowned at him. "So you don't believe in it?"

"Saffy did some digging around for me in her great-grandfather's research and journals on Briar Glen. From what he wrote, he believed there was such a thing as this unusual blue shade of rose that grew around here, but I'm sceptical."

Why didn't that come as any great shock to me?

I folded my arms, feeling protective of the pretty little town where I was born and grew up. "Of course, you are entitled to your opinion, Mr North. I admit it could be a tale perpetuated to bring in the tourists, but even so ... well, sometimes, it's good to let your imagination run free and escape for a while."

Xander eyed me from his deck chair. "Are you always so doe-eyed, Ms Harkness?"

Now it was my turn to cock an eyebrow. "And are you always so infuriating, Mr North?"

His mouth gave a momentary twitch. "Not always."

I watched him rise out of the chair and stretch, as though he had been trapped in a mediaeval torture device for six hours. "Dependent on how busy you are with this place, I wondered if you would be interested in meeting Saffy Clements."

"I thought you weren't interested in finding out more about that letter."

Light through the shop windows drizzled through Xander's hair, lifting strands of deep red. "You're right. I'm not. My interest is in the tea set."

How could he be so dismissive of that letter?

Xander indicated the empty painted shelves running around the walls. "When is your stock arriving?"

"Thursday"

"So, you're all organised and ahead of schedule?"

"Yes," I answered, wondering where this was leading. "I'm just waiting for my dad to arrive to help me put up that painting. Why?"

Xander North strode towards The Cup That Cheers' shop door, careful to avoid the dangling light fitting, and flicked it open. "Why don't you call your dad and delay him for a little while? No time like the present to go and speak to Saffy, is there?"

Chapter Twenty-One

S affron Clements' ceramics studio was on Glasgow's leafy south side in the basement of an old Edwardian solicitor's office.

It was stately grey stone and had a set of sturdy steps leading down to it, with two thrusting ferns either side of a glossy black door. A ceramic plaque beside the large sash window proclaimed, *Clements Ceramics*.

Xander led the way and pressed the intercom, saying his name into the speaker. There was a throaty laugh and then the door clicked to let us in.

It was a jumbly open-plan office space with mismatched chairs, a cluttered desk to the right and a couple of illuminated cabinets, highlighting an assortment of beautifully crafted glazed crockery, presumably made by the lady herself.

At the back was another door, which I assumed led to Saffy Clements' studio. This door eased open and a curvy, attractive brunette with milky skin and cinnamon freckles sashayed out.

She was wearing a loose-fitting T-shirt, splattered with clay, and tight jeans.

Her dark eyes glittered at Xander. "Hello, handsome. And to what do I owe the pleasure?"

As she neared Xander, she noticed the bruising on his forehead. "Oh my God, Xan! What have you done to yourself?"

Xander dismissed her fawning. "I haven't lost an eye, Saffy. I wasn't looking where I was going." He had the good grace to flick a long sideways look my way.

She reached up and brushed her fingers over his bruise. "Is it painful?" she enquired in a husky voice.

Then, noticing my presence, Saffy's big flirty smile withered. Was it just me or had the temperature in here plummeted?

Xander was oblivious. "Saffy, this is the lady I was telling you about. Sophie Harkness."

She pinned on a tight smile that didn't reach her eyes and extended a hand. "Nice to meet you."

"Likewise," I replied, shaking her hand. "I hope we aren't disturbing you."

Her gaze swivelled back to Xander. "Oh, I'm used to this one strolling in as though he owned the place."

But Xander was too preoccupied by one of Saffy's vases in the display cabinet to reply.

The look of adoration Saffy was bestowing on him was like a flower drinking in the sun on a spring day.

Xander returned his attention to Saffy. "I wondered if you could spare us a few minutes to look at the notes in your great-grandfather's journals? It's the notes he made about the Briar Glen area that we're especially interested in."

"Of course. Come with me."

She hooked hunks of her wild, dark curls back behind her ears and led us behind her reception desk, where an office computer sat amongst invoices and sketches. The door Saffy had come through had slipped open a little further and I could make out it was her studio. The sound of a radio seeped out. There was a long wooden table in the centre of the room and an electric pottery wheel, together with an assortment of buckets, an old refrigerator, a sturdy sink and a ceramic kiln in the corner.

Saffy pulled up a couple of electronic files on the screen and after a few moments, pictures of neat, considered handwriting appeared. Her great-grandfather's name, Victor George Prentice, was printed in bold type on the covers of each of the three journals.

"I don't know how useful some of this will be to you, "she admitted, increasing the size of the pages so that we could read them better. "What I did find strange though, is that my great-grandfather always seemed such a meticulous man – he was a librarian, so he was used to keeping records in good order – but there are sections of his notes that appear to be missing."

Her freckled hand closed around the mouse.

Xander and I leant in a little closer together towards the screen. Saffy's eyes narrowed at our close proximity. "I've read bits and pieces, but not as much as I would like. It's one of these things I keep promising I will do during my breaks, but work keeps getting in the way."

There were a number of paragraphs that Saffy's great-grandfather had written about Briar Glen's population and layout, together with sketchy notes on the rumoured blue rose. But it was as we were about to move on to the next page that an excited breath lodged itself in my throat.

"Could you go back, please?" I asked Saffy.

Xander turned to look at me. "What is it? Did you see Briar Forsyth mentioned?"

I shook my plait. "No. It wasn't her name I read." I scanned over the few lines again, to make sure I hadn't imagined it.

I pointed to the section up on the screen, written in the neat, confident black handwriting of Saffy's great-grandfather. "See whose name Mr Prentice has mentioned and why?"

I turned to Xander, hope and excitement tugging at me. "Jonathan. Jonathan Gray."

Xander shrugged. "Sorry?"

I jabbed my finger at the computer screen. "Jonathan was the name of the man this Briar Forsyth wrote to." My attention flew back to the images on the screen. "I think this Jonathan Gray mentioned here could be him."

Chapter Twenty-Two

Saffy peered at her great-grandfather's writing and read what he had said about Jonathan Gray. "Victor's not singing his praises, is he?"

Xander rubbed at his chin. I noticed it was carrying the faintest peppering of black stubble. With the light from the screen highlighting his concentrated expression, he began to read the journal notes for himself.

24th December 1899

Christmas Eve and yet the festive spirit seems to have eluded certain individuals.

I had the misfortune to come across Mr Jonathan Gray, as I travelled from the library in Briar Glen on my return journey to Darroch.

The snow was whirling itself into a frenzy and the trees appeared so forlorn, their heads heavy with ice.

I was preparing to board the carriage, when Gray appeared with a woman. He failed to notice me ascending the carriage steps. He was far too preoccupied, appearing to accuse this slight, distraught young lady of something.

I recall the haunting pain in her eyes, and the skirts of her gown being whipped about her ankles by the relentless cold.

The coach driver insisted we wait for another moment longer, in the hope that he might secure a few more travellers, and so I was able to sit within the confines of the carriage and witness the sorry spectacle of Gray and this distressed young lady exchanging words out in the snow.

I was unable to hear his words, but I could detect by his expression his fury and her visible heartbreak. There was one point in the conversation where he reached for her arm and gripped it tight in his gloved hand.

Infuriated at the sight of this aggressive behaviour, I started to rise from my seat, intending to intervene and put an end to what I was witnessing, when the carriage driver announced that we were to leave. He was concerned that the inclement weather would grow worse and he, his horses and myself could fall prey to the conditions.

As we set off across the cobbled town square, with the moon a frosty chip in the sky and the squeals of excited children echoing through the streets, I overheard Gray's voice, strident and sharp. "You tell anyone about this, you trollop, and I shall ruin you and that tawdry family of yours!"

I strained my head, clasping the scarf at my throat to keep out the chill wind. The woman gripped the ribbon under her chin securing her bonnet. Her eyes were almost childlike, and swimming with tears.

She reached out her gloved hand in an effort to appease him;

perhaps to make him understand. "But Jonathan, I want nothing from you, except that you acknowledge what has happened."

Our coach began to swing to the right, the horses' hooves plodding through the fresh snow.

The figures of Jonathan Gray and the young woman were slipping away from me, silhouetted shadows in the descending darkness, like pieces placed upon a chess board.

But as the driver of the coach eased us out onto the lane, Gray was marching away from his female companion. His top hat wobbled furiously as he moved. She appeared to say something else, before skittering after him in her shabby ankle boots.

Whatever she had said caused him to draw up, his dashing face contorted in fury. He swung round to confront her, his gold-topped walking cane winking like the decorations dripping from the Briar Glen Christmas tree in the church grounds. "Stay away from me, you hussy! And stay away from my parents, otherwise I shall wreak revenge on you, the likes of which you cannot begin to imagine!"

The last, resounding image in my head as my carriage departed, leaving this painful scene behind, was Jonathan Gray striding away towards his waiting coach and horses and the anguished young woman, sinking to her knees in the carpet of snow.

I let out a long, slow breath. Reading over Victor Prentice's version of these events was like being dragged there myself into the sparkling scene of Christmas Eve. I could see the distraught young woman, the chill wind biting at her bones, and the callous, well-dressed young man verbally berating her before striding away, leaving her on her knees with her gown clinging to her in the deep, crisp snow.

Even Xander fell silent for a moment. He turned to me. "So

you think the Jonathan in that letter you found is this Jonathan Gray?"

"I think there's a good chance. And if it is, this poor young woman he abandoned in the snow could well be Briar Forsyth, the lady who wrote the letter to him."

Standing behind Xander, Saffy observed us both. "There's more information contained in his other diaries and journals. He was a prolific notetaker."

She angled herself in front of Xander and presented him with a dazzling smile. "How about I email them over to you and if you have any questions, you can give me a call?"

"Thanks, Saffy. That would be very helpful. Oh, and if Sophie gives you her email address, can you send them to her as well, please? It's something we're checking out together."

I could feel myself shrivelling under her furious gaze.

"Sure," she managed after a moment. Her pale pink lips drew back in a cold smile. "I guess every Sherlock needs a Dr Watson."

Chapter Twenty-Three

25th September 1970, Briar Glen

Helena's love for her job grew.

Okay, so Sparkling Gifts didn't carry the same traditional old glamour that Carter's or Drury's did, but she woke up on those three mornings every week looking forward to seeing friendly faces from the local community and meeting new customers.

She assured herself that her enthusiasm for the little gift shop had nothing to do with Chris Auld.

Chris would drop in a few times a week, which always happened to coincide with when Helena was on her shift. He would chat to her about his mother, life in general and the three men's fashion businesses he had just invested in.

Helena found herself looking forward more and more to Chris's visits. She would make an extra effort with her hair and choose one of her smarter dresses or pretty, flower-sprigged shirts and flares.

She assured herself that it was because she wanted to be well turned out as she was representing Mrs Auld and *Sparkling Gifts*. Underneath the protestations, she knew better.

Mrs Auld had explained to Helena that Chris had decided to stay on in Briar Glen for a bit, rather than return to London and his rented flat. "He said there's more business opportunities up here at the moment."

Helena had nodded, a warm glow of delight lighting up inside of her. She didn't want to begin to imagine how empty and fragile her life would be without Chris there.

They fell into an easy pattern. Chris would drop by and time his visits so that he could escort Helena to the park across from the village for her tea break. They would sit on a bench, nursing polystyrene cups of washed-out tea and throw their heads back, laughing at something stupid that had happened in the shop, or Chris would regale her with stories about growing up with his indomitable mother and easy-going father. "It's a good job Dad was so malleable," mused Chris, grimacing as he took a mouthful of tea. "Heaven knows what life would have been like if he'd been a force of nature like my mother."

The September sun was playing hide and seek behind the trees and coppery leaves were cartwheeling around their feet. Helena glanced down at her watch. Her tea break was always over too quickly. She huddled deeper into her fake fur jacket.

"What do you want to do with your life, Helena?"

She drained the remnants of her tea and popped the cup into the bin beside their bench. "Wow! That's a big question!"

Chris's eyebrows arched. "Well?"

When he was looking at her like that, all interested, blazing tawny gaze, she struggled to have coherent thoughts. "I want to be a good mother to Marnie. I want her to look on me as a friend as she gets older, not just as her mum."

"You're already doing that," he answered in his assured but strange accent. "I mean, what do you want to do for you?"

She shot him a look. "You'll laugh."

"I bet I don't. Well, unless you tell me you want to become a professional footballer."

Helena grinned at him. "I might be very good at football."

"You could be. There's so many things I want to find out about you."

Heat charged through her and she found herself wishing she still had that silly polystyrene cup to play with.

Chris shuffled a little closer along the bench. His blond fringe was lifting in the breeze. "Go on. Talk to me."

She pulled a face. "All right. You did ask. Well, I would love to have my own crockery shop one day. I know it doesn't sound exciting or grand, but it has always been an ambition of mine."

When Chris didn't say anything, she let out a bark of embarrassed laughter. "See? I told you it was silly."

Helena let her gaze drift away from the autumnal horizon and back to Chris beside her.

"I'm not laughing and I don't think it's silly at all." He adjusted his leather blazer. "I think if you did something like that, it would be really successful." He fingered his empty cup. "What does your husband think about it?"

Helena blinked. It was an awful thought, but she felt like Donald was intruding on their conversation. "Oh, I don't talk about it much to him. Well, not at all. I did mention it once or twice when we first got married, but he just dismissed it."

"Why?"

Helena shifted. "He's a bit old-fashioned. He thinks once a woman gets married, they should stay at home."

Chris processed this. "Right. Well, everyone is entitled to their own opinion, of course, but I don't happen to agree with him."

She would have been very surprised if he had. She found herself smiling.

Looking down at her watch, she shot up from the bench. "Oh hell! I had better get back to the shop, otherwise your mum will be docking my wages."

"Helena." Chris's hand reached out and rested on her fluffy white sleeve. "You mustn't let him clip your wings. You're clever, you're ambitious and you're beautiful…"

Helena couldn't look at him. All these moments were moulding together into something that she was treasuring and didn't want to stop. "Chris…"

They stared at each other, the lazy golden sun glancing off their faces.

"It's just a pipe dream," she explained as they fell into step beside one another, Helena's long white lace-up boots clipping alongside Chris's buckled loafers. "I told you, Donald doesn't even know I've got this job. I don't know how much longer I can manage to keep that quiet, and once he does find out, which I have no doubt he will, he'll be furious."

Chris's handsome face tightened. "You shouldn't have to keep it a secret that you have a job."

She clutched her bag to her side. "Yes. Well… I almost got found out the other week. One of Donald's work colleagues came up to the village for a doctor's appointment and he told Donald he was sure he saw me working behind the counter in the gift shop. Luckily, Donald didn't believe him."

Chris gave Helena a sideways glance as they ventured out of the park gates and across the road. "I bet your husband wouldn't object if you had your own business that was making you a good income."

She shrugged. The lights from Sparkling Gifts spilt out onto the pavement.

"What time are you finishing up here today, Helena? Two-thirty as usual?"

"Yes. Why?"

"Meet me again at the park entrance as soon as you finish."

Helena's heart revved in her chest. "But I've got to collect Marnie from school."

"Don't worry. I won't keep you too long. Please?"

Helena couldn't resist. "All right, but I can't be late for her. What is this about?"

But Chris just winked, flapped his leather jacket and strode off.

All Helena could do was gaze after him.

Xander frowned across at me as we drove back to Briar Glen.

"You shouldn't be reading in a moving vehicle. It will make you feel queasy."

I glanced up from my phone screen as the scenery of swish office blocks and smoky-glassed, expensive restaurants gave way to the familiar woodland of Briar Glen that reminded me of broccoli clumps. Brown tourist signs announced, *"Welcome to our town, where the famous blue briar rose was said to grow in abundance and a warm Scottish welcome is always guaranteed."*

"Thanks, Dad. I'll bear that in mind."

Xander's brows bunched together. "Can't you leave all that reading till you get back home?"

I continued to scroll through the email of documents Saffy had forwarded to us both – albeit grudgingly to me. "I could," I admitted, my frustration growing. "But I'm keen to see if Saffy's great-grandfather has given any more details about that cad Jonathan Gray."

Xander flicked his indicator right, the light sparking against the windscreen of his sporty little Mazda. "Cad?"

"Well, how would you describe a man who abandons a woman in the snow on Christmas Eve?"

Xander flashed me a look from out of the corner of his eyes. "We don't know the whole story."

"No, I forgot," I added crisply. "It's a common occurrence to argue out in the street on Christmas Eve and threaten all sorts, before leaving the other person at the risk of the elements."

Xander offered me a withering stare, but said nothing.

I clicked away from the copious diary entries and scanned through my gallery of photographs. The ones I had taken of the peacock tea set popped up and I enlarged them for closer inspection. What part did the crockery play in all of this? Did it even play a part at all? Or had Briar's letter just been stuffed into the crockery case to conceal it?

Xander returned me to the car park behind The Cup That Cheers and watched me snatch up my bag from the footwell passenger side. "Thank you for taking me over to Saffy's," I said.

He gave a shrug. "Not a problem."

I clambered out. Whatever his reasons for helping me

unearth the background to Briar's letter, he was assisting. I ducked my head down to speak to him through the open car door. "The official opening of the shop is on the 30th at 10a.m. You're welcome to drop by. There will be warm scones and tea, as well as all my new stock on display. Something might take your fancy."

I realised what I'd said and cleared my throat. "I meant the crockery."

My cheeks stung as Xander's eyes stayed locked with mine. "I know what you meant."

"Well, anyway..." I said, hoping I sounded breezy. "Feel free to drop in."

He thrust on a pair of mirrored sunglasses which he leant over to retrieve from his glove compartment. "I might just do that, Ms Harkness. And let's agree to keep each other informed of any new developments with that letter, okay? Then we can move to auction."

He streaked off up the lane towards the main road, as I watched with renewed irritation and disappointment. Was that all that he was concerned about? Getting his commission and media space over the peacock crockery, rather than discovering the story behind it and why that woman had insisted on dumping it on me in the first place?

I fumbled about in my bag for my shop door keys, annoyed at myself for thinking that Xander might have had a shred of interest in Briar's letter, rather than simply been preoccupied with what he would gain financially from the tea set. That was the trouble with some people, I growled to myself. They had no soul.

It was like Christmas Day.

The floor of The Cup That Cheers was piled high with treasures. Everything from funky polka-dot designs to traditional Wedgwood flowers, Aynsley China sets, Portmeirion Water Garden and European Titanium in dark gold.

I hoped I had covered all the bases, appealing to every taste and budget. As I caught glimpses of arched spouts, gilded handles and glossy saucers, my heart sang with appreciation and utter fear. Gran would have loved all this.

Ewan had delivered the shop sign a short while ago, which Dad and one of his carpentry buddies were going to put up for me that afternoon.

As I had imagined, it was beautifully hand painted, with *The Cup That Cheers* scrolling across it in sweeping white lettering on a deep lilac background, with a teapot and a teacup and saucer on either side. It looked so artistic and elegant; you would never know the paints were waterproof PVC inks.

The smaller version of the sign, also created with waterproof UV inks, was to be suspended from the pole just above the shop door.

After erecting the signs, Dad had offered to put up a curtain pole at the front door to the shop, so that the smaller set of tie-back curtains I'd bought could be installed. They were made from the same Cunningham Clan purple tartan, and as soon I had glimpsed them online, I'd known they would look perfect, just as they did at the bottle-glass window. It gave the interior of the shop an extra cosy feel.

The whole concept and feel of The Cup That Cheers, with its window display, assortment of crockery and air of indulgence, was now finally coming together.

Cass was buzzing with enthusiasm as she helped Mum arrange some Day-Glo teapots and matching cups on a middle shelf. "Talk about being spoilt for choice," she said with a grin.

Mum smiled over at her. "I know. I think you girls are going to have a lot of customers struggling to decide what they want."

"Hopefully, they will be so undecided, they will opt for more than one set," I said, laughing, wiping my hands together and sizing up the empty window space. I had a rough idea how I wanted my first window display to look and had lined the windows with large sheets of purple canvas so as not to give anything away, and protect my artistic endeavours until Monday's grand opening.

Good grief. I couldn't quite believe that it was almost that time. I just hoped I hadn't forgotten anything.

As Mum and Cass hummed along to a Carly Simon song drifting out of the radio, I peered into some of the boxes of stock beside me. Adrenalin and anticipation, combined with a deep sensation of feeling frazzled, coursed through me.

In the last few days, I'd not only been preoccupied with making final preparations for the shop, but I had also been busy reading again through the substantial notes by Saffy Clements' great-grandfather, in the hope of discovering more about Jonathan Gray and Briar Forsyth. Could there be any other clues to what happened between them, that I might have missed?

I was convinced there must be more leads contained in those diaries and journals. It was just a case of being patient, wading through and locating them.

Xander had rung and texted on several occasions, explaining that his art-critic and assessment work had been taking up a lot of his time, but assuring me that he was still working his way through his crockery research and the journals, in the hope of unearthing something of value. As for Jake, there had been no further contact from him. I'd concluded from this that the flirting had been because I'd purchased one of his paintings. My pride had been stung a little, but oh well; I had far more important things to concentrate on.

I covered my hand with my mouth as I let out a most unladylike yawn.

Mum tapped up beside me in her boat shoes. "I hope you're pacing yourself, young lady. These past couple of weeks in the run-up to opening, you've been racing here and there like a demented thing."

I must have looked guilty, because she planted her hands on her hips and frowned. "As soon as we are done here, I want you to go home and relax in the bath. No shop business and no reading of diaries for the rest of the day. That's an order."

I reached for a lilac and white tea set, dusted with purple forget-me-nots, and began arranging it in the window on a matching gingham cloth I'd ordered from the fabric company that supplied the canvas for the windows. I'd bought some gorgeous and very lifelike blue roses from an on-line florists recommended by Cass, and I began to place them around the crockery. I thought that would be a nice homage to my home town ... if the rose story was true after all. Good grief! I was starting to sound like Xander North.

"Mum, I will take it easy for the rest of the day," I promised.

She gave me one of her gimlet looks. "Please make sure you do." She nodded her appreciation of my shop-window colour scheme.

Cass wandered over, holding a stripy red and white teapot. "That will look lovely."

I straightened up. "Thank you. I thought I should keep our first window display simple, by following the lavender and white colour scheme of the shop." Once the blue rose Briar Glen tea set had arrived, I intended to place that at the forefront of the display and prop a couple more of the fake powdery blue roses either side of it.

Warming to my theme, I went on to explain my ideas about having themed windows. "I thought we could go for red, russet and amber sets on display at the start of autumn, orange shades for Halloween, and really go to town at Christmas with ruby and green shaded crockery, tinsel, fairy lights ... the works!"

"And for spring, pale lemons and creams for a daffodil theme with Easter eggs and then for summer, maybe crockery featuring strong seaside yellows and blues, with perhaps the odd bucket and spade and toy sailing boat beside them?" suggested Cass.

I grinned back at her. "Absolutely! Oh, I can just picture it now."

Cass nodded her swishy brown ponytail. "I bet that Briar Glen tea set will look gorgeous. Expect to receive a lot of enquiries about it."

I leant towards the window space again to fiddle with a couple of the roses I'd placed there. "I hope so. I bet it generates extra commissions for the artist, Noah, as well. From what Ewan was telling me, the poor lad is the epitome of a struggling artist. He's in the third year of his ceramics course."

"Well, I'm sure you will both do well out of it." Mum whirled round at the sound of a brisk knock on the locked, shop door. "Oh! That might be the Briar Glen tea set being delivered now."

"That would be perfect timing if it is," I said. "It will be easier to get the rest of the display finished, if I have that set to work around."

But it wasn't the commissioned tea set. It was Xander.

Cass and Mum admired the tall, dark-haired stranger as he strode in.

Xander nodded at them in greeting and indicated the crockery beginning to occupy the shelves. "Busy, I see? How's it all going?"

"We are getting there. My dad is dropping by this afternoon to install a couple of small spotlights above each of the shelves."

He glanced over his shoulder at Mum and Cass, who had taken themselves further down the shop to clear away some bubble wrap. "I just came by to see how it was all going. It's looking good. I like the eclectic mix of..." He stopped talking, his attention alighting on the Jake Caldwell painting again, now adorning the far wall.

A pulse point throbbed in his gritted jaw. "I have to say I'm not keen on your taste in art."

I looked at the picture, with its battered farmhouse table, stout teapot and cups daubed in a myriad of watercolours. What was it about that picture – or indeed Jake Caldwell – that Xander had taken exception to?

"What is it?" I asked, confused and recalling his initial reaction when he saw it propped up against the wall. "Why don't you like that painting?"

Xander reached out and picked up a petrol-blue teacup from the shelf beside him. He studied it for a moment, turning it over in his hands before setting it back. "It's not the picture," he ground out after a few moments.

"Then if it's not his brushstrokes, what is it? You're looking at it as though you'd like to rip it off the wall."

Xander lashed me with a charged look. "It's nothing. Let's not talk about Caldwell or his pretty paintings anymore." He switched the conversation. "Have you got a moment?"

I blinked at him, not at all convinced. "Yes. Of course."

I encouraged Xander to follow me down to the office. Mum and Cass pretended to be occupied as we walked past them.

I closed the door as Xander sank into one of the two new black and chrome chairs. My curiosity was still piqued about his issue with Jake but I sat myself down behind the desk. He wasn't prepared to talk about it, whatever the problem was.

Xander chained me to my chair with his pensive expression. "Things have been rather hectic from my art interest point of view the last couple of weeks, but I've managed to read more of Saffy's great-grandfather's notes."

I shuffled forward in my chair, intrigued. "That's good. Have you discovered something?"

He gave the briefest of nods, making his dark, floppy fringe move against his forehead. "I think I might have." He leant forward too. "It's about Castle Marrian."

My eyes grew. "Wow. Okay. That's a little weird. I used to work there as a wedding planner."

"Really? Well, in that case you might be particularly interested in this."

"Why? What is it?"

Xander stretched out his long legs. "We will need to look into this, of course, to make sure it's correct, but according to the notes Victor Prentice made, Castle Marrian passed through the hands of several wealthy local families in the late 1800s and the early part of the 1900s."

"That's right." I screwed up my nose in recollection. "I know that there were two prominent families, the Masters and the Dayells, who owned it in the past."

Xander's eyes glinted. "That's right. But do you happen to know who one of the very short-lived owners was?"

I shook my head.

Xander moved even further forward, the sunlight from the office window behind me glancing across the top of my mahogany desk. "The family surname was Gray," he said with emphasis. "Leonora and Chadwick Gray."

"Gray?" I repeated, my mouth slipping open. "Are you saying that Jonathan Gray owned Castle Marrian?"

"That was the intention. Leonora and Chadwick Gray bought the property for their eldest son Jonathan to inherit."

I sank back into my chair. "They owned Castle Marrian?

His parents?" I let out a shocked laugh. "Well, there's no mention of the Gray family being part of its history. When I first started working there, I wanted to gen up on its background and they weren't mentioned."

"That isn't too surprising, given that they resided there for about five minutes, going by Victor's notes," replied Xander.

"What do you mean?"

"By the sound of it, living at Castle Marrian didn't work out for the Gray family and they sold it on."

I thought back to the letter written by Briar Forsyth, her pleading pain and anguish etched into every sentence.

My mouth grew grim. "And what's the betting that there was some scandal or trouble this Jonathan was embroiled in and that is why they had to leave Castle Marrian in such a hurry?"

Xander moved to speak but our conversation was interrupted by a brisk knock on the office door as Mum appeared. "Sorry to interrupt, sweetheart, but your dad is here to fix up those shelf lights for you."

Chapter Twenty-Four

E ven though my muscles were complaining on Thursday evening after all the bending, stretching, fetching and carrying, I also felt a sense of achievement and pride.

Once I had showered and slung on one of my off-the-shoulder jumpers and PJ bottoms, I rustled up a toasted cheese and tomato sandwich and some crisp salad.

Then I began to look over the excerpt of Victor Prentice's notes that Xander had flagged up for me.

I rubbed my gritty, tired eyes and persevered with reading my laptop screen.

I took a considered bite of my toasted sandwich. "I think you might well be right, Victor," I mused aloud, my lone voice bouncing against the walls of my sitting room. "I was thinking the same thing."

Monday delivered a June morning that carried tentative sunshine and a drifting blue sky, skittered with the odd cloud. I was relieved.

The Cup That Cheers, although a decent-sized shop, wasn't huge and I was concerned that all the inquisitive shop-goers who would (fingers crossed) arrive might not be able to fit in. Or perhaps that was wishful thinking?

We therefore decided to split the two trestle tables Mum had borrowed from Jill, one of her Women's Institute friends, so that one could be stationed outside the shop entrance and the other inside and further down the shop floor.

I'd set both tables with gingham tablecloths in readiness for delivery of the assorted scones from Innes, the local baker I had also set aside a few of the cheaper but still fetching tea sets to serve the complimentary tea in to my customers. If any of my first customers took a shine to them, I thought, they were reasonably priced, so that should lure them in…

The purple sheets of canvas remained on the windows, concealing my display. All the shelves creaked under the weight of the crockery for sale, with lilac price cards placed beside each of them.

Beside the counter, Dad had fitted a hook upon which hung the gift bags I'd had made for The Cup That Cheers, embossed with the shop name and the image of a little teapot and tied with the lilac Cunningham Clan tartan to match the curtains at the window and shop door.

Mum, Dad, Cass and I had been there since 7a.m., checking, sorting and arranging the final touches.

I stared around, taking in every detail, from the glossy teapots to Jake Caldwell's painting on the wall to my electronic cash register glowing on the counter. I had just about mentally prepared myself for dealing with my new piece of technology.

My thoughts tripped towards Gran and a grateful ball of emotion gathered at the base of my throat. I could not have done any of this without her. If she hadn't done what she did and had so much faith in me, I'm not sure at all what I would have done after deciding to quit my job at Castle Marrian.

I gazed around. Something told me Gran would have approved of The Cup That Cheers. In fact, with its hint of retro chic, I think she would have loved it.

Innes was due to deliver the job lot of warm scones – cherry and coconut, plain, fruit, apple and cinnamon, and cheese and treacle (I couldn't decide which ones and, in the end, erred on the side of caution and ordered a batch of each).

I darted into the shop bathroom and changed out of my shabby black cropped trousers and old T-shirt into the smarter outfit I had brought with me.

I threw on my pretty sky-blue sun dress dotted with daisies and my comfy white ballet pumps, before freeing my hair from its haphazard ponytail and scooping it into a side plait.

Once I'd squirted a spray of my favourite Jo Malone perfume and applied some beige eye shadow, black mascara, a flash of rose blusher and my favourite candy-pink lipstick, I gave over the use of the staff bathroom to Cass, who had also brought a change of clothes with her.

Mum and Dad had shot home in the car to freshen up and returned just as Innes was showing up in the rear car park and off-loading huge Tupperware boxes of scones that were steaming up the sides of their plastic containers. My stomach let out a loud growl of appreciation.

Cass appeared in a floaty beige skirt and lacy cream top, with her conker-brown hair styled in an up-do, showing off her big eyes. "Oh, my goodness!" She laughed at the sight of Innes traipsing through the back door of The Cup That Cheers, clutching the boxes of scones. They were permeating the air with a warm, sweet, floury scent. "Do you think we have got enough there?"

Dad rolled his eyes and ran self-conscious fingers down his silky claret tie. "Just like her mother, this one. Catering for ten thousand when fifty will do."

"You didn't have to wear a tie, Dad," I said with a smile, knowing he was far more comfortable in his polo shirts.

Dad pulled a disgruntled expression. "Try telling that to your mother. She had to crowbar me into this suit."

"Well, you look very smart."

A clinking sound travelled out to the car park from inside the shop. Mum emerged in her peach shift dress and matching linen jacket. Her red bob swung around her face.

"Dora from the WI has just dropped off those huge urns for dispensing hot water." She gave a wide but somewhat nervous grin. "It's almost time for you to open that door, sweetheart."

I gestured to Cass, my stomach exploding like a nest of butterflies. The hands on my watch were creeping towards 10a.m. This was it. This was the day I had been working towards. This was the moment my Gran had wanted for herself and now for me. I took a sharp breath. "Right, ladies and gents, let's do this."

The footfall was enthusiastic and brisk, once I peeled away the canvas from the shop window to reveal the display, complete with the specially commissioned Briar Glen tea set taking centre stage.

Scones were devoured, teacups rattled and there was a polite but enthusiastic buzz of conversation.

I was delighted to see a few of my former work colleagues from Castle Marrian in attendance; they had come along to support me, and waved at me from the back of the throng. I had sent them an email, inviting them to the opening of The Cup That Cheers, and sure enough, Derek, Connie, Ivy and Stacey clapped and smiled along with the rest of the locals as the shop opened its doors for the first time.

I'd spotted Xander amongst the crowd too, head and shoulders above everybody else, but there was no sign of Jake yet. Thank goodness. I hoped that whatever the problem was with him and Xander, it wouldn't erupt in a shouting match at our inaugural opening. Seeing as I hadn't heard from Jake lately, perhaps he wouldn't come or had forgotten about the shop opening being today anyway.

I was finishing up serving another customer, who was buying the Astley tea set in rose gold as an engagement present for her niece, when Xander emerged inside the shop, holding a cup and saucer.

"Congratulations," he said.

Cass took over at the counter, while I stepped to one side. Mum, I noticed, had switched the music on the iPod to play her favourite, Michael Bublé. As his velvety tones sang about only having eyes for you, Xander took a considered sip of his tea.

Every so often, Cass flicked him a discreet look of pink-tinged appreciation while she rang through purchases. I had to admit he did look very handsome in his open-necked lemon shirt and black silk waistcoat, even if he was a grouchy sod.

I had come to notice the way his dark brows arched whenever he was talking about something serious...

"So," I announced, trying to stay focused. "I'm going to read more of Victor Prentice's diaries tonight. I know you think I have a fertile imagination, but from where I'm standing, I think this Jonathan Gray must have done something awful for his family to up sticks and sell Castle Marrian like that."

Xander fixed me to the spot with his gaze. "A woman with a mission, eh?"

I felt my back go ramrod-straight. "Are you teasing me?"

Xander's eyes were difficult to read. He opened his mouth to say something, when there was a movement at my shoulder. Xander's mouth flat-lined.

"Hey! Sophie. Sorry I'm late. Things to do, people to see, you know?"

I buried a wriggle of annoyance at Jake's languid excuses. It sounded as if he thought it was hardly worth coming along. Beside me, Xander's expression was thunderous.

So much for them not spotting one another.

Jake's easy smile swivelled away from me. When he noticed who I was chatting to, he grinned wider and swept Xander from head to toe with a gloating expression. "Well, look who it is! Hi, Xander. How's it going?"

Xander placed his cup and saucer down on the counter. He couldn't bring himself to make eye contact with Jake. "Well, thanks. You?"

There was something provocative about Jake's demeanour. "Oh, you know. Commissions going well. Very busy. How is the world of the art critic?"

Xander lifted his eyes to Jake after a moment. "Very rewarding. Well, it is when you're confronted by beautiful work that is genuine and heartfelt." Xander let his gaze travel across the bobbing heads of the customers admiring the crockery-filled shelves and settle on Jake's painting. "Still, we can't be fortunate all the time, can we?"

Ouch! Dear me! If the temperature plummeted any more in here, there would be polar bears and penguins arriving.

I remained standing between the two of them, my head turning as though I was at a tennis match. My diminutive stature was dwarfed by their towering frames. What on earth was going on between them?

Xander straightened his silky black waistcoat and snatched his mobile out of his back trouser pocket. He ignored Jake again and trained all his attention on me. "Thank you for the invitation, Sophie. Your shop looks terrific and I wish you every success."

I felt a pang of something that I could have sworn was disappointment. "You're leaving already?"

"I'm going to the opening of a new artist's gallery exhibition in Edinburgh."

He stalked past Jake, his mouth carrying a disapproving flicker and ignored him. "I'll catch up with you later."

Jake's face broke into a self-satisfied grin. "Bye, Xander. Good to see you again."

I noticed Xander's retreating shoulders tense under his shirt as he departed.

I turned to a smug Jake. "How have things been? Busy?"

"Very, lots of commissions," he answered airily. "Sorry I haven't been in touch the last couple of weeks but you know how it is."

I frowned up at him. That was a vague explanation. I gestured over my shoulder after Xander. "What was all that about?"

Jake's eyes widened with faux innocence. "I don't know what you mean."

The cash register let out a series of satisfying rings and dings behind me. I studied him. "Please don't think I'm being nosey, but the atmosphere between you two was dreadful. What's going on?"

Jake leant against the corner of the counter as if he owned the place. He furnished himself with a fresh cup of tea from the nearby trestle table, then glinted at me as he took a languid sip. "I didn't know you knew Frozen North."

"I have got to know Xander through an acquaintance of my late grandmother's. And what did you just call him?"

Jake's mouth was twitching with scorn. "Frozen North. The guy is incapable of showing any emotion. Don't tell me you hadn't noticed."

I surprised myself by rallying to Xander's defence. "I think that's unfair. I mean … okay … he can be a bit guarded but…"

Jake let out a bark of laughter that made a couple of ladies hovering by the Wedgwood spin round in surprise. "That's an understatement." He moved in a little closer to me. "The guy is an emotional vacuum." A loaded smile appeared on his face. "So, what's the story with you two?"

"There is no story," I insisted in a crisp tone. "Xander and I have been working on a—" I drew myself up. I didn't want to tell Jake about the peacock tea set or the letter. It seemed private somehow. The fewer people who knew about it, the better.

I gave what I hoped was a casual shrug. "Xander was helping me with a couple of old tea sets of my Gran's. You know, getting them valued."

"Oh, right." Jake accepted my hurried explanation. He shot me a look out of the corner of his eye. "Just be careful of old Frozen, okay?"

"What do you mean?"

Jake dragged a pensive hand over the top of his cropped haircut, which shone like spun gold in the sunshine sliding through the shop window. "Oh, just forget it. I shouldn't have said anything."

An unsettling sensation quivered through me. "No, come on. Please tell me. What is it?"

He didn't say anything.

"Jake, you can't say something out of the blue like that and then not explain."

He rubbed at his shaved chin. "Look, we can't talk properly here. What are you doing this evening?"

"This evening?" I repeated like a parrot, as Mum eased past me, clutching a box containing one of the sunflower-sprigged teapots for a young mum and her baby in a pushchair.

"Yes. I thought we could go out to dinner. I can tell you all about old Northy boy."

I considered Jake's invitation. "Look, thank you for the invite but after such a hectic day, I'm going to be exhausted. All I will want to do is relax with a glass of wine."

"Well, in that case, I'll come round to yours with a takeaway." Jake's slash of white smile dazzled. "Give me a note of your address and I'll see you around 7p.m."

A small voice inside my head insisted that whatever it was Xander was supposed to have done, I didn't want to know, but that wasn't satisfying my burning curiosity. I couldn't leave things like this.

Chapter Twenty-Five

"So, what is this all about?" I asked Jake, scooping some shreds of lemon chicken and pineapple chunks onto my warmed plate in the kitchen.

"Sorry?"

"What you wanted to discuss with me? About Xander?"

Jake helped himself to a heaped tablespoon of egg fried rice and a portion of crispy shredded beef. "Oh yeah. That." We were sitting opposite one another at the kitchen table. He took a sip of white wine, looking concerned. "Well, it's a bit delicate."

I rested my knife and fork on the side of my plate. "Look, Jake. Please just tell me, whatever it is. You can trust me."

He abandoned his dinner and sank back in his chair. "Okay. So, it was a couple of years back and I was starting to get noticed by the art world. It had been one hell of a slog. Anyway, I met this girl and fell for her. What I didn't know was that she was the girlfriend of Xander North." Jake let out a painful sigh and continued. "Their relationship was all but

201

over. She was miserable with him. But as soon as he found out, he was determined to ruin my career even before it started."

He must have noticed me frowning. "Oh, I know you might be struggling to imagine him being a spiteful sod, but he's good at the Jekyll and Hyde stuff." He took another gulp of wine.

"So, what happened?" I asked, feeling trepidation.

Jake's shoulders sagged under his dark shirt. "The review he gave me was malicious. Full of vitriol. Then there were others. When you take into account the number of valuable contacts he has in the art world, I'm sure I don't need to tell you that my career took a nosedive."

I pushed my food around my plate with my fork, my appetite beginning to wane. "And then?"

"I had no option but to make a complaint – to the newspaper he was working on at the time."

"And did Xander admit to what he'd done?"

Jake gave a brief nod of his head. "He had to."

My head was struggling to slot and slide all of this into place. I thought about Xander. I realised I didn't know him all that well, but to maliciously go after someone like that, in the hope of destroying their career... It just didn't seem like him at all. "What happened with his job on the paper? And the girl?"

Jake's mouth contorted into a smirk. "Old boys' club. They let him keep his art critic column at the paper, once he had apologised to me and assured me that his stupid vendetta would stop. As for the girl – her name was Nadia – well, after all that, I think she'd had her fair share of the both of us and decided to move back to Croatia."

I forked up a piece of lemon chicken. My understanding of Xander, or at least what I knew of him, was tilted on its axis. It didn't seem like he would be capable of doing something so spiteful and unprofessional. It was understandable that he would be hurt that his girlfriend had fallen for someone else. But to go after Jake in such a savage and public way was not something anyone should be proud of. Then I recalled his dismissive attitude towards the Briar Forsyth letter and his remarks about only being interested in the value of the peacock tea set. Perhaps there was a ruthless side to him that I was unaware of.

I lowered my fork again and took a sip of water, my thoughts zooming all over the place.

Jake tilted his head to one side. "Sophie? Are you okay?"

I forced a smile. "Yes. Yes, I'm fine, thanks. I'm just a bit surprised."

Jake rubbed his forehead. "Shit! I knew I shouldn't have said anything."

"No," I faltered, my voice becoming more insistent. "No, I'm glad you did. And I'm sorry about Nadia."

Jake was resigned. "I believe in things happening for a reason. Don't get me wrong. It hurt like hell at the time when Nadia told me she was going back to Croatia. But now..." He let his hands rise and fall. "I'm moving on with my life."

And I felt myself blush as he winked across the debris of Chinese takeaway cartons.

I considered what Jake told me about Xander, while I rinsed out the plastic takeaway containers and stacked them up in one of my kitchen cupboards.

Even though Jake had been chatting about his up-and-coming commissions, I had only been half listening. Confusion gnawed at me. I could see Xander's crashing expression when he saw Jake's painting up on the shop wall. I could hear the growl in his voice when he spoke his name.

"Coffee?" I called through to the sitting room, distracted.

Jake shouted back an enthusiastic "Yes please."

It was while I was filling the kettle that I thought I heard my mobile let out its recognisable sharp ring through in the sitting room. I set down two mugs and padded through to answer it. Jake was lounging on the sofa, his head propped back. "Everything okay?" he asked.

I glanced at my mobile sitting on the coffee table. "I thought I heard my mobile ring."

Jake twisted round. " "Oh, it was mine. We must have a similar ringtone."

"Oh, okay."

Jake offered me a winning smile. "It was nothing important."

"Thank you for a lovely evening."

I blushed up at Jake as he lingered in the doorway, all sharp cheekbones and confident swagger.

"You're welcome."

He bent his lips to mine and grazed them with a kiss. Then

he jumped back, checking himself. "Sorry. I hope I wasn't too forward then."

"There's no need to apologise."

He made a move to leave, signalling below to the waiting taxi driver. A thought seemed to occur to him. "I know you've got a lot on at the moment with the shop, but maybe we could go out at the weekend? There's a gorgeous tapas bar in town."

My head dragged up a fleeting image of Xander. I forced it away. "That would be good."

"Great. I'll give you a call during the week."

I closed the door behind him, blotting out the shard of buttery moon and the June darkness, laced with the inviting, fresh scent of summer.

Jake was very attractive and that kiss was pleasant.

Oh God! Pleasant?! That was how I would describe the weather.

There just wasn't that exciting zing there when he kissed me – no buckling of my knees or the thud of my heart in my ears. I rolled my eyes at myself. I sounded like one of Gran's romantic novels she would devour from the library.

But then that was how I felt about Callum at the beginning and look how that turned out. I was doing it again: overthinking everything and analysing it all with my emotional microscope.

Chapter Twenty-Six

25th September 1970, Briar Glen Park

"S ay that again."

Chris's amber eyes glinted at her. "I said I want you to manage my new business."

Helena's arched black brows flew up to her centre parting. The afternoon sun was shifting through Chris's hair, lifting the kaleidoscope of blond tones, as they sauntered through the wrought-iron park gates. It gave him an almost angelic appearance, although Helena knew he was anything but.

"But what business?" she managed.

They strolled along together, side by side. The breeze was crisp, ruffling up the grass.

Helena was aware as they walked along that their steps mirrored one another's. She reached up and fiddled with her jacket. She had taken care to ensure her winged kohl liner and frosted baby pink lipstick were perfect, before she said goodbye to Mrs Auld for the day and hurried across to meet Chris.

Oh God. She couldn't drag her eyes away from him. This was ridiculous! Her stomach was swooping all over the place. She was a married woman with a little girl and yet,the last few weeks, Helena hadn't been able to stem the excited tingles of anticipation every Monday, Wednesday and Friday. She found herself agonising over her outfit for each workday and experimenting with her hair.

Part of her hated feeling like this, all on alert, as she tried not to stare out of the bull's eye shop windows of Sparkling Gifts, wondering whether Chris would happen to drop by.

She recalled the stab of fear when Mrs Auld had remarked that Chris might be returning to London at some point. A sudden hollow emptiness had formed within her heart and she'd been forced to avert her eyes to disguise the pain.

"Helena? Are you listening to me? You're miles away."

Helena huddled deeper into her pink fluffy jacket. "Sorry."

Chris delivered one of his charming, lopsided smiles that made her chest fizz. "I'm saying that I'd like you to manage my new business. Well, once it's off the ground, that is."

Helena blinked at him. So, she hadn't imagined it. That was what he'd said after all. "But I don't understand. I work for your mum."

She felt herself cringe – why was she stating the obvious?

Chris indicated for them to sit down again on another bench. As soon as they did, he reached over and seized hold of her hand. The sensation triggered a gasp that Helena tried to disguise with a forced laugh. "I already have a job," she managed.

If Chris noticed how awkward she was, he didn't show it. His dark blond hair ruffled. "I know you do. But, no disrespect to my mum, you are wasted there."

Helena watched him shuffle a little closer to her. In truth, she was willing him to. His knee glanced against her thigh. She steadied herself. Oh, for pity's sake! *Get a grip, she scolded herself.* You have a husband and six-year-old daughter. *"But your mum has been so good to me." She found herself drinking in every detail of Chris's golden good looks. "What business are you talking about? I mean, I'm very flattered and I love clothes, but I'm not an expert on fashion…"*

Chris held up one hand, a smile flickering around his mouth. "My new business is nothing to do with fashion."

"Sorry. You've lost me." Helena could feel herself beginning to submerge in Chris's gaze. She set her spine straight. This was crazy. She shouldn't even be here, let alone listening to Chris's offer of a job. She knew what she should do. She should thank him for thinking of her and walk away; rise up from this park bench, where the leaves were beginning to pirouette around her long lace-up boots, and go home.

She knew she was falling for him. Every time she saw him, her heart twisted in on itself. She had to stop it. She had Marnie to think of. But what was this? *whispered another voice.* It wasn't an affair. *The thought of it made Helena's freckle-tipped cheeks zing with colour. She wasn't doing anything wrong, was she?*

Before she could stop herself, Helena was blushing to the tip of her tilted-up nose. "What sort of business is it, if it isn't to do with fashion?"

Chris searched her face for a reaction. "A crockery shop."

Helena pulled herself upright. "Are you joking?"

"Do I look like I'm joking?"

Helena could feel her brows gathering in confusion. "But why would you want to do that? Your mum already stocks crockery."

"Well, of a fashion," conceded Chris with that mischievous smile of his that always made her stomach squirm.

A small boy trundled past on his scooter, followed by his harassed-looking mother.

"And she already knows, so there's no need to get yourself all worked up about it."

Helena's stunned mouth dropped open further. "What did she say?"

Chris shrugged his broad shoulders. "She was fine about it, especially when I pointed out that as I was starting a new business here, that would mean I wouldn't be heading back to London for a while."

Helena was sure there was a charged emphasis in his voice.

Her thoughts skittered in all directions. This was good. This was great. Wasn't it?

The autumn sunshine washed across the grass, spilling over the empty swings and roundabout.

"I've already bought some premises here in Briar Glen. Actually, it's very close by. The owner was selling up and it won't take much to bring it up to date."

Her head was on autopilot. If she didn't know any better, she'd think she had climbed onto the kids' roundabout and spun herself round several times. "Blimey. You haven't hung around then."

"Mum thinks you do a great job, Helena. Please don't think she doesn't. But she admitted to me that the space in Sparkling Gifts is limited and she knows you get frustrated at times, that you can't expand that part of the business for her."

Chris gave a delicious smile that, had Helena been standing, would have knocked her clean off her feet. "So, I put it to her that if we were to open a crockery shop, she could return to concentrating on her usual stock and she could hand over the crockery she has just now to us."

A thrilled sensation tripped up her spine. Then the cold chill of reality, mixed in with a wave of guilt, gripped her. "But Marnie... I..."

Chris dismissed her concerns. "I'll be appointing staff. You'll be the manager, so don't worry about Marnie. That won't be an issue."

Helena found herself succumbing. She enjoyed working in Sparkling Gifts and she had grown fond of Mrs Auld, with her battleship persona, which contained a kind and caring attitude underneath the bluster. But the prospect of working with Chris... It was like he had ignited something in her that she didn't even realise existed.

Helena swallowed, her tongue all at once feeling too large for her mouth. "This shop," she managed, a blush rising in her cheeks. "Which one is it?"

I shuffled into my PJs and nestled in bed, balancing my laptop on a breakfast tray. I sipped my mug of camomile tea as I began to read the next few pages of Victor Prentice's notes, rather than keep examining what Jake had told me about Xander. I didn't want to believe that he was capable of being so spiteful.

I shoved the festering feelings of disappointment in Xander to one side and concentrated on the Prentice diaries. They would be a good distraction.

A Scottish Highland Surprise

1ˢᵗ February 1900

It was a rather uneventful morning at the library, until Police Constable Doolan arrived.

Mrs Mortimer was scurrying towards me, very flustered, when she located me sorting the apothecary section. "Oh, Mr Prentice. PC Doolan is here. He wishes to speak to you about a criminality."

When I stared back at her and prepared to maintain my innocence of whatever misdemeanour I was rumoured to have committed, she flapped her pale hands. "You misunderstand me. His enquiries are not connected to you." She dropped her voice lower. "PC Doolan informed me there has been a crime committed up at Castle Marrian."

"Of what nature?"

"A theft," delivered Mrs Mortimer, her cheeks as rosy with excitement as the cameo brooch at her throat. She beckoned me to follow her and I obeyed.

PC Doolan was standing to attention at the bureau, his large, meaty hands clasped behind his back and the oil lamps highlighting the impressive sheen of his buttoned uniform.

After exchanging a few pleasantries, PC Doolan explained the purpose of his visit to the library.

"A tea set?" I repeated. "A tea set has gone missing from the Castle Marrian estate?"

Mrs Mortimer continued to linger behind the bureau, her piled-up, burnished curls bent. She pretended to address an issue in the ledger, but one discreet flick of my eyes and she vanished to continue attending to the apothecary section on my behalf. She was a reliable and hard-working colleague, but had a propensity for gossip.

I watched Mrs Mortimer swish away in her ankle-length gown of salmon-pink.

I indicated to PC Doolan to follow me through to the library office, where we took up our respective seats. The air carried the scent of beeswax, and looking out at the shelves of books, their spines shining with expectation, never failed to raise my spirits.

We carried a total of two thousand volumes, which although respectable for a small town in Scotland, fell far short of the rumoured eight thousand that the Dundalk Free Library possessed.

I had read this with what I have to admit was a burning feeling of envy. It was my intention to encourage as many folks into Briar Glen Free Library as I was able. The joy of books and the education and escapism they provided were not and should not be exclusive to the more educated and privileged in society, in my humble opinion.

All deserved to savour and enjoy the beauty of reading and that was why I was so grateful to Leonora and Chadwick Gray for their generous donations to the library.

We were not busy, but three of the mahogany booths were occupied by members of the public. However, the heavy tread of a police officer's boots across the polished wooden floor had drawn attention.

It was much better therefore to conduct any conversations in private.

"Mr and Mrs Gray reported the theft yesterday evening," explained PC Doolan from under his impressive grey moustache. "It's of great sentimental value to them, especially Mrs Gray. I understand Mr Gray commissioned the local artist Ernest Telfer to craft the tea set as a birthday present for her last year. Therefore, it is extremely valuable."

I listened with interest, feeling resentment and anger on their behalf.

PC Doolan fixed me with inquisitive eyes. "Mr Prentice, you are a well-respected member of the Briar Glen community. You also possess considerable knowledge about the people who live here. I was hoping you may have been witness to something unusual related to this crime? Or perhaps happened upon some gossip or information in regards to the missing crockery?"

I shook my head. "My apologies, PC Doolan, but this is the first I have heard of it. Do the family have their suspicions on who may have been responsible for taking it?"

PC Doolan shook his head, on which sat his military-style police helmet. "No. Well, not at this juncture. However, in my opinion, the most conceivable explanation is that a member of their staff must have found themselves in a financial predicament and felt the only avenue open to them was to take the tea set in the hope of selling it."

I frowned at PC Doolan's hypothesis. Leonora and Chadwick Gray were a respected couple. On the few occasions I had been invited to Castle Marrian to attend to their private library, it was apparent that they treated their employees with the utmost consideration and that their staff looked upon them with fondness and respect.

"I realise I am not aware of the details as you are, PC Doolan," I began as tactfully as I could manage. "But from what I know of Mr and Mrs Gray and the relations they have with their staff, I find it difficult to imagine any of their employees undertaking something so unsavoury."

I let out a gasp and sat bolt upright against my pillows,

almost upending my mug of camomile. So, I had been right! The peacock tea set had been stolen.

I gawped at my laptop screen, my bedside light casting a peachy glow across my bedroom. But who had taken it and why?

I re-read the last few paragraphs again, Victor Prentice's handwriting skittering across the page. PC Doolan had made the assumption at the time that it was a member of the Castle Marrian staff who was guilty of taking it. But what if they weren't? What if that was what someone wanted the police to think?

I moved on to another diary excerpt;

2nd April 1900

Rumours in the town are rife that Castle Marrian perhaps may change hands again in only a matter of months.

It may be idle talk, but there are tales circulating that Leonora and Chadwick Gray, the current owners of the grand house, have experienced a sudden and unexpected change of heart over not only remaining in Briar Glen, but also over residing in Castle Marrian.

The gossip is that their intention is now to sell the property and locate elsewhere.

I cannot help but reflect on the ugly scene I witnessed on Christmas Eve, with their son verbally berating that poor young woman and abandoning her to the elements.

Perhaps I am allowing my imagination to dominate my common sense, but I cannot help but speculate their abrupt decision may well be connected in some way to that Christmas Eve night, Jonathan

Gray and whatever misdemeanours he seems more than capable of committing.

I thought again about the letter written to Jonathan Gray by the distressed Briar Forsyth, insisting she didn't want any treasures, just to be recognised and granted respect. Was the treasure she was referring to the tea set itself?

And why the sudden decision by the Gray family to move away from Briar Glen and leave Castle Marrian behind? It just all seemed rather rushed and impetuous.

My imagination was going into overdrive. What if the supposed theft of the tea set had been orchestrated deliberately? What if it hadn't been an employee that had stolen the tea set after all – but someone closer to home?

An idea pulled at my thoughts and wouldn't let go.

What if their son, Jonathan, had been responsible?

Chapter Twenty-Seven

My mind was still churning the next morning, as I arrived at The Cup That Cheers.

I strolled up to the shop door, after having enjoyed the walk from my flat, to see that there were already signs of life inside.

Cass was drifting about the shop floor, in preparation for opening up at 9a.m. She beamed at me as I entered. "Good morning, boss," she said cheekily. "Yesterday was great, wasn't it?"

"It certainly was. Far better than we could have hoped!"

I was greeting an elderly lady and her well-dressed daughter, when my mobile chirruped from the depths of my shoulder bag.

It was Xander.

I pointed down to my office, indicating to Cass I would take the call there, and she nodded.

I closed my office door behind me and tugged open the hopper window. A zingy breeze wafted in and there was a

216

sudden fizz of birdsong. It was the first day of July and there was the promise of summer holidays in the air.

I switched on my computer. "How are you?" I asked him, mentally running through what Jake had said about Xander last night.

"I'm okay, thanks." I noticed his rumbly, deep voice seemed somewhat off-kilter this morning. He didn't *sound* okay.

"So, what can I help you with?" I asked, realising I sounded every bit as odd as he did.

Xander appeared to detect the sudden inflection in my voice. There was a weighted pause before he cleared his throat. "I've been reading more of Saffy's great-grandfather's diary. I think you were correct about the tea set."

I paced up and down my office, my mobile clutched to my ear. A kernel of optimism started to grow.

"It seems that one of the staff up at Castle Marrian took it to begin with and then goodness knows what happened to it after that."

My indignation kicked in. He had read the same journal entries as me and yet he was viewing it all from a loftier, opposite position. "Does it?"

"What do you mean?"

"You're making assumptions, Xander."

He let out a grunt. "It's far more likely for a member of staff to have taken it. Perhaps they had money worries."

I shook my high ponytail, even though Xander couldn't see me. "I admit that it doesn't look good, but it's not for certain." Warming to my theme, I continued talking. My voice was heavy with disappointment. "Often people can surprise you, and not in a good way."

Xander listened to my loaded comments, but didn't reply.

"I think it's quite conceivable that anyone, not just a member of Castle Marrian staff, would be capable of stealing that tea set."

Xander started to disagree, but I carried on. "I'm not saying that is what happened, but I wouldn't be at all surprised if it had."

"Let's assume you're right and that it wasn't one of the Gray's employees that stole the tea set. Who else could it be and what motive might they have for doing it?"

I pictured Briar Forsyth's letter. "Whoever this Briar is, her letter suggests Jonathan Gray treated her very badly, so if he was capable of abandoning a woman in the snow, I'm pretty sure stealing a tea set from under the noses of his parents wouldn't make him bat an eyelid. And we don't know what they were arguing about when Victor Prentice spotted them on Christmas Eve."

Xander digested this. "I suppose it's possible, but unlikely. Quite a risky thing for the likes of Jonathan Gray to do. I still think it's a member of the household who stole it."

I pulled a face at the phone. Well, hopefully we would be able to find out for certain. I really wanted to disprove his theory.

While I was mentally mulling things over, Xander's voice cut through my thoughts. "I have a confession to make, Sophie."

My eyes widened. "Oh?"

"The real reason I rang was to apologise for dashing off yesterday straight after your shop opening."

I rubbed at the edge of my desk with one finger. "I was a bit surprised when you left like that." Was Xander going to confess to me what had taken place between him and Jake?

"Yes. Well." There was a frustrated growl. "The truth is, I can't stand to be in the same room as Jake Caldwell."

My eyebrows rose to the heavens. I hoped I sounded surprised. I didn't want Xander to realise Jake had told me about what happened between them. My stomach rolled. "Oh? Why is that?"

It was as if I could hear Xander deliberating with himself whether to confide in me about it or not. In the end, he decided not to. He let out a resigned breath. "Let's just say our paths have crossed in the past."

Part of me had hoped what Jake had said about Xander had been exaggerated or was even untrue. But Xander's reluctance to talk about what had happened between them fanned my growing suspicions.

I gripped the phone tighter, my fingers flexing. Why was it so important for me to know Xander wasn't the person Jake had portrayed him to be? Was Xander really vindictive? Petty? Had he deliberately tried to sabotage someone's career?

That description didn't fit with the Xander I thought I was growing to know. And yet I couldn't be unaware of my track record of trusting people who didn't warrant it. The way Callum had dumped me and moved on, drowned me in lies and lurid stories, always had his eye on "bettering himself" by being with someone who had her own detached five-bedroom house and a healthy bank balance... I suspected something wasn't right, but thought that if I turned my back on it, it would slink away.

I swore to myself I would never do that again.

"Sophie? Sophie? Are you still there?"

I dragged myself out of my own, deep thoughts. "Yes. Sorry." I rubbed my finger again at the imaginary smudge on my desk. "I've been thinking more about the tea set. I'm going to post a couple of those photographs I took of it, on the shop social media accounts. You never know. One or two of the locals might have some information about it."

"That's a good idea," agreed Xander. "The sooner we can get some more background on the crockery, the better."

I knew what he was implying again. I also knew my voice had adopted a sharper edge, but I didn't care. "What you mean is, the sooner we can get to the bottom of its history and Briar's letter, the sooner you can arrange for it to be sold at auction."

Xander started to say something else, but I ended the call. "I'll let you know how I get on."

He appeared taken aback. "Oh. Okay."

I slid into my desk chair, with a sinking feeling like that of a child who has just been told that Father Christmas doesn't exist after all.

Chapter Twenty-Eight

E ven after a steady stream of customers and a bus load of enthusiastic day trippers, keen to see the area where the rumoured blue briar rose once flourished, I walked home deflated.

Cass had done a sterling job of shifting a couple of our extravagant Kate Spade sets to an indecisive customer, as well as a shedload of our funky, more reasonably priced sets to a group of student friends preparing to move away to university. I was so grateful to her for all her hard work, but I found myself trudging back into my flat, changing and eating my stir-fry like a robot.

Jake's comments about Xander had really got to me. I felt cheated somehow, and deceived. And the fact I was feeling like this annoyed me.

After devouring a bowl of peanut butter ice-cream I hadn't wanted, I sat cross-legged on my sofa and fired up my laptop. I logged onto The Cup That Cheers' website first, in all its white and purple glory, and posted two of the best photographs I'd taken of the peacock tea set on there, as well as on the shop's Twitter, Facebook and Instagram accounts. I also included the following message to accompany the photos;

Does anyone have any knowledge of the peacock tea set
featured in these two photographs, please?
All responses will be treated in the strictest confidence. Please
email me, Sophie Harkness, at the shop website address.
Any information, however insignificant you think it may be,
would be much appreciated.
Thank you.

I licked my dessert spoon, which was dripping with the remnants of my ice-cream, and clattered it back into the bowl. In my appeal for information, I decided not to mention the well-dressed lady who had chosen to abandon the tea set with me in the first place. I figured that if I didn't refer to her and she read my plea, she might have a change of heart, realise she could trust me and decide to make contact. If I mentioned her, it might make her reconsider and cause her embarrassment.

I wandered into my bedroom and fetched the tea set from the bottom of my wardrobe. I set the now familiar discoloured white leather case on top of my bed and opened it.

I gave the crockery a brief smile, as though greeting an old friend, before reaching into the pouch stitched into the lid and pulling free the letter. It was odd. At the beginning, I had considered the peacock design and the mix of blues and greens rather garish, but the more I looked at it, the more I found myself appreciating the sweeps of colour and the extravagant detail in the peacock's fanned tail.

I opened up the letter again, my eyes sweeping across its contents. Briar Forsyth and I had something in common, I concluded to myself as I folded the letter up and slid it back inside the case lid. We had both trusted someone who had not been the person we believed them to be.

Jake phoned the next morning, as I was leaving for work, and we made a date for Saturday. As I drove past the flower-strewn gardens and sweet little cottages of Briar Glen, I knew I should have been looking forward to going out to dinner with Jake. Excited even. He was a successful artist, talented and Viking-handsome.

Except I wasn't. It wasn't that I wasn't looking forward to going out to dinner with him. I was sure it was going to be very nice. I just wasn't frothing over with anticipation about it either.

Then why did you say you would go out with him? hissed a voice inside my ear. *Do you find him attractive?*

I blinked as I indicated right, past a line of heavy-headed oak trees. Of course, Jake was attractive. He was intelligent. He was flirtatious. It was just … just…

I ordered the muttering voice to bugger off. I refused to examine why my stomach wasn't performing cartwheels whenever I thought about him. I was preoccupied with The Cup That Cheers, I decided.

No, Saturday would be fun, I persuaded myself with a mental shake. Jake was fun, charming and loved tapas. What was there not to like? Far better to be going out to dinner with someone like him than with a grumpy pottery lover.

Another day of brisk business unfolded, including three more requests for the commemorative Briar Glen tea set.

Noah, Ewan's student friend and talented ceramic artist, was delighted when I emailed over the three additional commissions after lunch.

I received a "Whoop! Whoop!" in reply, followed by three celebratory emojis.

Mid-afternoon swung around and I was showing Cass an *Alice in Wonderland*-inspired tea set that had caught my eye in a supplier's catalogue when the shop phone rang. Cass hurried behind the counter to answer it. She waggled her eyebrows at me as she spoke to the person at the other end of the line. "Do you mind me asking your name, Madam?"

She gestured to me. "That's fine, Mrs Dunsmuir. I'll pass you over to Sophie now."

Cass cupped one hand over the receiver, her hazel eyes sparkling with optimism. "It's a Mrs Ivy Dunsmuir on the line. She says she thinks she may have some information for you about the peacock tea set."

"Ivy?" I sprinted away from the counter. "Oh, that's great. Thanks, Cass." I eagerly accepted the receiver. We didn't have any customers in the shop at that moment, so Cass pottered around, dusting the shelves and the crockery, while I took the call.

"Hi, Ivy. How are you? This is a pleasant surprise."

"It certainly is," she replied. "I hope you're doing well. You're much missed up at Castle Marrian, you know." She hesitated. "I'm actually ringing you about something else, pet. It's that tea set you posted pictures of on Facebook."

My heart begun to thud faster. "What about it, Ivy? Do you recognise it?"

"Anything interesting?" asked Cass when I finished talking to Ivy and put the phone down.

"It might be. I used to work with Ivy up at Castle Marrian and she says she recognised the tea set from my photographs on Facebook."

Cass lowered her duster. "That's great. But she's not the lady that left the tea set here in the first place?"

I shook my plait. "No, she isn't." I tapped my pen against the edge of the counter, trying to stem the tide of growing optimism inside me. "But she did say she thinks she knows who did."

Chapter Twenty-Nine

I arranged to go and speak to Ivy at closing time.

The footfall began to peter out by quarter to six, so Cass and I decided to close ten minutes earlier than usual.

She insisted on locking up so I could get away. I think Cass could tell I was brimming with hopeful anticipation, from the way I was hopping from foot to foot like an agitated five-year-old requiring an urgent visit to the bathroom.

Ivy lived in one of the detached cottages up by the swooping rise and fall of the Briar Glen hills.

The house was very compact and presentable, built of cream and toffee brick, with a beech door and plumes of trees in the well-tended front garden.

Ivy came bustling to the door and beckoned me in, with her inquisitive, friendly bitter-chocolate cockapoo at her heels. She led me into a sitting room with honey-coloured walls and squashy tan furniture strewn with hessian cushions.

As we sat down opposite each other, me on the sofa and Ivy

taking up residence in her armchair, she apologised for her dog. "I'm so sorry about Cooper. He's very sociable."

"Please don't apologise," I grinned, as Cooper plonked himself down on his bottom by my feet for an extended ear rub. "He's gorgeous."

She gestured to her galley kitchen through from the sitting room. "Give me a second and I'll make us some tea."

A few minutes later, Ivy returned with a tray set out with Cath Kidston crockery, which I recognised straightaway. I smiled, pointing to the white porcelain splashed with images of wildflowers in primary colours. "That's familiar."

Ivy poured the tea out of the matching pot. "I couldn't resist it when I came into your lovely shop the other day."

"Thank you." I scrutinised her open, friendly face. "It couldn't have been me that served you. I would have given you a very generous discount!"

Ivy laughed and explained that it wasn't. "It was an enthusiastic young lady with a bow in her hair."

"Cass," I replied. "Yes, she's great."

There was a pause in our conversation while we both took a sip of excellent tea.

"Ivy," I began. "You said you knew the—"

But before I could speak again, Ivy shuffled forward, balancing her saucer on her lap. Her floral blouse shimmered. "I believe I know who may have deposited that tea set with you."

My heart did a hopeful leap.

She set her cup and saucer down on a coffee table positioned beside her chair. "I have a close friend. Her name is Ophelia Walker. She lives on the outskirts of Briar Glen."

She laced her hands together in her lap. Her wedding ring glittered. "Ophelia was a schoolteacher at Briar Glen Primary for years. She retired last year. She'd seen a couple of TV programmes about tracing your family tree and she mentioned to me she wanted to do that, now she had more time."

I nodded, taking another pull of tea.

Ivy smiled. "Sorry. I'm digressing a bit." She took another sip of tea. "The upshot is, I have seen that tea set before, in Ophelia's home."

I craned forward in the armchair, my expectation growing. "So, your friend – Ophelia Walker – she owned the tea set?"

Ivy nodded. "Her sister Annabel did. When she died last year, Ophelia discovered the tea set stashed up in the attic. I remember her telling me about it at the time." Ivy frowned. "That's what I don't understand – why all at once she has decided she doesn't want it."

She flicked me a look. "When I saw your post on Facebook and recognised the crockery, I was in two minds whether to contact Ophelia straightaway and ask her about it, but she has had a tough time coming to terms with losing her sister and I didn't want to embarrass her or make her think I was prying."

Ivy studied me with her misty grey eyes that fanned out with fine lines at the corners. "When she first found it, she was so enamoured with it. So why try to give it away now?" She looked confused. "When I saw the photographs of the tea set and read your appeal for information about it, I was taken aback. Goodness knows why Ophelia had a change of heart and decided she wanted rid of it. Especially with an old letter inside…"

I was giving Cooper another rub behind his floppy velvet

ears. He let out a satisfied grunt, just as my hand stopped petting in surprise. "So, Mrs Walker discovered the letter beside the tea set?"

Ivy nodded. "Yes. Well, not at first. I think it was a day or two after finding the tea set and she took a closer look at it. She didn't go into great detail about what was in the letter. She was a bit guarded about it all, which isn't like her."

So, was it because of the letter and its contents, that Ophelia Walker decided she didn't want to keep it? Perhaps she knew more about the letter than she was leading Ivy to believe?

I shuffled further forward on the sofa, eager to obtain as many answers as I could. "You said Mrs Walker had wanted to look into her family tree. Did she ever tell you whether she managed to do that or if she had discovered anything interesting?"

Ivy picked up her cup and saucer again. "That's the strange thing. She was so enthusiastic about delving into her past, she would give me a running commentary on how she was going to do it and how excited she was about it."

"And now?"

"She hasn't mentioned it for weeks – not the tea set, not the letter, her family tree … nothing." Ivy frowned. "I tried to ask her about it all the last time we met for coffee a couple of weeks ago, but she was very evasive. She side-stepped my questions and changed the subject."

Ivy gave Cooper a fond smile as he continued to bask in my attention. "I didn't want to appear nosey or upset her, so I didn't mention it again."

I patted Cooper's curly coat. It felt solid and warm under

my hand. "Do you think you could give me Mrs Walker's contact details, please? I'd really like to talk to her."

Ivy considered my request, the early evening light spilling across the hills outside the sitting room window.

After a few more moments, she agreed. "Yes. Of course. Whatever it is that is bothering her about that tea set or the letter, Ophelia needs to confront it. I hate the thought of her troubled."

Ivy rose out of her armchair and drifted over to a bureau by the window. She located a pen and a piece of paper and noted down her friend's address and phone number. "Here, Sophie. Good luck. I think you are going to need it."

Chapter Thirty

My thoughts tumbled around my head, as I thanked Ivy for all her help and returned to my car.

Even though my stomach let out a demanding growl for dinner, I decided not to set off for home straightaway. The element of surprise in this case might be the best option.

If I rang Ophelia Walker, forewarned was forearmed and there was a good chance she would refuse to speak to me over the phone. But if I just turned up at her house and attempted to talk to her face to face, she might be a little more amenable.

Surely it was her that left the tea set with me and then vanished.

I checked the address again on the piece of paper that Ivy gave me and set off for Ophelia Walker's house.

I was getting closer to discovering the story of the tea set and Briar Forsyth's letter. I could feel it.

Ophelia Walker lived in one of the old cottages on the outskirts of the town.

They were in their own mini community, in a cul-de-sac, facing out towards the nest of hills that cradled Briar Glen.

The evening sky was morphing into a pretty evening kaleidoscope of tangerine and violet as I pulled up in front of Ophelia's cottage. It featured glittery sash windows with silky buttercup curtains, hanging baskets and a small, square, lush garden, powdered with flowers.

There was an engraving of the blue briar rose a stonemason from long ago had carved into the brickwork above the heavy, burgundy door. I heard a dog from another garden let out a series of half-hearted barks.

I made my way up the crazy-paving path and knocked at the door. I thought there was a flicker of movement inside and sure enough, a distinguished older man answered the door, his expression expectant. "Can I help you?"

"Good evening, sir. I wondered if I could have a quick word with Mrs Ophelia Walker, please? I'm Sophie Harkness and I own the new crockery shop in the town."

He nodded his sweep of side-parted silver hair, but there was something about his demeanour that changed in a flicker when he discovered who I was. "Ophelia?" he called over his shoulder. "There's a young lady here, asking to speak to you."

"Who is it?" travelled an inquiring voice from somewhere down the hall.

Mr Walker relayed back to her who I was. She didn't answer.

"I promise I won't take up too much of your time," I insisted, my voice carrying itself down her hallway. "Please.

I'm trying to get some information on an unusual peacock tea set that was..."

She emerged at her husband's shoulder.

It was her. I recognised her straightaway. It was the same woman who had arrived at The Cup That Cheers in an expensive burgundy coat, clutching the tea set. The same woman who had deposited it with me, before fleeing.

We regarded one another with questioning eyes. She scooped a stray lock of shoulder-skimming white hair back behind her ear. Her expression was tense.

She shot a loaded glance up at her husband, before wrapping her arms around herself in a protective gesture. "Why do you want to speak to me?"

This was ridiculous. It was obvious from her expression that she recognised me.

A seed of worry started to grow. She wasn't delighted to see me hovering on her doorstep. Any moment now, she could slam the door in my face. What was it Ivy had said? *"Good luck. You're going to need it."*

I smiled at her, hoping to ease her concerns. "I've just come from speaking to a friend of yours, Mrs Ivy Dunsmuir. She told me you might have some knowledge of a peacock tea set that was left with me recently?"

Ophelia Walker remained composed. "Sorry, I don't know what you're talking about."

Right. So, she had decided for whatever reason not to make it easy for me. I offered her what I hoped was a gentle smile. Her poor husband, standing beside her in the doorway, was observing us both with a bemused frown. "Mrs Walker, I just wondered why you brought the tea set to my shop? Or perhaps, if you don't know anything about the tea set, Mrs Walker, you might know more about the letter that I discovered with it?"

Her cerise lips twitched. She swallowed.

"There was a letter from March 1900 that I found tucked inside the case that the tea set came in."

Ophelia Walker composed herself. She raised her chin in an act of defiance. "I don't know anything about tea sets or old letters. Whoever told you I would hasn't got a clue what they were talking about. Now if you'll excuse me…"

Panic began to set in.

Ophelia Walker was lying. But why?

I blinked at her, scrambling around inside my head about what to say next. I had to persuade her to talk to me. To be honest with me.

"Mrs Walker," I began in desperation. "I think the crockery set and the letter might be linked."

Her husband flicked her a charged glance, but Ophelia Walker pretended not to notice.

"Your friend Mrs Dunsmuir mentioned that you found a tea set in your late sister's belongings when she passed away and that you were looking into your family tree. If I could just have a quick word with you, please?"

She didn't reply.

"That letter was written by a lady called Briar Forsyth … and I think this poor woman might have been accused of something that she didn't do…"

I took a step back in surprise as Ophelia Walker barged past her husband. Her face was contorted with frustration and anger. "It sounds as though you don't need to speak to me. You seem to know so much about me already."

"Ophelia," warned her husband.

She took no notice. "I can't help you. Now, can you please leave?"

And with that, she banged her panelled burgundy front door shut in my face.

Chapter Thirty-One

11ᵗʰ December 1970, Cup of Joy, Briar Glen

T he shop was like a Christmas grotto.

Helena knew she had gone berserk with the decorations, but she wanted to impress Chris so much and let him see she was serious about making the business a success.

She had arranged the bevelled windows with gold and silver tinsel from Woolworths to match the dangling baubles of the tree stationed there. She had even secured strands of the tinsel along the edges of the shelves. Their crockery stock glowed almost every bit as much as Helena's slew of decorations; everything from vintage Denby to Kilncraft Bacchus teacups and saucers and more unusual and expensive designs like Royal Copenhagen.

Mrs Auld had been so supportive of Helena's decision when she had told her she was accepting Chris's job offer. She hadn't seemed at all surprised. In fact, she admitted she had been expecting it. She had also been very helpful, surrendering the limited crockery stock she had to Chris, delighted that her only son would be staying in Briar Glen for the time being.

The whole process had been enthralling and bewildering, from Chris showing her around the shop (once a bicycle repair business, now transformed into this festive cornucopia) to recruiting staff, to their opening on 1st December, just in time for Christmas.

Helena had not been able to keep her new job quiet from Donald. She had chided herself for not telling him at the start. He had launched into a diatribe at first, going on about him being the breadwinner and Helena the homemaker. That was the way of things.

Helena's fists had balled by her sides as she mentally compared her unambitious husband with charismatic Chris.

It was only when she discovered her voice, after the last few months of having been thrown in at the deep end of business, that Donald observed in astonishment that his wife had morphed into another woman. He realised this with a quiet but grudging admiration.

"I'm still going to be here to take care of Marnie," pointed out Helena. "My mind is made up. It's not up for discussion."

Donald had stared back at his wife across their chintz-ridden sitting room, with her pretty tilting nose and defiant air. He had never seen her like this before. If he was being honest, it was rather attractive.

But before he could tell her as much, she had spun away on her wedged heel and vanished into the kitchen to prepare dinner and watch Crackerjack with Marnie.

Helena had changed. But was it for the better?

Right now, he wasn't sure.

But whether her husband was pleased with her new status as a working mum or not, Helena was too delirious with happiness to care. Although nothing had happened between her and Chris, she could sense the increasing tension and atmosphere.

It was wrong to will something to happen between them. She knew that. In some ways, she was relieved when Barbara and Angela, her two members of staff, were in the shop. It kept things safe and controlled.

Helena and Chris had exchanged stories of their past before but now that she was working for him in Cup of Joy, she felt as though each day she was discovering something new about him. He supported Rangers and Arsenal. He liked Elvis and Sweet. He loved spaghetti Westerns. They were peeling back deeper layers of each other's lives and sharing moments that she treasured.

It was only a matter of time until something happened. They both knew it and they refused to ignore it. They didn't want to.

It had been a brisk Friday afternoon of trade and the centre of Briar Glen was drizzled with a light flurry of snow. Locals had decided not to venture into town and so local businesses had been able to capitalise on keen Christmas shoppers.

Marnie had gone round to her friend Joanne's for tea straight from school. That had meant Helena was able to work a few extra hours and give Angela and Barbara a helping hand in Cup of Joy.

Helena was winding her crimson crocheted scarf around her neck, when Chris appeared from the stock room. "You dashing off? I thought Marnie was at her friend's?"

"She is."

"Well then. You can let me buy you a Christmas drink."

Helena fiddled with a strand of hair. "Oh."

Chris cocked his head to one side. "That wasn't exactly the response I was hoping for."

Helena's face broke into a grin. "And what were you hoping for? Bells? Whistles?"

"A full marching band at least."

Helena watched as the retro fairy lights strung against the back wall cast an angelic glow around Chris's head. She wanted to laugh. Angelic wasn't how she would describe him.

"And the answer is? I have to give you your Christmas present, Helena."

Helena was glad she was wearing her scarf. She could feel heat travelling up her neck. "If it's not a pink diamond, I'm not interested."

Chris smiled and reached into his jacket, which was hanging up on a nearby hook. He plucked a small jewellery box out of it, all glossy maroon wood and topped off with a lime-green bow. "Here. This is for you."

Helena's fingers fluttered to her neck. Her scarf was wrapped around it like a cobra and she had no idea what to do with her hands. "What is it?"

"I'm not telling you that. You have to open it."

Helena shot Chris a charged glance. She turned and reached under the counter. She had bought Chris a gift a few weeks ago and had hidden it in one of the locked compartment drawers she had a key for. She hadn't even been sure she was going to give it to him. But now she was so glad she had bought him something.

She had wrapped it in electric-blue foil paper sprinkled with Christmas trees and she'd tied a navy bow around it. A pretty gift tag, in the shape of a glittery snowflake, was attached.

They both let out flirtatious laughs, as the streetlamps outside cast a soupy glow.

"You first," insisted Chris.

They exchanged playful smiles, before Helena removed her thick scarf and deposited it on top of the counter. She felt self-conscious under Chris's intent hazel gaze.

She focused on her present, her fingers fumbling and pulling at the ribbon. She eased open the lid.

Nestled against the cream cushion inside was a hand-crafted brooch in the shape of a teacup and saucer, made of porcelain and decorated with the daintiest pink tea roses. Helena couldn't pull her eyes away from the dainty beauty of it. "Chris," she breathed after what seemed like an age. "It's … it's stunning."

"You like it?"

"I love it. Thank you so much." She allowed her fingers to trace its flower decoration again and again.

She snapped her head up. "Right. Your turn now."

There was so much intimacy captured between them at that moment. The two of them together, alone in Cup of Joy, with the Christmas weather swirling outside, shoppers huddled against the elements and clutching their purchases as they made their way home.

Chris smiled again at her as he tugged off the wrapping paper and deposited it on the counter beside her scarf. He slid open the oblong white box and admired the black marble and gold pen Helena had bought him.

"You're always losing them," she said in a rush, feeling gawky and self-conscious.

Chris's expression melted with appreciation. "Well, I can assure you that I won't be losing this one. Thank you. It's lovely."

Helena's throat constricted as she watched Chris's fingertips run up and down the pen. "So, how about that Christmas drink?"

The lights winking all around her, Chris's golden good looks, and the knowledge that Marnie was safe and having fun round at her school friend Joanne's – no doubt munching her way through platefuls of tuna paste sandwiches and watching Scooby-Doo – made Helena agonise over what to do.

One drink. One drink with this gorgeous man to celebrate Cup of Joy and the impending Christmas holidays and then she could catch a taxi home. "All right," she breathed, before she allowed herself to scrutinise what she was doing. "Just give me a moment."

Chris broke into a delighted grin. "Great. I'll just switch everything off."

Helena darted past him to the staff bathroom located at the rear of the shop. She closed the door behind her, before slumping against it. Adrenalin and longing rocketed through her.

Refusing to analyse what she was doing, she scrambled about in her fringed shoulder bag and retrieved her frosted pink lipstick. She slicked it on, her wide light blue eyes asking questions she was intent on ignoring.

She blew out a cloud of air, flicked her straight hair back over her shoulders and reached for the door handle. She was clipping her way back towards the shop floor, when muffled voices travelled towards her.

Helena drew up, gathering her belted winter coat tighter about her. Was that a last-minute customer? It was when the other person spoke again that realisation struck her in the chest. No. It couldn't be. It couldn't be Donald.

Helena pressed her rigid spine against the nearest wall. Her shoulder bag was digging into her side.

"So… I just wondered if you could reserve the… oh, hang on a second…" There was the noise of scrabbling around and crinkling paper. "It's the J&G Meakin Poppy tea set."

What? What was Donald doing here in Cup of Joy and why was

he asking about that tea set? Helena's head was whirring with guilt and confusion. She forced herself to take a deep breath.

From the shop floor, the conversation continued, much to Helena's horror and swirling guilt. "Sorry," followed up Donald, "I should have introduced myself. I'm Helena's husband."

Helena forced her eyes shut, willing this crazy, awkward situation away. What did he think he was doing? Why was he here? Was he suspicious that something was going on between her and Chris?

Chris's silence was tearing into Helena.

"You're her husband?" Chris managed after a pause. "Oh. Right. It's good to meet you at last. I'm Chris Auld. I own this place."

Helena forced herself away from the wall and risked a peek around the corner. The two men were exchanging polite smiles and handshakes.

"Helena is such an asset to this shop," said Chris. "She really has worked wonders."

Donald took in the shelves of crockery and the swathes of Christmas decorations fringing everywhere. "Helena has always been obsessed with crockery. Never understood it myself, but..." As though detecting Chris examining him, he corrected himself. "Sorry, it's just she has mentioned this particular tea set so many times at home since it arrived, I would like to buy it for her for Christmas."

Helena felt like she was watching the events play out through some sort of enveloping mist. She gripped her handbag tighter to her side.

Donald cast his ghostly grey gaze around. "Is she still here? Only that's her scarf and I wanted it to be a surprise."

"She's through the back," answered Chris. "She won't be long."

"Right."

Helena rubbed at her face, willing herself anywhere but here. This was awful. And that Meakin tea set Donald had mentioned... He couldn't afford that, so why was he even asking about it?

Helena felt embarrassed and clumsy, hiding behind the connecting door. She slumped her head back against the wall

"Price is no option," insisted Donald, his voice stinging her again and again. "I've been saving up for it."

No. No! This was all wrong. Guilt gnawed at her. She couldn't let him do this.

Jutting out her trembling chin, Helena made her way back out to the shop. Her legs trembled in her long boots. She drew on all her acting reserves to appear surprised at the sight of her husband standing there.

She didn't dare risk looking over at Chris, at least not straightaway.

Helena struggled to push out a smile at her husband. "Donald. What are you doing here?"

Chris watched, his jaw clenched through a forced smile.

"Oh, just thought I'd drop by and give you a lift home. We can collect Marnie from Joanne's on the way. It isn't great weather at the moment."

Helena snatched up her coil of red scarf, resting on top of the counter like a slumbering snake.

She was trapped in an agonising limbo. Chris was to her left, wearing a look of hurt that was etched into the angles of his handsome face. To the right, Donald was loitering there, hands stuffed into his pockets and his shoulders hunched over as usual.

The snow was spiralling down now.

Why did Donald want to buy her that tea set? She knew she had been going on about how beautiful it was at home, but he had given her the clear impression he wasn't even listening. Whenever she spoke about Cup of Joy or crockery, his eyes would glaze over.

Helena's hand reached to the top of her bag and brushed against the box containing the brooch Chris had just given her. Chris noticed. His mouth slid into a resigned ghost of a smile.

As Helena and Donald reached the shop door, Donald tugged it open and a blast of crisp December air pummelled her cheeks. She found herself almost barrelling into her husband's donkey-jacketed backt. "What we were just talking about," said Donald in cryptic tones to Chris. "Can you put it aside for me?"

"Sure. No problem. Goodnight, Helena. See you Monday."

Chris delivered the Meakin Poppy tea set on Saturday to her address, as Donald had requested. She and Marnie were out in the back garden, building a snowman and promising themselves a hot chocolate afterwards

What Helena didn't know was that Chris refused to charge Donald for the Meakin she had fallen in love with the first day it arrived at the shop. She had glimpsed its ruby-red Poppy pattern emblazoned over it like exploding hearts. It was ironic, as that was what her own heart felt like now.

As Helena listened to Marnie's excited chatter about putting one of her daddy's old bobble hats on top of the snowman's crooked head, a growing sense-of realisation shook Helena over and over.

What had she even been thinking? The sight of her red-nosed daughter dancing about in front of her brought the whole situation screaming into focus.

Visions of Donald standing there in Cup of Joy opposite Chris, prepared to bankrupt himself to buy her that tea set.

Chris was everything that her husband wasn't – confident, charismatic, dangerous – but what about Marnie?

She felt her leather-gloved hands working by themselves, disembodied, moulding and patting the snow into a rotund body. "You're doing a great job, Mummy," said Marnie, beaming up at her, her lashes spiked with cold.

Helena never returned to Cup of Joy on Monday morning. Her explanation to Donald was that she had experienced a change of heart about not being around at home as much and that she felt like Marnie was suffering. She knew that was a lie, but that was all she had.

Donald's initial surprise at her decision soon gave way to secret delight that his wife had seen sense in the end. He realised he couldn't extinguish her feelings for that flash idiot Chris Auld overnight, but arriving at that ridiculous shop out of the blue like that had been a stroke of genius on his part.

Donald congratulated himself again as he recalled his stunned wife standing there. Throwing in mention of that tea set she had been raving about had been a great idea too. And it turned out he hadn't even had to put his hand in his pocket for it. That poser Auld had insisted it was a leaving gift for Helena. No need to reveal that to his wife though.

She would be pining after him even more if she knew that, and he couldn't risk it.

Donald gave another self-congratulatory grin. Over before it even *started, thanks to him. And he had his wife back where she belonged. At home.*

_____

Helena avoided the town centre from then on. She couldn't face the prospect of seeing Cup of Joy, let alone Chris. The mere thought of it made her heart deflate.

Three weeks later, she was told by Mrs Docherty in the corner shop that Cup of Joy was closing, the shop was being sold and Chris was returning to London. "Don't think he could hack it up here," remarked Mrs Docherty with a dismissive sniff. "No doubt too quiet and parochial for the likes of him."

Helena bundled her shopping into her drawstring bag and escaped the stuffy confines of the shop before tears slithered down her face.

She never saw Chris again, but his parting gift was four of the most expensive tea sets in their stock, with a note that just said, For you – from me X.

That was all he left her, together with the memories she carried around on repeat in her head.

Cup of Joy was sold within a matter of weeks and became a florist's...

_____

It came as no surprise that Ophelia Walker made no attempt to contact me and I was struggling to decide what I should do next.

I did consider contacting Xander for advice, but he had

been even more aloof than usual since our last phone conversation. I didn't want to say anything either, for fear of igniting the issues between him and Jake again. I just wished Xander had told me himself, rather than letting me hear all the details from Jake.

What did please me was the feeling I was growing closer to piecing together the mystery of the tea set and letter. I knew I was getting somewhere, albeit more slowly than I had hoped and without help from Ophelia Walker. All the little threads leading back to the tea set and Briar Forsyth's letter had separated and frayed, but it was as though I could see what their destination could be now and how they might tie together.

Nevertheless, I knew I had to try and speak to Ophelia Walker again. The recognition on her face when she saw me standing there on her doorstep had been evident, yet she didn't want to discuss the tea set, the letter or why she had felt compelled to leave it with me in the first place and vanish.

But without speaking to her, I knew there were vital pieces of the puzzle missing and she was in possession of far more knowledge than I had at my disposal.

Saturday swung around and before I knew it, it was time for my dinner with Jake.

"Looking forward to it?" asked Mum, popping her head round the door of the shop that afternoon.

I nodded. "Yes. Of course."

It would be lovely, I assured myself. A dinner date on a

Saturday evening with a very attractive man. Of course I was looking forward to it. Why wouldn't I be? I fished out my ankle-length summery dress in ice-blue, decorated with pink roses, and secured my hair in a messy topknot.

Jake was half an hour late collecting me. I waited for an apology, but it didn't come. Instead, I opened my flat door to be greeted with a laconic smile. "Had an urgent phone call, but I'm here now."

My eyebrows arched with disapproval. He could have rung me and let me know. I bit back my irritation. I felt I should give him the benefit of the doubt.

As we drove towards Glasgow, leaving behind the scooped inlets of cottages and tended gardens for the glinting spires and thrusting blocks of the city, I filled in Jake about the situation with Ophelia Walker.

"I wouldn't give the old dear any more thought," he said with a dismissive raise of one hand. "If she doesn't want to talk to you, you'll just have to suck it up."

His blond profile concentrated on the road ahead. "If I were you, I'd sell that crockery and pocket the cash. This woman, whoever she is, left the tea set with you. If she loses out on the cash, that's her problem." He gave me a charming smile. ""She shouldn't have parted with it in the first place."

I studied his smiling profile. *But I'm not you.*

"Anyway, forget all about that tonight and let's enjoy this fish restaurant. It just received another five-star review in that broadsheet supplement."

"Fish? I thought we were going to that tapas bar."

Jake eased his growling white Audi TT into a parking space

in front of a lit-up, smoked-glass restaurant, proclaiming its name as Sea Scape.

His voice was brisk. "Change of plan. Thought this place would be better." He switched on his megawatt smile. "It's more expensive, but you're worth it."

He bounded out of the driver's side, leaving me to stare at his vacant black leather seat.

We were greeted by a fawning maître d', who directed us to a table by the window that overlooked the sprawling Botanic Gardens and its sea of impressive domed glasshouses. The colours swished across the sky and the sloping roofs bled together in the pastel July-evening light.

The menu was sensational, an elaborate affair of everything from seafood linguine and clam broth to cod and chorizo stew and smoked trout salad.

"What do you recommend, seeing as you have been here before? I can't make up my mind." I looked across the table at a distracted Jake. He was holding his leather-bound menu but wasn't paying any attention to it. He seemed preoccupied, shifting in his high-backed chair for a better view of the restaurant car park.

"Jake?"

He adjusted the collar of his stripey Paul Smith shirt. "Sorry?"

I followed his absent gaze out of the windows beside us. "I asked you what you would recommend from the menu."

"Oh. Yeah. Sorry." He dragged his attention back to the menu and gave the pages a cursory glance. "How about the stir-fry prawns with peppers and spinach, or the Thai-style steamed fish?"

Then he transferred his attention back to the car park, scanning the vehicles already there with his keen, light eyes.

I lowered my menu. All around us, there were tables occupied by couples exchanging conversation, discussing what they wanted to eat or sharing an intimate moment. "Jake? Are you all right?"

He blinked back at me across the table, the flickering glow from the candle centrepiece wavering like an exotic dancer. "What? Oh, yes. Sorry."

I twisted round in my seat, following his gaze out of the window and down to the unremarkable car park. "You seem very distracted."

Jake snatched up his menu again. "No. I'm fine. Really. Just struggling to decide what I'm going to have."

"Well, I think the menu will help, rather than the car park."

Jake let out a loud, theatrical laugh that drew curious glances from a couple of other tables. What the hell was the matter with him?

I examined him across the top of my menu. *Oh, for pity's sake!* He was doing it again, gawping out of the window and not communicating with me at all. I could have been exchanged for the Madam Tussaud's waxwork of Kylie Minogue and he wouldn't have noticed.

I sat for a few more moments before his rude behaviour ignited my indignation. I thumped down my menu beside my polished cutlery and angled myself further round in my chair.

But this time, Jake shot out his hand and seized mine. I gave a jolt of surprise that almost made me bang my knees against the underside of the table. His charged expression was swivelling between me and the restaurant entrance.

I could hear the effusive maître d' behind me, greeting more guests who had arrived. Jake continued to hold my hand in a tight grip across the table. It was beginning to feel rather uncomfortable. I think I preferred it when he was ignoring me to admire the car park. "Jake. Do you think you could release my hand, please?"

But he wasn't paying any attention to me. Again. His expression was contorting from anticipation to smug expectation. He was focused on something over my right shoulder.

Now what was he looking at? I made a move to follow his gaze and prepared to twist around in my chair again, but Jake stunned me a second time, by leaning across the table and snatching my lips with his in a prolonged kiss.

It took a few seconds for my brain and my lips to realise what was happening. Once the weird situation registered, I sprang back, breathless and stunned. My cheeks were zinging with heat.

I fluffed at the hem of my dress, aware of bemused diners looking over.

Then came a flicker of movement at my elbow.

I looked up, expecting to see a member of the waiting staff hovering there. But it wasn't.

It was Xander.

Chapter Thirty-Two

J ake grinned up at Xander with a look of triumph.

Behind Xander hovered a stern-looking Saffy Clements, dressed in a pillar-box-red shift dress, her corkscrew dark curls springing past her shoulders. She looked gorgeous.

With Xander sporting a dashing black satin waistcoat, charcoal shirt and trousers, the two of them were a very good-looking couple on a night out together. That thought made my insides twist.

I swallowed.

"Good evening, Xander." Jake grinned. "What a coincidence this is."

The way he said it – his words dripping in sarcasm – made me sit up straighter. I stared across the top of the flickering candle decoration at him. My eyes narrowed with suspicion.

Xander's chilly expression fell on me. "Isn't it just?" He ignored Jake. "Out on a date?"

I opened my mouth to speak, my mind zig-zagging. "Yes. No. Well. Kind of."

Saffy's attention travelled from me to Jake and back again. She gave me an odd look as she started to move past us in a pair of pointed heels. "Well, have a nice evening. Come on, Xander. Let's go to our table."

But Xander didn't move. He remained standing at my shoulder, his eyes searching mine. They carried an echo of something akin to disappointment. Dragging them away, he transferred his attention back to Jake, who sat there, his mouth twitching with amusement.

"Let's go somewhere else," ground out Xander after a few moments.

Saffy pushed out her bottom lip. "But I thought you wanted to try this place."

Xander's jaw was stiff. "There's always another time." He placed one hand at the small of Saffy's back and the simple, intimate movement made my heart deflate. He turned his broad back on Jake and me, throwing an "Enjoy your evening" over his shoulder.

I swivelled around in my seat, watching them leave the restaurant, with the confused maître d' hurrying after them, asking if they were all right and insisting he could find them an alternative table closer to the alcove, if they would prefer it.

I swung back to face Jake, who was grinning like a Great White.

"Well, what do you know? It's a small world, isn't it?" His demeanour was victorious. Gone was the tense body language and fascination with the restaurant car park.

"Sorry about being so distracted earlier," he oozed. "Now,

let's take a look at this gorgeous menu, shall we?"

While he persisted in reeling off small talk and exclaiming at the array of seafood dishes on offer, I found my fingers reaching up to touch my lips. Jake was now describing how wonderful the Scottish salmon was said to be here, but my brain was too preoccupied with what had just taken place.

The sudden and unexpected change of restaurant venue; Jake's constant monitoring of the car park; his surreptitious observation of the restaurant entrance; then that theatrical kiss and the sudden hand-holding, which just happened to occur as Xander and Saffy were coming through the door…

Jake was pointing to something else on the menu. "I am rather partial to prawns, as well. What do you think, Soph?"

The way he called me "Soph" made my fingers ball in the lap of my dress. It was all so obvious and contrived. He had used me to get one over on Xander. I struggled to keep my voice level. "You must think I'm stupid."

"Sorry?"

I leant in closer to the edge of the table. "You planned this, Jake."

He was sitting in his chair, chest puffed out with self-congratulation as though he had discovered a cure for the common cold. "Planned what? I don't follow."

"I do," I ground out. "You wanted to annoy Xander, so you arranged for us to come here."

I folded my arms across my chest, making the silky material of my dress rustle.

A waiter appeared at the table to take our order, but Jake dismissed him with an arrogant jerk of his head. "Not now. In a minute."

The waiter gave him a chilly stare and vanished again. Jake flipped back to his charm offensive. "Oh, don't be silly. It was just a coincidence, that's all."

He reached one hand across the gleaming white tablecloth, gesturing for me to take his, but I didn't. Instead, my teeth clamped together.

My bracelets rattled against my wrist, as I tightened my folded arms. "That's why you've been all jumpy and that's why you kissed me. You did all this to rile Xander."

Jake let out an unconvincing laugh. "Of course I didn't. How would I know Frozen North and his lady friend were going to stroll in here?"

"You tell me. It's very odd you changed our restaurant venue at the last minute."

Jake's shoulders stiffened under his stripy shirt.

"Is that why you were late picking me up tonight? Because you were busy ferreting out where Xander and Saffy were going and wanted to make sure we happened to be at the same place?"

Jake shuffled in his chair, like a mischievous child. He opened his mouth to protest and then snatched back whatever excuse he was about to make, when he picked up on my blazing anger. There was a resigned sigh, which fuelled my embarrassment and annoyance even more. "Yes. All right. You got me."

I fought to control my annoyance, keen not to make an entertaining scene for the surrounding diners. "I thought as much. I know you have history with him. You told me so yourself."

My thoughts travelled back to Xander's eyes searching

mine when he saw us sitting here. He must have seen Jake kiss me. It would have been difficult not to, the way Jake lunged across the table. The thought of him seeing that made my heart wither. "There was no need to involve me in your stupid games."

"It was only a bit of fun," snorted Jake. "The guy is so full of himself, he deserves taking down a notch or two."

He shot forward in his chair again, a pleading edge to his features. "Look, I admit I did time that kiss so North would see it, but if it's any consolation, I enjoyed it."

There was that testosterone-filled smile again. "Come to think of it, I wouldn't mind a re-run, if you have no objections."

He had to be joking. Was this idiot for real? Couldn't he hear what an utter knob he has? It was like he had no filter. What the hell was I doing, still sitting across from him?

Catching sight of a taxi gliding into the car park below, I jumped to my feet and snatched up my purse from the table. A family of four were preparing to disgorge from it. I was aware of inquisitive looks from a couple of tables around us, but I didn't care.

I wanted out of this restaurant and I wanted to get away from this imbecile.

Jake stared up at me. "What are you doing? Where are you going? Sit down, Soph."

"Stop calling me Soph," I hissed. "Whatever juvenile games you want to play, Jake, you sure as hell are not involving me in them."

"Aww, come on. No harm done."

That's where you're wrong. There was harm done. Xander's reaction was testament to that.

My fingers dug deeper into the soft leather of my small bag. "Well, if you can't see that, then I pity you, Jake." I picked up my copy of the menu and turned to where there was a description of the chef's specials. An older lady at the next table was drinking in the scene playing out beside her, with her forkful of salad half suspended before her lips.

I turned to Jake and waggled the menu at him. "I recommend the sea bass. It sounds delicious."

And then I was clattering out of the restaurant and down the steps towards the taxi in my heels, stinging with hurt and embarrassment about it all.

I arrived home, anxious to clamber into bed and sleep away this evening.

God, what a car crash that had been! Jake had turned out to be manipulative, with all the maturity of a five-year-old.

I was tempted to ring Xander and try to explain what had happened, but my pride stopped me. What on earth could I say to him? He was out with Saffy this evening anyway and I was sure she wouldn't want her night out with Xander interrupted by me. I could sense I wasn't one of her favourite people anyway.

Maybe it was best just to leave things as they were. It was a tangle of rivalry and resentment between Jake and Xander, and me wading in could make things even worse.

I changed into my PJs and gave the baked beans an aggressive stir in the saucepan, before fetching a huge hunk of Cornish Cove cheese from the fridge. Once my toast was golden, I drizzled the baked beans over the toast and completed it with a dusting of grated cheese over the top. You could never have too much cheese when you felt an utter tit and needed a plateful of comfort food.

I sat at my kitchen table and ate, dissecting how I could have been so stupid as to let my guard down. I cut a square of toast. After Callum, I swore I wouldn't be manipulated again. Talk about déjà vu!

I kept receiving images of Xander's wounded expression when he saw me with Jake. Why did he look so hurt? Maybe it had brought back memories of his ex.

I tried to distract myself with thoughts of the tea set and Briar's letter, but as for Ophelia Walker, that promise of a development seemed to have screeched to a dead end.

I picked up my mobile lying in front of me on the kitchen table as I ate. I grew annoyed at myself when I realised I was checking my messages, to see if Xander had tried to ring me.

But why would he?

There were three missed calls from Jake and then one dramatic message from him, which aggravated me even more. "Come on, Soph! I didn't mean any harm by it. But you have to admit, Xander North has a poker up his arse." I listened, my mouth drawn into a tight line. "After what happened with Nadia and the crap reviews he gave my work..." He paused, before his message became more petulant. "I don't know why you got so aerated over it all anyway. Unless you fancy old Frozen North yourself..."

My fingers dug into my phone, as his muddled Scots-

Transatlantic ramble continued. "Well, just a warning. If you do have any ideas, you ought to know that he and that woman he was with tonight have become an item. I hear it's serious."

My stomach twisted in on itself. Pictures of Xander and Saffy together lodged themselves in front of my eyes. I'd had enough of this. I'd heard enough. I deleted the message, my fingers jabbing at the buttons on my phone. Why did it matter so much to me what Xander thought or what he thought he saw?

He was with Saffy, for pity's sake!

I would not be part of their squabbles. I didn't want to be caught up in their mess.

I took another savage bite of my toast, even though I no longer felt hungry. Xander North. Frozen North. He must have recovered from Nadia and was now moving on with Saffy – and who could blame him? She was very attractive and talented too.

A swift emotional punch landed in my stomach. I clattered my fork down onto the plate and stared off into the distance. What with losing my gran, resigning from Castle Marrian, and the sudden and dramatic acquisition of the shop, there had been so much going on in my life. A tsunami of events which I had been trying to control, but which had left me knocked breathless on the shore.

My thoughts insisted on conjuring up more pictures of Xander, even though that was the last thing I wanted or needed right now. Perhaps Frozen North had thawed after all and Saffy had been the one to do it.

Chapter Thirty-Three

Monday morning brought a sombre sky. But that didn't deter the tourists, who still appreciated and exclaimed at all the beautiful flowered gardens Briar Glen had to offer.

The local schoolchildren were enjoying the last month or so of their summer holidays, so there were the usual demands for ice-cream or a bus trip into town as frazzled parents herded them past the door of The Cup That Cheers.

Cass was busy extolling the virtues of a dainty set of Theodore Haviland Apple Blossom China to two elderly ladies, who were explaining they were here visiting their eldest sister at the residential care home. "We just had to pop in," beamed the one in a bright blue rain jacket. "We've heard so many lovely things about this place."

Her sister, who carried the same proud profile, indicated one of our farmhouse-style teapots, a vintage Lingard, all painted and gilded English floral pottery. "I'm a bit more of a traditionalist."

"Well, hopefully we have something to suit all tastes," smiled Cass. "The Haviland Apple Blossom pattern was discontinued after 1989, so we think these were made some time between 1940 and 1989 in New York. Or perhaps you would like to take a look at something a little more modern?"

She gestured to a couple of open boxes littered with polystyrene, which had been delivered only ten minutes before. "You can see we haven't even unpacked these yet."

The two sisters admired the vintage Sadler teapot, with its pink lid and cherry blossom pattern, which Cass had lifted out of its box.

I smiled over at Cass and mouthed, "Good work," while the two ladies continued their discussion. Someone had been doing their homework!

My attention travelled to Jake Caldwell's painting on the wall and I could feel my admiration and appreciation of Cass waning and my eyes narrowing. I was in two minds about whether to remove it and stash it in the store room. I stung with embarrassment and anger at the thought of Saturday night. Then I pictured Xander's expression as he saw Jake and me sat together.

They are as bad as each other, I concluded to myself, winding each other up. I could understand why Xander must have felt betrayed by Nadia, but crucifying Jake's art career like that – and then Jake using me to stick two fingers back up at Xander. Bloody hell! It was like witnessing two warring toddlers!

A flicker of movement made me turn around, causing me to forget Jake and Xander's rivalry.

My eyes widened.

It was Ophelia Walker.

She continued to linger there in the shop doorway, shadows of uncertainty crossing her face, despite the confident way she was dressed in a pale biscuit linen suit and a floaty printed scarf draped around her shoulders.

It was like one of those tense scenes in a spaghetti Western with Clint Eastwood. All that was missing was rolling tumbleweed and one of us chewing on a matchstick.

I took tentative steps over the wooden floor, worried in case any sudden movement or the wrong word would make her change her mind and vanish again. "Hello, Mrs Walker."

She gave a brief nod of her silver hair. "Do you have a few minutes to talk?"

Cass was occupied with the two ladies, who were now debating the finer points of porcelain versus ceramic.

Had she decided to talk about the tea set? What had made her change her mind? I tried not to feel too optimistic. I had no idea why she was here – yet. "Yes. Of course. We can chat in my office."

Ophelia Walker tugged her long jacket tighter around herself, despite the cosy atmosphere in the shop and the muggy summer temperature outside. She scanned my office as I invited her to sit down. "Would you like a cup of tea or a coffee perhaps?"

"A tea would be very nice, thank you."

I slid back out of my office and chose two of our prettiest pastel-green Tuscan China cups and saucers from the kitchenette, which we had converted out of a corner of the store room. Well, this was unexpected! And even though I'd only just promised myself that I wouldn't speculate on why Ophelia was here, I found myself doing it anyway.

My excitement mounted as I watched the kettle boil and prepared a pot of tea in my and Cass's matching Tuscan China teapot. It felt indulgent and satisfying to use something pretty and with an air of the antique for ourselves. My grandmother would have been proud.

I fetched a matching plate from the cupboard above my head, together with a packet of chocolate digestives. I set everything out on a tray and negotiated my way back to the office. I could hear Cass and the two elderly sisters sharing a giggle about "solid bottoms". I presumed they were talking about teapot bases.

Mrs Walker was sitting in the same pensive position when I returned. I set the loaded tea tray on my desk and proceeded to pour the tea. Mrs Walker accepted her cup and saucer with a murmured "Thank you." She flicked me a reserved look over its rim.

There was a charged pause, before she blurted, "I'm sorry. I should have spoken to you when you came to see me." She took an embarrassed sip of her tea and set the cup and saucer back down on my desk. It gave the faintest chink against the mahogany.

I offered an understanding smile and tried to appear calm. "So, you do know about the tea set?"

On seeing Mrs Walker's small, embarrassed smile and nod, my stomach performed an excited "Whoosh!"

"It was the discovery of the tea set that made me decide to investigate my family tree – well, that and the fact I'm now retired. Lots more time on my hands." She clasped her fingers together in her nervous lap. "I was adamant I wasn't going to speak to you but Hal, my husband, talked me round."

She rolled her lined, dark eyes. "When I first found the tea set amongst my late sister's belongings, I was going to keep it."

I sat forward. "And was that when you discovered the letter?"

"Not immediately," she confessed. "It was the next day, when I investigated the case the crockery was in, that I found the letter in the pouch." Mrs Walker reached out for her teacup and took another sip. She replaced it on the saucer and let her attention drift to the couple of A5-sized paintings of teapots decorating my office wall.

"I'm a bit obsessed," I remarked, following her gaze.

Mrs Walker responded with an absent smile, before continuing with her explanation. "After you visited, Hal reminded me how sad and desperate that letter sounded. He said it wasn't like me to turn my back on helping someone or trying to right a wrong." Her serious mouth glided into another small smile. "My husband knows what an interfering old busybody I can be. He also knows only too well how to play on my conscience."

"Well, I really appreciate you coming to speak to me." My brain was bubbling over with so many questions I wanted to ask her. "Mrs Walker, may I ask you what you know about the tea set or what you have been able to find out?"

She raised her plucked brows almost to the top of her silvery hairline. "It's true what they say, you know. Sometimes, ignorance is bliss."

I blinked across my desk at her. Through the closed officer

door, I could make out the chirpy murmurings of Cass, the laughter of the two elderly sisters and the happy bleeps from the cash register. Cass's affable, warm personality was securing yet another sale.

Mrs Walker's voice interrupted my thoughts. "About looking into my family tree – I had been procrastinating so much about it and I think I was driving poor Hal to distraction." Her eyes softened. "Annabel – my sister – was fascinated by Scottish history and was particularly keen to read up about Briar Glen, what with all its supposed connections to the blue rose, the lovely gardens the locals have and, of course, Castle Marrian."

I asked Mrs Walker if her sister had been able to discover anything interesting about Briar Glen or any of its previous inhabitants.

She sighed. "If only she had been able to. She died suddenly a year ago, not long after she began researching the local area."

"I'm so sorry," I said. "I lost my grandmother a few months ago. That's how I came to open this place."

Mrs Walker appraised her pretty, flower-speckled teacup and the teapot paintings on my office walls. "Well, I'm sure your grandmother would be very proud of you."

I gently steered our conversation back to the family tree investigations she had mentioned. "May I ask what *you* found out, Mrs Walker? About your family tree, I mean?"

She let out a dry laugh. "I didn't discover I was related to a Nobel peace prize winner or a doctor who saved millions of lives, if that's what you mean. If only that were true."

I offered her a gentle smile of encouragement, willing her to explain. The suspense was draining.

She let out a resigned sigh and, taking another sip of her tea, settled herself to explain. "It's more to do with the rattling of skeletons."

I sank back in my swivel chair, conjuring up images of Briar Forsyth's letter and wondering who or what these skeletons were.

"I think what was most hurtful was discovering that my mother had kept something from us – from Annabel and me." Ophelia Walker regarded me. "I suppose all families have a secret or two, but to find out like this was the greatest shock of my life."

And with that, she began to tell me.

Chapter Thirty-Four

"It turns out that my late great-aunt Isadora was married twice. We weren't aware of that at all."

"Right. I see."

I hoped my eager expression was convincing Mrs Walker to continue with her explanation.

She clasped and unclasped her hands. "Her first marriage we knew about, of course. That was to my great-uncle, Sydney Morrice."

"And the second?"

She fixed me with her gaze. "It transpires that her second husband was Jonathan Gray."

I blinked at her in shock. "As in *the* Jonathan Gray, who was named in the tea-set letter?"

Ophelia Walker's pink slicked mouth grew grim. "The very same."

I leant forward. "And you didn't know about this up until then?"

"Not a word. My mother never said anything about Isadora

being married twice, let alone who her second husband was. Nor did the rest of my family, come to that."

She glanced up at my office paintings again, before returning her attention to me. "I can't say I'm surprised they didn't want it to discuss it. Jonathan Gray's name was dirt around here. From my research, he could be charming when he wanted to be, but he had no scruples whatsoever."

"Mrs Walker, how much do you know about this Jonathan Gray? Up until that letter, I'd never heard of him."

"He wasn't a pillar of the local community. I'm sure that marriage wasn't one that Isadora would have been proud of. Bad enough that she was considered a bit wild, let alone another marriage to the likes of him."

I sank back, digesting all of this. "And he was the son of Leonora and Chadwick Gray, who owned Castle Marrian?"

"That's right. The very same. A spoilt, audacious individual, if ever there was one. Goodness knows he must have charmed my great-aunt though, when she married him."

"And what happened to Isadora?"

"All I could find ou, was that after their marriage foundered, she took off to London in 1898 and was never seen or heard from again."

I thought of the peacock tea set concealed in the bottom of my wardrobe and the letter to Jonathan Gray from Briar Forsyth nestling in beside it. "I worked as a wedding planner up at Castle Marrian before opening my crockery shop and I never even knew that his family once owned it."

Mrs Walker hitched up a brow as she finished the remnants of her tea. "Oh, did you? It's such an impressive place. I can't say that surprises me that you weren't aware of the Grays' links to it. I think the folks around here have airbrushed them out of the history books."

I eyed her. "Is that why you didn't want to keep the tea set? Because it belonged to Jonathan Gray's family?"

Ophelia Walker nodded. "I didn't want any connection to that man – not after what I discovered about him."

I hoped my silence might encourage her to expand, and after a few moments of inward debate, Ophelia Walker gave a resigned sigh. "When I discovered he had been married to Isadora, I did some more digging. It would seem that our Mr Gray was rather partial to the young ladies of Briar Glen and ended up fathering several children; well, when I say fathering…"

I blinked at her. "You mean getting these young women pregnant and then abandoning them?"

"Exactly. The local librarian was very helpful. He pointed me in the right direction when it came to birth records."

Well. It sounded like Isadora had had a lucky escape in the end. "This lady who signed the tea set letter," I began again, "Briar Forsyth. Do you happen to know anything about her?"

"Not as yet," she admitted. "But I'm hoping to remedy that."

"Would you like some help?" I offered. "That letter she wrote to Jonathan Gray touched me and … well … it sounds as if she could very well be another casualty of his."

Mrs Walker's lips pursed. "I don't doubt that for a second." She inclined her silky, silvery head and a glimmer of a smile emerged, banishing her usual stern veneer. "You must think I'm a silly old fool, abandoning that tea set the way I did and then hurrying away. But after losing my sister so suddenly and then discovering the link that tea set has to the likes of Jonathan Gray, well, I don't think I was thinking straight. Grief can do some very strange things to you."

My thoughts strayed to my grandmother. "There's no need for you to explain, Mrs Walker. Losing someone you love, well, it's like a part of you dies with them and all rationality goes out the window."

She gave a watery smile. "I'm so sorry I didn't do this before. Thank you for being so understanding." Her powdered cheeks pinged with gratitude. "I would be delighted if you were willing to help me, Sophie."

I watched her rise to her feet, scooping up her leather bag and pushing it under one arm. "And please call me Ophelia."

Chapter Thirty-Five

Before she left, Ophelia suggested we meet up at her house at the end of the week. "That will give me a bit of time to sort out Annabel's notes. I just wish she had been given the chance to do more of what she loved before she…" Her voice tailed off into a whisper.

I reached out and patted her on the arm. "Are you sure you feel up to this? The last thing I want to do is upset you or distress you."

Ophelia smiled and jutted out her chin in an act of defiance. "In a lot of ways, it will be comforting. It will be giving her research the attention it deserves. She was so enthusiastic about her history." Her face melted into a wistful expression.

We arranged for me to pop round after I closed The Cup That Cheers on Friday.

"We'll have dinner," she insisted, brooking no argument. "Then we can get going over a glass of Hal's homemade wine."

I decided, after the mention of Hal's delicious-sounding

libation, that I wouldn't drive to Ophelia's after work on Friday, but that I would take a taxi there and home instead.

The two elderly sisters had departed, clutching their purchases, by the time Ophelia left.

"They even bought two of the Royal Albert Polka Rose cups and saucers," explained Cass with satisfaction. I noticed her cast her eyes to the floor for a second. "I hope it's okay, but I noticed a tiny chip on one of the cup handles, so I gave them a discount of fifteen per cent."

"Of course, that's okay," I insisted. "That's what I want The Cup That Cheers to be all about: excellent customer service. You did great!"

Cass's elfin face glowed with satisfaction, but our conversation was interrupted by the insistent ring of my mobile.

I frowned down at my phone. "Oh. It's Xander."

Cass took herself off back towards the counter.

I straightened my back, willing my voice to sound detached, but noticing straightaway that he appeared odd and distracted. "Hi, Sophie. I was just ringing to see how things were going."

"With me or with the tea set?" I closed my eyes for a moment, realising I sounded rather mardy. But I couldn't help it. I had no idea what was going on here. This was the first time we had spoken since the fiasco with Jake in the restaurant two nights ago.

I smiled out at a couple of backpackers who were pointing to our summery window display of yellow and blue crockery.

There followed an annoying silence until he spoke again. "Any developments about the tea set or the letter?"

So, this call wasn't about me – he wasn't going to ask me whether I had felt awkward at all, caught up in his and Jake's feud, or tell me that he might have experienced a pang of jealousy, seeing me sitting there with Jake Caldwell in the first place.

Frozen North indeed.

I pressed my lips together, concealing a bolt of hurt. I was admitting to myself that I had felt irked at seeing him with Saffy, all curves and curls in her red dress. I'd fought to ignore it, but there it was.

I forced myself to speak again. I sounded crisp and matter-of-fact. "Things are moving in the right direction. It's a bit of a long story, but I've discovered the identity of the lady who left the tea set here at the shop. It turns out her late sister was really into local history and she was compiling notes about Briar Glen before she passed away."

I watched the two blonde backpackers make their way into the shop.

"That sounds promising," said Xander. "Will you keep me posted on how things go? I have a friend of a friend in France who is an avid collector of vintage crockery. He is very interested…"

Frustration overtook me. The sight of him with Saffy, and the way he was acting all bristly, stoked my annoyance, prodding at it like a sharp stick. "Of course. It's all about the money, isn't it?"

"Sorry?"

Cass moved to welcome the backpackers as I marched towards the rear of the shop. Spools of honey sun were splashing across the wooden floor. "There are lives tangled up in that tea set and with that letter: histories, relationships and families. It's not just about profit, Xander."

He surprised me by cutting through what I was saying. His tone was strained. "Hey! Hang on a second. What do you take me for? Some sort of heartless idiot?"

I clamped my mouth shut and looked around the shop.

"Did you have a good time on Saturday night?"

I clutched my mobile, surprised by his sudden question. A flame of jealousy lit up inside me, as I pictured Xander and Saffy strolling into the restaurant together, like one of those glamorous couples in a Christmas perfume ad. "I could ask the same about you."

"Pardon?"

"Well, you were out to dinner with Saffy."

"Just as friends."

I pictured her in her slinky dress. I was certain Saffy was harbouring hopes of much more than that.

"You're a grown woman, of course, and it's up to you what you do and who with, but I should warn you that he's bad news, Sophie."

I blinked at Xander's growling tone down the line. "Oh, I know all about the history between you and Jake Caldwell."

A crackling silence ensued for a moment. "You do?"

"Yes. He told me everything."

Xander was wrong-footed. "You're kidding? He actually told you? And you're okay with it?"

Right now, I didn't feel like I owed him an explanation. The fact I had discovered Jake was an arrogant, childish prat was my business. "I'm sorry, but I have to go. We have customers."

I gripped my mobile to my ear. "I'll keep you updated on

how things go with the notes Ophelia Walker's sister compiled and if there is anything useful in there."

Xander was distracted. "Who?"

"The lady who left the tea set with me."

I could sense his momentary confusion down the line. What was going on with Xander? He didn't sound like himself at all. He was normally so composed. Whatever it was, Jake telling me what had happened between them clearly hadn't been something he had expected. Even from a distance, I could hear the calm and cool Xander North was lost for words.

I politely terminated the call but for the rest of the day I had a ball of unsettled frustration rolling around inside my stomach. In one way, it would have been far better for me if Xander had remained incommunicado.

The fact that he had been in touch had upset the rhythm I was hoping to achieve again in my life.

I did remove the Jake Caldwell painting though, with the assistance of Cass, who frowned at my decision to take it down but didn't ask any questions.

Once we'd stashed it in the store room, I threw a spare sheet of purple canvas over it.

That made me feel a little better.

Chapter Thirty-Six

After a gorgeous dinner of roast chicken with all the trimmings, followed by a slice of warm apple pie and lashings of creamy custard, Hal insisted I sample some of his homemade red wine. "I know you're supposed to have red with red meat, but I don't think the Etiquette Police will be coming to arrest me any time soon."

I slumped back against their sofa and took a sip of the wine. It was ruby-red, with a fresh, tangy taste that reminded me of warm fields of sunshine. It was glorious. "After all this, I won't be able to move," I joked.

Ophelia laughed as she reappeared from the kitchen and set down a tea tray. "You don't need to. I'll bring through Annabel's notes in a jiffy."

I set down my drained wine glass and eyed Ophelia's tea set with appreciation. It was white porcelain and clotted with red poppies and butterflies

When she noticed me admiring it, I blushed. "Sorry. I can never switch off. Is that Victorian, by any chance?"

"It is," replied Ophelia, impressed. "How did you know?"

"The cups and saucers have a particular wavy edge to them, which was indicative of many of the Victorian crockery sets. It's lovely."

"It was my mother's. She received it as a wedding present from her parents and passed it down to me."

Once Hal took himself off with a topped-up wine glass of his homemade brew into the conservatory, Ophelia vanished to retrieve the box of her late sister's research into Briar Glen.

She bustled back a few moments later, carrying a large brown cardboard box that contained what appeared to be an array of exercise jotters and fancy patterned notebooks.

I jumped up from the sofa to assist her and took the box from her, setting it down on the fawn carpet.

"There isn't a huge amount here," she said with a ring of concern. "So, I don't know how lucky we are going to be finding out anything more about Jonathan Gray, let alone any mention of Briar Forsyth."

"Don't worry," I assured her. "It's worth taking a look anyway. It will be very interesting, I'm sure."

Ophelia sank down beside me on her mink chenille sofa and then we began the process of looking through the material.

I noticed her start as she picked up the first notebook, which was a quilted, jewelled affair. "This is the first time I've been able to go anywhere near these things since Annabel passed. I didn't have the heart to before."

Annabel's handwriting filled the lined pages. It was small, neat and controlled, in a mixture of black and blue ink. "At least my sister used headings. That might help us a bit more."

Sure enough, headings breaking up the paragraphs, such as

Local churches, History of the town clock and *The Blue Briar Glen Rose*, provided some sort of rough guide.

I read with interest Annabel's notes on the Briar Glen Rose:

The powder-blue Briar Glen rose was said to have grown in abundance in the area.

Although no actual evidence of it exists, the image of this beautiful flower became closely associated with Briar Glen. It also provided an attractive emblem for the local stonemasons to use when the cottages were built.

Almost all of the local cottages possess an engraving above their door, depicting the mysterious blue Briar Glen rose in full bloom.

The blue rose was said to represent something impossible to comprehend or a dream that may never be fulfilled.

When falling in love, roses of this shade are said to bring hope when love may be unrequited.

Xander's serious, dark features materialised in my head, but I pushed him away and riffled through a few more pages. This was ridiculous! Could I have chosen a more difficult man to have a crush on?

"Are you all right, Sophie?"

I turned with a start to look at Ophelia beside me. "Oh yes. Sorry. I'm fine."

Ophelia set the notebook she had been flicking through down on her lap. "You're tired. You've been working all day. It was selfish of me to suggest we do this tonight."

I shook my ponytail vigorously. "Not at all. Come on. Let's finish that pot of tea and carry on for a little longer."

———————

The July night sky had surrendered to darkness and the soupy streetlights were splashing across the cul-de-sac outside Ophelia's sitting-room window. She rustled around, clicking on her table lamps.

Between us, we had gone through a number of the notebooks now and the more innocuous orange exercise books, but there had been nothing of note, apart from interesting enthusiastic mentions about a couple of local church ministers from ninety years ago, who had shared a deep attraction to an enigmatic widow.

There were also, according to Annabel's research, rumours of a blue briar rose appearing in 1925 in the garden of a young woman who was in love with her piano teacher.

I passed across this section to Ophelia to read. She blinked, her lined mouth twitching with amusement. "Well. I had no idea our little town was such a hotbed of passion and lust."

She noticed me stretch my arms behind my head.

"Let's call it a day," she suggested." We can make arrangements to resume this another day."

I angled my feet away from the pile of notebooks slipping over each other by our legs. "Are you sure?"

"Absolutely. Would you like a coffee before you go?"

"No, thank you. I'll ring and order my taxi home now. I'm working tomorrow. Thank you for such a delicious dinner."

Ophelia beamed at me. "You're welcome. I'm so sorry we can't give you a lift home. That's my husband's homemade wine for you!"

I was about to propel myself up from the sofa to assist

Ophelia with returning her tea set to the kitchen, when something caught my attention further down in the cardboard box.

At first, it appeared just like the other notebooks. It was when I leant forward to examine it further that I caught sight of something scribbled across the front of its red velvet cover.

Castle Marrian & The Grays.

I picked it up and turned the notebook round. My heart leapt with hope. "Ophelia. Look at this."

Her hazel eyes widened. She hurried to sink back down on the sofa beside me. "Oh, my goodness. Well spotted! Let's take a look."

I passed the notebook to her and she opened it, so that it lay between our laps. Unlike the other notebooks we had looked at, this one contained grand black and white photographs of Castle Marrian pasted into its pages.

We exchanged excited glances.

The first few pages consisted of bullet points: dates of when Castle Marrian was built, who tended to its sprawling grounds, how many rooms it possessed. It was odd to see my former workplace captured at that particular point in time. It was still impressive, but there was something more formal about its appearance then, compared to now.

Perhaps my memories of its modern, lavish, confetti-strewn weddings were colouring my view.

Ophelia studied the pictures. "How long did you work there for?"

"Three years, but I left in April. That's why I opened the crockery shop." When Ophelia raised her brows in an enquiring manner, I smiled. "It's a bit of a long story. Remind me to tell you about it next time."

"Oh, don't worry. I will!"

It was only when Ophelia turned a few more of the pages that we both stopped.

We stared down at Annabel's capital-lettered heading before scanning the scribbled paragraphs that followed.

We swapped wide-eyed stares and read on.

Chapter Thirty-Seven

T his particular section was headed *LIST OF STAFF EMPLOYED AT CASTLE MARRIAN.*

I pointed to the entries and both Ophelia and I began to read her late sister's account, the notebook flipped open between us, under the cosy flicker of her sitting-room lamps.

From what I have read during my initial research, the Gray family seemed to have a revolving door policy when it came to employing staff.

These are just a selection of the names I have encountered, having been employed at the Grays' residence:

Oliver Barmwell – Stable Hand – July 1899 – December 1899
Angus Cairns – Head Gardener – June 1899 – September 1899
Charlotte Evans – Kitchen Maid – June 1899 – February 1900

A Scottish Highland Surprise

Briar Forsyth – Scullery Maid – July 1899 – March 1900

My finger began to jab at that entry. "Oh my God! Ophelia! Look!"

Ophelia reached towards her white spectacle case on the table beside her. "Hang on a second. Annabel's writing is a little scribbled here. Let me put on my reading glasses."

She slipped on a pair of fetching gold and white spectacles and followed my excited finger. "Oh, my goodness! Briar Forsyth. There can't have been many ladies around here with a name like that."

"And look at the month Annabel has listed for Briar Forsyth ending her employment at Castle Marrian: March 1900." I recalled the date Briar had written that letter to Jonathan Gray was 31st March 1900.

Ophelia swiped off her reading glasses and waggled them. "That's if that cretin Jonathan Gray didn't have a hand in ending her employment for her." She let out a long, slow breath. "Goodness. I think we finally might be getting somewhere with all of this." Then she frowned down at her late sister's handwritten scribbles. "From what Annabel has documented here, Briar Forsyth was only employed with them for a matter of months as a scullery maid."

As if pre-empting what she was about to say, I nodded. "And that was a very familiar and impassioned tone Briar Forsyth used when writing to the son of her employers."

Ophelia set down her reading glasses on the table and gave a decisive clap of her freckled, long-fingered hands. "Exactly. So now we just need to know what the connection is between

Jonathan Gray and Briar Forsyth and where that tea set comes in."

She pulled a relieved face. "Thank goodness my great-aunt had the good sense to leave that man."

She gestured to the few more notebooks nestled at the bottom of the cardboard box. "Tomorrow, I can continue…" Her expressive face collapsed as a thought came to her. "Oh bugger! I was going to say I could do some more reading of this lot, but I'd forgotten my son, daughter-in-law and my two little grandsons are coming up from the Lakes for a few days."

I held up one hand, halting her concern. "Don't worry about that. Would you have any objections to me taking these home with me? I can continue to look through them over the next few evenings."

Ophelia shone with appreciation. "Oh, Sophie, are you sure? I love Jamie and Logan to bits, but they are only six and four and, going by previous experience, I'll be lucky if I have time to go to the bathroom, let alone sit for a few minutes to look anywhere near any of this."

I laughed and dismissed her apology. "No need to explain. I will take good care of these and providing tomorrow isn't a hectic Saturday in the shop and I have the energy, I'll continue looking through more of Annabel's research tomorrow night."

I slapped my hands down on my summery white trousers. "Right. I had better call a taxi now, otherwise I'll be nodding off on your sofa."

As it turned out, Saturday evolved from a steady morning at The Cup That Cheers into a hectic afternoon. There were a couple of local families bringing in friends to see the shop straight after lunch, which resulted in a few sales, followed by a coach load of Italian tourists.

They meandered around in awe, advancing on the shelves and flitting from one teapot to another, one tea set to another, deliberating and agonising over what they would buy. A few of them then darted back outside the shop, to take pictures of the shop window.

Once we had waved them all off with an effusive "*Grazie*" and "*Ciao*", Cass and I slumped into our chairs behind the counter.

"I think I need a lie-down in a darkened room for the next half an hour," I joked, glancing over my shoulder at the glossy yellow and blue crockery adorning our current window display.

Cass spotted me. "Already thinking about ideas for autumn?"

I pulled an apologetic face. "Was it that obvious?"

Once the children returned to school in a month's time after the summer holidays, the number of visitors to Briar Glen would start to dwindle, and in just a few weeks the surrounding gardens and parks would begin to wrap themselves in russet and amber colours. "I was thinking of sorting out any red, amber and orange tea sets," I mused. "We could get some coppery crepe paper and some leaf stencils as well."

Cass smiled with enthusiasm. "That would be lovely. I can

just picture it now. If you like, I could start looking through the stock and flag up any pieces I think might be suitable?"

"That would be a big help. Thanks, Cass."

I rose from my seat to go and make us a well-deserved cuppa. "Oh, and once Halloween approaches, I thought we could inject the display with a few pumpkins, witches' brooms; mix it all up a bit."

Cass agreed that was a great idea.

"Right," I exclaimed, tapping away from her in my open-toed, jewelled pumps, "I am going to make this pot of tea for us, before we both pass out from dehydration."

But the shop doorbell had other ideas. It was already tinkling, bringing with it a wide-eyed older American couple, who were animatedly chatting about our window display.

Cass jumped up from behind the counter, wreathed in her most welcoming smile. "No rest for the wicked," she hissed out of one side of her mouth. "You had better throw in two sugars for me."

The American lady, in her linen beige trousers, gold trainers and belted jacket, admired the tartan teapot. "Oh, Larry! I can't make up my mind between this one and that one over there. No, not the one with the thistles!"

I buried a grin. "I think I might join you."

Something told me we were both going to need an infusion of sugar.

I arrived home that Saturday evening with weary feet. I was craving a simple dinner before flaking out on the sofa in front of some mindless TV, but the box of Annabel's notebooks threw me meaningful glances from the hallway. I set it down by the edge of my sofa and picked out a couple more notebooks, including the one Ophelia and I had been halfway through on Friday evening.

I snuggled up against my scatter cushions and turned first of all to the notebook we had been reading the other night, the one that contained details of Castle Marrian's former employees.

As it turned out, the list ran on for pages. Most of them were just like Briar Forsyth: their employment with the Gray family lasted for only a matter of months. Seeing as the Gray family occupied Castle Marrian for less than a year, something told me being in their employ would not have been an enjoyable or rewarding experience. Despite the claims in Victor Prentice's journal extract that the Grays were reported to be kind and considerate towards their staff, nothing was pointing to that, if their fast turnaround of employees was anything to go by.

After a few more pages wading through names, the dizzying list of employees started to become a hazy blur:

Charles Hesketh – Butler – June 1899 – February 1900
Annie Mason – Head Cook – July 1899 – January 1900

I muttered a "Good grief!" to myself. If this had been a modern-day organisation with a revolving door of staff, questions would have been asked.

I could feel myself blinking at the lined pages and streams of black handwriting. The combination of feeling so cosy, with the summer rain slapping against my sitting-room window and the dreamy, languid music as I switched on my CD player, began to entice my eyes to shut themselves for a few moments.

Sleep was pulling at me and I began to succumb against my cushions, the exercise book flopping open on my lap.

It was only when it tumbled to the floor that the fluttery noise of the pages startled me. I pushed myself upright, swiping at my tangle of ponytail.

Maybe I should stop for the day, I thought, reaching down to retrieve the exercise jotter. It had fallen open on the carpet, spine upwards like a mini tent.

I was about to close it and return it to the top of the pile in the box when my attention locked onto the pages it had fallen open on. I peered down at Annabel's swooping handwriting.

The weather was now dark and moody outside, so I reached for my brass table lamp and fired it on.

The light spilt across the open notebook, bringing Annabel's notes even more vividly to life. I stared in surprise at what I was reading, before a thrilled, raspy noise escaped from the base of my throat. I pushed myself poker-straight and swiped at my eyes with the back of my hand, before reading over the notes again.

I stared into the distance for a moment, focusing somewhere between my silky curtains and my fluted vase of yellow roses.

My emotions sky-dived from excitement to indignation while I processed what I'd just read, before returning to read it over once more, just to make sure.

Chapter Thirty-Eight

I t was a copy of a newspaper article, dated 5th February 1900, from the *Briar Glen Informer*.

It wasn't formal in its tone. It was more gossipy and pretentious and appeared to have featured in the local paper's version of our modern society column.

Annabel had photocopied it and pasted it onto the right-hand page. It read:

> *It is reported that an employee at the spectacular stately home that is Castle Marrian has departed from their employ in haste, after the alleged theft of a valuable bespoke tea set belonging to Mrs Leonora Gray.*
>
> *Although it is understood that the Gray family have requested the local constabulary halt their investigations into the unfortunate situation, which took place on 31 January, a female employee was dismissed shortly after the theft became apparent.*

*The Informer understands that the dismissed member of staff
is a Ms Briar Forsyth, aged twenty, who resides in Briar
Glen.*

I stopped reading, my emotions spiking in a carousel of surprise and indignation on behalf of Briar. So, Briar had been accused of stealing the tea set after all and was dismissed from her job at Castle Marrian. But what happened to being innocent until proven guilty?

I reached for my phone and called Ophelia. I remembered she had her two young grandsons visiting, but I knew she would want to be made aware of this latest discovery.

Once Ophelia had managed to bribe the boys with a chocolate digestive each and a promise that "Nanna would read them an extra bedtime story," she managed to secure a few minutes' peace so that I could read the article Annabel had attached inside this notebook.

"It doesn't make any sense," I remarked, once I'd explained my latest discovery to her. I eyed the article lying face up in the notebook. "Why didn't the Grays want the police to continue investigating the theft, if they believed a member of their staff had stolen from them?"

Ophelia made murmurs of agreement.

"And that letter stashed inside the tea-set case – if you were guilty of stealing from the family of the man you loved, surely the last thing you would do is write a passionate letter to him?"

I imagined what I would have done if I had been in Briar's position and guilty of what I was accused of. Most people would have put as much space between themselves and their former employers as they could, have gone somewhere far away and sold the tea set, before pocketing the proceeds and vanishing into thin air. I was sure you wouldn't want to maintain any sort of communication with him or his family. Not to mention that if Briar sent the letter to Jonathan Gray, she wouldn't have been able to keep it with the tea set.

Ophelia clicked her tongue as she considered what I was saying. "Quite so. If you were guilty of something like that, especially in those days, I would have thought you would have vanished with your spoils too."

I chewed my lip. "Something doesn't ring true about all of this."

"I agree. And from the little I do know about Isadora's ex-husband, I think Jonathan Gray would be capable of just about anything. If he was capable of fathering and then abandoning a number of his own children, I'm sure having an employee blamed for stealing would be nothing in his eyes."

I paced backwards and forwards in my sitting room, watching the rain shimmer and sliver down the window. "We need to find out what happened to Briar Forsyth."

If we could locate a thread back to Briar, then perhaps we stood more of a chance of finding what happened between her and Jonathan Gray.

Before we ended the call, Ophelia informed me that her son and daughter-in-law were planning on taking the two little boys to Edinburgh Zoo for the day on Monday. "So, I can drop by the library first thing on Monday morning and do some digging about Briar Forsyth."

"Are you sure? Don't you want to put your feet up and have a rest?"

I swore I could almost hear Ophelia shaking that silver crown of hair. "We've got to get to the bottom of this!" she assured me. "And anyway, it will be rewarding, carrying on the research Annabel never had the chance to finish."

I went to bed that night, buzzing with anticipation.

I travelled to The Cup That Cheers as normal on the Monday morning, with Ophelia's promise to drop by with any information she might find swirling around my head.

Drizzly July rain brought with it a slow start so I decided to set up my laptop on the counter and update the shop's social media accounts, while Cass was on the office PC, placing another stock order.

I turned to The Cup That Cheers' website first, to launch a "Who would you like to have afternoon tea with and why?" competition. The best entry would win a £25 gift voucher to spend in the shop.

After I typed up the blurb, I included a few pictures of famous faces such as Marilyn Monroe, Barack Obama and William Shakespeare, which might give potential entrants some ideas.

I also posted an update and photos that Cass had taken of a selection of our latest crockery arrivals, with the enticing heading "Just In! How Can You Resist?!", on the Twitter, Facebook and Instagram accounts.

I had chosen a perfect eclectic mix of funky, student-y sets, with sunflowers, multi-coloured triangles and rainbow stripes. I'd also included something for more conservative tastes, from teapots sprinkled with discreet daisies to plain tea sets in the palest duck-egg blue and vanilla.

Monday morning brought a few sales and a brief but productive meeting with a sales representative for a new crockery company, keen to have their ceramics, featuring gorgeous paintings of Scottish wildlife such as Highland cattle and birds of prey, stocked in the shop. I was very enthusiastic and was sure the tourists to Briar Glen would be drawn to them.

The sales representative had just left the shop and we were limping towards lunchtime when a glittery-eyed Ophelia came bursting through the door, sending the silver bell into a frenzy. She was struggling to contain herself. "Morning, Sophie," she breathed, hitching her quilted white shoulder bag further up her shoulder. "I've just come from the library."

I beckoned her over. A slow, hopeful smile spread across my face. "What is it? What have you found out?"

She dumped her bag on top of the counter beside my opened laptop and rummaged around inside for her mobile. "Well," she began, searching her phone for something, "I went up to Briar Glen Library first thing. I didn't know what I expected to find, but anyway..." Her voice vanished and she thrust her phone screen at me. I took a step closer. "It's a marriage certificate," she babbled. "For Briar Forsyth."

I leant forward, eager to see what was on the screen, but a thought occurred to me as I did. My anticipation contorted into a feeling of dread. "Oh God, don't tell me she married Jonathan Gray!"

Ophelia rolled her eyes, as if that idea had never even

occurred to her. "Let's give the girl some credit. No, I'm relieved to say she didn't."

I examined Ophelia's outstretched phone screen again, but I was struggling to make out the details. "Thank goodness for that. Then who did she marry?" Then I started to laugh. "Ophelia. I don't think that's what you were looking for. Then again, it might be." I nodded towards her phone. A photo of Hal was on the screen; he was topless, lounging on a sunbed and raising a pint of something cool beside some palm trees.

"Bloody phone!" mumbled Ophelia, jabbing at it with a shell-pink-painted fingernail. "That was on our last holiday to Majorca." Impatience took over. "Never mind. It will be quicker if I tell you." She fixed me with her expectant gaze. "What would you say if I told you Briar married Ernest Telfer?"

My jaw grew slack. "Ernest Telfer? As in Ernest Telfer who crafted the peacock tea set? The tea set that Briar was accused of stealing?"

Ophelia nodded, struggling to contain herself. "The very one."

Chapter Thirty-Nine

I opened and closed my mouth for several seconds.

So, Briar married the artist who created the peacock tea set for Jonathan Gray's mother Leonora? The same tea set that had reportedly been stolen from the family by Briar herself?

"Well," I gasped. "I definitely didn't see that one coming."

Ophelia was bristling with anticipation under her sunshine-yellow and blue nautical jacket. Raindrops were sliding down the sleeves, but she was oblivious. "And there's something else," she said in a thrilled whisper, despite there being no one else in the vicinity. "Briar gave birth to a little boy, George, in November 1900 but she and Ernest only married in the June."

I rubbed at my forehead, mentally pushing these latest developments together like pieces of a scattered puzzle. Maths had never been my strong point, but even I was able to calculate that didn't add up. "Wow! So, the likelihood is that George wasn't Ernest's?"

"That is what I was thinking," agreed Ophelia. "If we're

right, Briar would have already been pregnant when she met Ernest and he married her when she was four months gone."

I glanced around at the loaded shelves of the shop, my mind whirring. "So could this little boy have been Jonathan Gray's?"

Ophelia frowned. "I wondered that." She scrolled away from the marriage certificate, which she had now managed to retrieve on her phone, to George's birth certificate, and set her mobile down on the counter. "Another possible child of Jonathan Gray's to add to the long list, perhaps? In fact, I wouldn't be at all surprised. He isn't named as the father on George's birth certificate, but that is probably to be expected. Ernest Telfer is."

All the loose ends were beginning to intertwine.

What if Jonathan Gray, heir to Castle Marrian, had got Briar, the family scullery maid, pregnant and then dumped her? But what about the tea set? Had Briar threatened to tell Jonathan's family about her pregnancy? Perhaps she had said that unless he publicly acknowledged her and the baby – even married her – she was going to make sure that not only his parents but the entire town knew?

Maybe that was why Jonathan Gray had Briar accused of stealing his mother's tea set. Had he pretended Briar stole it from the family home, in order to blacken Briar's name and therefore cast doubt on her claims that she was pregnant with his child?

And then there were those scenes with an enraged Jonathan Gray and a distressed young woman out in the snow in Briar Glen on Christmas Eve, that Saffy's great-grandfather had made an account of. Was the young woman Victor Prentice had seen a desperate and upset Briar Forsyth? Maybe Briar wanted him to publicly acknowledge their relationship, and then, when he discovered she was expecting his baby, he was determined to banish her from his life? Had he engineered the theft so she would be blamed?

I relayed all my reeling thoughts to Ophelia.

"That all sounds perfectly plausible to me," she answered.

Sympathy for Briar and George's situation rose higher and higher inside of me. I swivelled my laptop further round, so that Ophelia had a clear view of the screen. "You said that George was born in November 1900, is that right?"

Ophelia picked up her phone and checked the boy's birth certificate. "Yes. He was born on the 8th. Why?"

My fingers jabbed my laptop keyboard, pulling up the Castle Marrian website. It was strange being confronted with my former place of work, especially now the ghosts who once lived there seemed to be haunting my thoughts.

I bypassed the colourful glossy website photographs of it, with its whipped-cream turrets like extravagant meringues, and chandeliers dripping from its ornate ceilings.

I located the section which detailed the history of Castle Marrian and gestured to the second paragraph. Ophelia read the few lines I pointed out to her.

Castle Marrian was the treasured home of the Masters family for many years, until Lady Eliza Masters lost her beloved husband Lord Alfred Masters in a tragic riding accident in the spring of 1899.

Unable to face the prospect of living in Castle Marrian

without her beloved "Alf", Lady Masters insisted that the property be put up for sale.

From June 1899 to April 1900, it was rumoured that another family briefly occupied this splendid estate, but such was their unpopularity amongst not only the locals but also their staff at the time, they failed to settle in Briar Glen.

Castle Marrian found herself placed on the market once again, but was eventually purchased by the respected Dayell family in January 1901.

Ophelia straightened up. "That must be the Grays they are referring to. Who else could it be?" I could practically see Ophelia's mind going into overdrive. "So, Jonathan Gray's parents occupied Castle Marrian until April 1900 and then the three of them did a runner."

I raised one eyebrow. "A bit of a coincidence, don't you think? They sell the property and move on, just as Briar Forsyth's pregnancy will have started to show?

She digested what I was saying. "But would they just up and leave like that, over a dismissed maid? The Gray family sound a rather brazen bunch to me. I'm wondering if something else took place that cemented their decision to leave the area?"

Ophelia was charged with intent as she left the shop, promising to go home, have lunch and see if she could unearth anything else.

I thanked her for all her help and she brushed it aside. "It is making me feel like I'm carrying on Annabel's work. I'm also every much enjoying it."

I waved her off and began shutting down my laptop. Behind me, the shop doorbell let out its sparkling tinkle. I wondered if it might be Ophelia having forgotten something but, when I turned around, I was confronted by a stony-faced Saffy Clements. Her feline green eyes flickered over me.

Before I had even managed to gather myself and say hello, she crossed her arms across her black leather jacket. "I think we should have a chat."

Chapter Forty

S affy drifted past the shelves, her gaze sweeping from the white ceiling to the lilac walls.

Her fingers ran over the array of Royal Worcester and Spode, with its recognisable blue and white willow pattern. The spotlights in The Cup That Cheers gave the shop a cosier feel, as the rain continued to splatter against the windows. They also highlighted the shots of burgundy in Saffy's cloud of curly dark hair.

She swivelled on her wedged heels, which she had teamed with cropped denim trousers a belted, scarlet raincoat and a candy-striped shirt. "Look. I'm going to come straight to the point here, Sophie. What the hell are you doing with Jake Caldwell?"

I wasn't sure what I'd expected Saffy to say. I was too taken aback by her sudden and unexpected arrival in the shop to have thought that far ahead.

I gathered myself. "Why? I mean, why do you ask? I don't mean to sound rude, but I don't think who I go out with is any of your business." Images of Jake's behaviour and me stalking out of the restaurant shimmered in front of my eyes. I had no intention of having anything more to do with him, but I failed to see why I should explain this to Saffy.

She flicked back her halo of curls. "Well, it is my business when it comes to Xander." She eyed me. "So, you are going out with Jake?"

"No. Well, I was going to. I mean, I thought we were going out for dinner."

Good grief. I was even beginning to confuse myself, so Lord knew what Saffy was making of my bumbling, incoherent explanation. "Look, I can understand why Xander would want to get one over Jake after what happened with his girlfriend, but I'm not interested in getting caught up in their games." I let my hands rise and fall in a helpless gesture. "I know there are always two sides to every story, Saffy, and I realise Xander must have been so hurt over Nadia, but I don't think trying to ruin someone's career is the way to go about it."

Saffy stared at me for a couple of seconds and then let out a bark of dry laughter. "What are you talking about? What did Jake tell you exactly?"

Without being asked, she sank down on one of the two stools behind the counter and dropped her shoulder bag to the floor. She looked like a moody French model sitting there, appraising me.

I remained standing. Her loaded expression was making me feel uneasy. "Jake told me Xander has never got over Nadia dumping him for Jake and has had it in for him ever since."

Saffy threw her head back and laughed, displaying small

white teeth. "Dear me. You would have thought by now Caldwell could have come up with something more original."

My cheeks flared as trepidation nibbled at me. "What do you mean? What are you talking about?"

Saffy gestured for me to sit down, so I took up the stool opposite her.

She clasped her ringed fingers together in her lap. "Two years ago, Xander was with Nadia Gates, a fashion journalist." As she said it, her pretty, freckled features clouded over. "He was crazy about her. At the time, he was also involved in researching a series of painting frauds for the paper he writes his art review column for."

She pinned me with her intense eyes, her lashes casting little shadows on the tops of her cheeks. "It turned out that Jake Caldwell was copying the work of another artist, long since gone, and was passing these so-called 'originals' off as his own work and charging innocent punters extortionate amounts."

I stiffened as I sat there, processing what Saffy was saying. I felt my throat dry with embarrassment. "Seriously? Jake was copying someone else's paintings?"

Saffy hitched up one brow. "Except he wasn't going under his real name at the time. He signed himself as James Deighton."

"What happened? Was Jake held accountable for it?"

Saffy's wry smile told me the answer. "Not our Jake. Too slippery for that. He made sure his copies stayed just on the right side of legal. He incorporated tweaks here and there to keep him out of trouble. The other issue was that the artist he was ripping off had been some poor, struggling individual in the 1930s who nobody had heard of."

Saffy's red slicked lips curled at the corner. "I bet if he had been ripping off someone high-profile, it would have been a different story."

"So, what happened?"

Saffy toyed with one of her ornate dress rings as she spoke. "Well, rumours soon got around the art world about what Jake AKA James Deighton had been up to. It can be pretty incestuous; everyone knows everyone else." She paused before continuing again. "And though nothing could be proved outright, the Deighton brand became tainted. Nobody wanted anything to do with him. It affected his sales too."

I conjured up an image of Jake sitting across from me in my flat, all smarmy charm, feeding me poison about Xander. My stomach tightened at the memory.

"Anyway," carried on Saffy, "it soon got back to Jake about Xander's involvement in investigating what he had been up to. The fact that Xander was also a respected art critic made Jake furious and lose all sense of perspective."

I was beginning realise where this was leading. My cheeks burnt with shame. I had believed all Jake's crap. I had thought badly of Xander and all the time... Talk about gullible.

I let out a long, low breath. "And then?"

"Then Jake decided to get his revenge on Xander. He discovered the one thing that mattered to Xander more than anything."

I experienced an unsettling chill as I anticipated the answer. "You mean Nadia?"

Saffy cast her eyes around the shop before glancing to her left at the rain-drizzled window. "Yep."

Her mouth twisted into a firm line. "I'd heard stories about her being materialistic and having a thing for bad boys, but Xander adored her, so it came as no surprise when Jake lured her away with designer handbags and luxurious weekends away." Saffy gave the briefest shake of her head, as if still struggling to comprehend what Nadia did to Xander. "I think she got off on draping herself off the arm of art's biggest bad boy, if you know what I mean."

My heart plummeted to the floor for Xander. How the hell could she do that to him? I rubbed at my face. Worse than that, I had believed all the crap Jake told me. It had been poor Xander who had been hurting all that time. He was the one who had been doing the right thing. He was the one who had stopped Jake ripping off unsuspecting art buyers and, in an act of twisted revenge, Jake had taken Xander's girlfriend away from him.

My jaw clenched. I felt so gullible. So stupid. I dragged both hands down my face. "What a bastard! Did they stay together? Nadia and Jake, I mean?"

Saffy's mouth curled. "No. It only lasted a matter of months and once the novelty of winding up Xander wore off, Jake dropped her." She made a snorting noise. "Do you know that woman had the bare-faced cheek to then try and reconcile with Xander? Needless to say, he told her to forget it. Xander is a very proud man."

The softening of her mouth as she talked about Xander. The way her eyes glowed when she spoke his name. The uncompromising way she had looked at me the first time we met in her studio... I scanned her cinnamon-freckled face. It was even clearer to me now than it had been before. Saffy was in love with Xander herself.

A myriad emotions surged through me.

I opened my mouth to say something, but nothing came out. If Saffy noticed, she didn't comment on it. She simply carried on with her explanation, burying any hurt she might be harbouring, so that I could understand.

"Xander was so cut up over Nadia, I did wonder a few times if he would ever allow himself to open his heart to anyone ever again."

"But it isn't – it wasn't – what you or Xander think," I said. "Jake lied to me from the start. He told me that Xander's girlfriend fell for him and when Xander found out, that was when he started a vendetta against him and his artwork. He was so plausible..." Now it was my turn for my voice to vanish. "I don't even know why I went out to dinner with Jake. I was flattered, I suppose, but that was as far as it went."

I recalled Jake stealing that kiss and his smirk of triumph at Xander. My stomach lurched in embarrassment and anger. It was important for me to stress to Saffy what really happened. She had chosen to come to the shop and talk to me and I felt I owed her an explanation; she had come here to defend Xander, to make sure I knew the truth. It was important to her. I understood that.

"What you saw and what Xander saw... I wasn't kissing him back. He reached across the table to kiss me when he saw you and Xander enter the restaurant. It was all engineered on his part."

I felt a movement to my left. An elderly couple had paused

outside the shop window, sheltering under their giant umbrella. I returned to my explanation of what happened. "I got up and walked out on Jake moments after you and Xander left, but not before giving him a right mouthful."

A flicker of a satisfied smile toyed at Saffy's mouth.

"That's why Jake was so preoccupied at the table. He was too busy checking the car park every five minutes, to see if you and Xander had arrived." I let out a sigh of exasperation. "He was late picking me up too. He fed me some lies about an urgent call, but he must have been onto someone, finding out Xander's movements for that evening."

"No doubt Xander's PA," supplied Saffy with a knowing look. "Lorna is a lovey girl, but she can't hold her own water, let alone manage Xander's diary with discretion."

Saffy drank in my expression. "I believe you," she said after a pause. "I do."

An image of smug, blond Jake sitting across from me, spouting lies, wavered in front of my eyes again. "But his art career," I asked. "How did he manage to resurrect that?"

"He hasn't," confided Saffy. "I know his website is an all-singing, all-dancing affair, but it's all show and no substance. As soon as he realised Xander was onto him, Jake dropped his James Deighton persona and fled to the States for several months. He hid out there until it became yesterday's news. I hear he's doing the odd bit of lecturing work now."

I nodded. "It was the art student son of one of the tradesmen I know who recommended him."

Saffy rolled her eyes. "He got off lightly, all things considered. Because his plagiarism couldn't be definitively proved, he's still managing to just about keep his cheating head above water, now that he's back from the States." She offered me a look. "Don't tell me you haven't noticed the subtle but still evident American twang?"

She reached down for the strap of her handbag by her feet, then rose on her wedged sandals and moved towards the shop door, just as the elderly couple with the big umbrella were about to come in.

I accompanied Saffy to the door, my head reconciling everything she had just told me. "Thank you for coming to see me and for explaining everything. You didn't have to do that."

Saffy pushed her hands into the pockets of her trendy scarlet jacket. "Yes, I did. How could I not? Xander is very special to me and what sort of friend would I be if I didn't look out for him?"

I watched Saffy's spiral curls head out of the door. She paused and spun round. "I think you should speak to him." She acknowledged the couple as they made their way past her, flapping their wet umbrella and complaining about the rain.

She adjusted the strap of her shoulder bag. "So anyway, I just wanted to tell you the truth. Don't believe a word that snake Caldwell has told you." She gazed at me levelly. "Xander is worth a million of him. He's not the guilty party in all of this."

Then she was gone.

Chapter Forty-One

My head was scrambled after Saffy's departure, but I managed to keep my professional demeanour together long enough to sell the endearing elderly couple a new teapot to replace their broken one. "We've had our Sheridan Staffordshire for years," sighed the lady, her bright, silvery button eyes shining. "But it was beginning to leak all over the place."

"So, time for a new one," chipped in her husband.

As soon as I had thanked them, Cass reappeared, having placed our latest stock order; my office was now vacant again.

I excused myself for a few minutes with my mobile and shut myself in my office. Snapshots of the shocked, crestfallen look in Xander's eyes when he saw me with Jake revisited me again.

The compunction to talk to Xander, to explain to him, was all-consuming. Saffy's words echoed in my head while I sought out his number. It must have taken so much for her to come here and talk to me. The way she spoke about Xander and the softness in her voice just confirmed to me the depth of her feelings for him. Even from the first time I met her at her studio, I could tell she thought much more of him than she cared to admit.

I deliberated for a moment about what to do. I didn't want to put Saffy in an awkward position, but the idea of Xander thinking I was with Jake was intolerable. I wanted him to know the truth.

I located his number and it gave a series of urgent, energetic rings that seemed to last for ages.

I had no idea what I was going to say to him. All I knew was that I had to let him know that I wasn't like Nadia; that I had been harbouring growing feelings for him, but after the pain of what happened with Callum, I'd shared his reluctance to open up and trust someone else again.

I wanted to tell him how despicable I thought Jake Caldwell was and how stupid and naïve I felt after being manipulated by him. I should never have listened to Jake's lies or believed him in the first place.

Xander's phone rang out a few more times and then there was the click of my call being answered. "Xander," I said in a rush, my breath catching at the base of my throat. My heart was jumping about in my chest.

"Hello?"

My spine turned to ice. It was a female voice. "Er…" I shot out of my office chair. "Hi. Sorry. I was looking for Xander."

There was a questioning lift to her words. "This is Nadia Gates speaking, Xander's girlfriend. He's on a Zoom call at the moment, but won't be long. Can I take a message?"

My legs stiffened under my pinstripe trousers. *Nadia*? My

mind homed in on her description of herself as his girlfriend. Did this mean Xander had forgiven her? Had he decided to rekindle his relationship with her?

My mouth turned to ash. If Nadia had turned up again, begging for forgiveness and convincing Xander they could make a fresh start…. My thoughts tumbled over each other.

I searched the teapot paintings on my office wall. I was fighting to speak. "It doesn't matter," I struggled, biting back the pain. "I'm sorry. Sorry to bother you."

Then I hung up.

Chapter Forty-Two

I managed to force conversation and smiles for the remainder of Monday morning.

Cass knew there was something I was struggling with. Every so often, I would catch her eyeing me with concern. She asked me a couple of times if I felt all right and I pretended an unsettled night's sleep was the reason for me being reserved.

I didn't want to talk about it. I felt stupid and frustrated with myself.

As I wrapped a purchase of a simple but pretty white porcelain teacup and saucer, emblazoned with a thistle, in a sheet of purple tissue paper, I made a decision. I would have to accept the messy situation for what it was and move on.

Xander, despite Saffy's protestations, must have decided he could forgive Nadia after all and that he wanted her back in his life. Perhaps he had been attracted to me, but that must have been as far as it went. Maybe I had been some sort of temporary diversion and he had been waiting and hoping for Nadia to realise how stupid she had been.

"Sophie? Sophie?"

I stopped folding the tissue paper over and over and turned to look at Cass.

She was frowning at me. She aimed a brief glance at the customer, a well-dressed young woman in her thirties, who was clasping the hand of her little girl.

Cass switched on a pleasant smile. "Sophie, I think you've wrapped that enough. Any more layers and Houdini wouldn't be able to escape from that."

I stared down at my hands and the sheets of rumpled tissue paper. "Sorry. I was miles away then."

Cass waited until the bemused customer and her daughter had vanished out of the door, the little girl carrying the glossy The Cup That Cheers drawstring gift bag with the weight of responsibility shining out of her saucer-like cornflower-blue eyes.

"Please don't think I'm prying, Sophie," began Cass, swivelling all her concern towards me. "But you haven't been yourself for the last couple of hours."

"I'm fine, thanks," I insisted. "Just feeling a bit off-colour."

"Then why don't you take yourself off home? I can manage here, and if things get hectic, I can give you a call. Or maybe your mum could come in and give me a hand?"

The prospect of rattling around the flat on my own, thinking about Xander, was an even worse option than staying to work in the shop. At least there was noise and buzz outside, now that the rain had dissipated.

I patted the arm of her lacy white shirt. "Thank you. That's really kind of you, Cass. But I'm fine."

Cass opened her mouth to argue the point, but was

interrupted by the shop door swinging open, bringing with it a bubbling, effusive Ophelia. She was flapping a sheet of paper in her hand. "I have some more positive news."

She grinned at Cass and me, as though she were auditioning for a toothpaste advert. "I was trawling through the Gray family tree and I came across this."

She thrust the paper towards me.

I scanned what Ophelia had written in her elegant, big, looped handwriting. "Mr Carson Gray?" I stared up at her. "As in Carson Gray who owns the local bookshop, Cover to Cover?"

Ophelia nodded. "He's a descendant of the Gray family, as you might have guessed. You'll also notice his home address and that he lives locally, just up past St Barnaby's Church."

I glanced down again at Carson Gray's details and then back up at her. "I don't mean to sound pessimistic, but he might not know anything about his family or about Jonathan Gray."

Ophelia folded her arms. "Well, that did cross my mind at first. That was until I did a bit of digging on Carson Gray himself."

I couldn't help but smile, despite my emotional bruises. "You'll be giving Columbo a run for his money!"

Ophelia laughed. "I think my sister would be impressed, that's for sure." She gestured to the sheet of paper I was still holding. "It turns out that Carson Gray is an amateur genealogist. He worked for years as a history teacher at a private school in Glasgow." She arched her brows expectantly. "You can bet he has looked into his own past. That would be like a manicurist not taking care of her own nails."

Cass laughed. "That's a great analogy and very true."

Ophelia grinned at Cass, grateful for her support. "So, I hope you don't mind, but I took the liberty of calling Carson Gray on the way from the library and he said he would be happy to speak to us this evening."

She pulled an apologetic face. "Is that okay with you, Sophie? Please say if you have other plans."

Visions of me drifting around my flat, trying to find things to do and not dwelling on my missed opportunity with Xander, weren't appealing. The best thing for me to do right now was to keep occupied.

I shook my head and waggled Carson Gray's details in my hand. "No," I smiled, "I'm not busy tonight."

Chapter Forty-Three

Carson Gray was struggling to contain his enthusiasm as he greeted Ophelia and me at his Charles Rennie Mackintosh-inspired front door. He was a tall, wiry man with an abundance of salt and pepper hair and a long, friendly face.

He ushered us into a hectic but cosy sitting room, cluttered with heavy, ornate wooden furniture. I noticed a bookshelf at the rear of the room, packed with a jumble of books.

Carson Gray gestured to both of us to sit down in each of the two claret armchairs, while he took up residence on the opposite sofa once he'd made us all tea. "My wife is out at her book club this evening, so please don't feel you're taking up too much of my time." His slightly lopsided mouth flipped into an endearing smile.

"Thank you, Mr Gray," I said, smiling with appreciation.

"It's Carson. Please." He leant forward on the sofa. "So, you're interested in Briar Glen and the Gray family." He raised his bristly brows in expectation.

315

Ophelia began first, explaining the full story, including how shocked she was when she found out her great-aunt Isadora had been briefly married to Jonathan Gray.

I took over at that point. "Ophelia and I had been intending to find out about Briar Forsyth, once we had discovered the letter from her to Jonathan Gray tucked in beside the tea set."

We'd decided as we pulled up in front of Carson Gray's detached bungalow that we wouldn't mention Ophelia wanting to rid herself of the tea set and therefore dumping it on me. We weren't sure how he would take that and we didn't want to appear rude.

Carson's expressions were a picture as Ophelia and I took turns to describe what we had discovered so far, thanks to Annabel's hard work. It was as though he couldn't make up his mind, between the two of us, which one he found more arresting.

Once Ophelia had explained about the alleged theft of the tea set, I reached down to my feet and set out the leather case. With one swift click, it eased open, the peacock design and rich colours greeting Carson Gray. "Bloody hell!" he gasped. "Is that it? Is that the actual tea set that was taken?" He let out another sound of appreciation when I slid my hand inside the pouch stitched into the open lid and eased out the yellowing letter from Briar Forsyth to Jonathan Gray. It let out the gentlest rustle and smelled of warm vanilla. I handed it to him.

Carson Gray's smoky grey eyes almost fell out of his head. "Oh, my word!" He read it over a couple of times. "This is ... this is the final piece of the puzzle."

Ophelia let out a husky laugh. "If only that were true."

Carson blinked across at her. "What do you mean?"

Ophelia explained about Briar Forsyth and how she had been wrongly accused of stealing the tea set.

Carson appraised both of us. There was a look of anticipation shifting in his eyes. "Well, I'm glad you have come to talk to me in that case."

I flashed a hopeful smile at him. "Oh, and why's that?"

He clasped his large, knotted hands together. "Because you're right. Briar Forsyth didn't steal that tea set." His absorbed gaze flickered over the open case and the tea set resting by my feet.

Ophelia thumped her hands down on her lap in triumph. "I knew it! So, what happened between them? Did Jonathan Gray get Briar pregnant and pretend she stole it to blacken her name?"

Carson stretched out his long, pipe-cleaner legs in front of him. "You are partly right."

My attention was drawn to his hesitation. "Sorry, but I don't follow."

Carson's angled cheeks picked up streaks of colour. "This isn't something I tend to relate about my dear ancestors at dinner parties."

As the gold carriage clock ticked on top of the grey stone fireplace, Carson looked thoughtfully at Ophelia and me. "Yes, you are right in a sense. Jonathan did steal the tea set and try to frame Briar for it." His rumbling voice continued to command our attention. "That is what this letter is all about." He gestured to the aging document as it lay unfolded on the coffee table.

"But why did you say we were partly correct?" I asked.

Carson's next sentence made me sit up straighter on his sofa. "You are right that Briar Forsyth did fall pregnant, but you're wrong about who the baby's father was."

Chapter Forty-Four

Ophelia's mouth fell open.

She delved into her rose-gold handbag and produced her phone. She located the copy of George's birth certificate and pushed the phone with its image towards Carson. "The named father on this certificate is Ernest Telfer, but Jonathan Gray was the boy's biological father. He must have been. Why go to all that trouble of trying to frame the girl for stealing?"

I remembered Saffy's great-grandfather's diary entry about that icy Christmas Eve, with Jonathan Gray verbally abusing a distressed young woman, and told Carson as much.

Carson held up his hands in mock surrender. "That's true. She did have a son called George and Ernest Telfer was named as his father on the birth certificate. I've also no doubt Jonathan Gray was more than capable of humiliating a woman in freezing conditions like that." He shook his head. "It's very clear that young man had no moral compass."

I could feel my forehead creasing. "So if Jonathan Gray wasn't George's biological father, then why did he attempt to blame Briar for stealing and try to get rid of her? Why have her accused of taking this?" I pointed down to the tea set resting on Carson's loud Paisley carpet.

"And why try to bribe her with it?" interjected Ophelia. "At least that is what we assumed he was doing, going by Briar's reference in her letter to something beautiful and a treasure."

Another thought crept across my brain. One that made the possibility of this poor young woman being manipulated and treated like a major inconvenience prickle my skin.

Carson eyed us both. He pointed to the tea set winking out of its dark velvet interior. "Jonathan was incensed when he found out Briar Forsyth was pregnant and wanted to protect his own interests, so he thought having her blamed for theft and dismissed from Castle Marrian would solve all his problems."

Ophelia wrinkled her long regal nose in concentration. "So what are you saying?"

My heart heaved in my chest. I thought I could guess and Carson's next sentence proved me to be correct. "Jonathan Gray wasn't the father of Briar Forsyth's son. Chadwick Gray was."

Ophelia made a rasping, shocked noise. "What?!"

"I tracked down archived charge papers from the local police at the time. Chadwick Gray was accused of raping Briar Forsyth one evening in the run-up to Christmas when his wife and son were attending a local function. Old man Gray had a drink problem, which the family were desperate to keep under wraps."

The disgust and venom I felt for Jonathan Gray and his father intensified. "The poor young woman." I swallowed. "So what happened then?"

"Jonathan Gray found out what his father had done, when Briar discovered she was pregnant. He panicked. He had images of his inheritance and Castle Marrian slipping away from him, if there was a half-brother or sister in the mix."

Ophelia toyed with one of her stud earrings, still processing this revelation. She opened and closed her mouth a few times. "So he had Briar blamed for stealing the tea set to protect that father of his?"

"That was the plan," said Carson. "But in the end, it transpired Briar Forsyth wasn't actually working on the morning of 31st January when the tea set went missing. She had an alibi and his story fell apart."

Waves of delight on behalf of Briar washed over me.

"From what I then discovered," carried on Carson, "Jonathan Gray knew he had to do something. I get the impression Briar was a brave young woman and wasn't prepared to be bullied."

He paused before picking up the story again. "Briar didn't want to continue working at Castle Marrian, not after what had happened with Chadwick Gray, and with his devious son lurking around every corner. And who could blame her? But she wasn't prepared to be bullied out of town either, especially as she was the innocent party in all of this."

"Did she refuse to leave Briar Glen?" I asked, my admiration and sympathy for her growing ever deeper.

"She did indeed," answered Carson. All Briar wanted was justice, and the Gray family had no intention of giving her that.

"So Jonathan Gray then came up with the idea of trying to bribe her with the tea set, which he had accused her of stealing in the first place. It was especially commissioned by Chadwick Gray for his wife Leonora's birthday."

"And Ernest Telfer made it," I added, giving the tea set another glance.

Ophelia frowned. "But didn't Leonora question where it had gone?"

Carson's long mouth tightened. "Reading between the lines, both Chadwick and Leonora were in on it. They wanted Briar gone from their lives, together with the baby."

"Good grief," I muttered. Leonora knew what her husband had done. She knew he had attacked a young woman in their employ and made her pregnant and yet she had gone along with her son's devious plan to have Briar accused of something she was innocent of, just to protect the family.

"But still Briar stood her ground," murmured Ophelia, her admiration for Briar Forsyth shining in her hazel eyes. "Good for her."

Carson indicated the letter. "She tells Jonathan Gray where he can stick his tea set."

My thoughts whizzed again to Briar and Ernest Telfer. "And when the Grays refused to accept the return of the tea set, for fear of the truth being exposed, Briar took it to Ernest Telfer, who crafted it in the first place."

"Exactly!" proclaimed Carson with relish. "It didn't take long for Ernest to fall in love with Briar. They got married and he raised George as his own and they lived out the rest of their days in Briar Glen."

That gave Ophelia and me some comfort, knowing that this courageous young woman and her little boy at least found happiness and contentment with a decent, caring man like Ernest Telfer.

"And what about the Grays?" asked Ophelia, enthralled. "From what Sophie and I unearthed, they departed from Castle Marrian and moved away from Briar Glen in the spring of 1900."

Carson nodded, confirming that was true. "According to the records I saw, they moved to some crumbling old estate in the Lake District, which swallowed up most of their cash, and they ended up living on fresh air. Rumours swirled about Chadwick Gray's penchant for drinking and his attraction to young women. Like father, like son in this case. The stories about old man Gray affected his stables business. Customers vanished." Carson pulled a face. "The landed gentry didn't want to be associated with anyone who didn't have two pennies to rub together."

"They were shunned?" I asked, shocked, surprised and captivated by all this every bit as much as Ophelia was.

"Leonora and Chadwick Gray passed away within months of one another in 1904; she from tuberculosis and he from a heart attack."

"And Jonathan?" asked Ophelia. "Whatever happened to him?"

"If it is any consolation, I think your aunt had a lucky escape."

Carson rose up from his chair and moved towards his jumble of books. He rummaged in a bureau alongside and produced a bland-looking punch-holed folder. He flipped it open and rifled through the pages.

His serious face split into a triumphant grin when he located what he was searching for. "Ah. Here it is."

He moved back towards us, proffering the open folder. It was a copy of Jonathan Gray's death certificate, stating that he died on Boxing Day 1910, in Stirling Prison, aged just thirty-two, from pneumonia.

I snapped my head up. "Prison?"

Carson remained standing and thrust his panhandle hands into the pockets of his trousers. "I located a few paragraphs about his court case in the local paper. It seems he was up to his old tricks."

"Stealing?" asked Ophelia, her dark eyes bouncing between the open page and Carson.

"He broke into a nearby church and stole some gold ornaments and the collection." Carson shook his head in dismay. "He got caught by one of the church elders out walking his gun dogs." He moved towards his sitting-room window, with its display of lilies and cream roses springing out of a long, thin vase. "So, you see, I don't have much of an impressive ancestry to boast about."

Ophelia and I set the open folder down on the coffee table in front of us. I offered him a sympathetic smile. "Well, the way I see it, you've rescued the reputation of a desperate young woman and her child. "

Ophelia agreed beside me. "If that isn't something to boast about, I don't know what is."

Carson's slanted cheeks creased with appreciation. "Thank you.

We smiled, filled with delight and relief at having been finally able to uncover the truth.

Then Carson winked. "I run a genealogy training course at night school. Are either of you two ladies interested at all?"

Chapter Forty-Five

I suspected Ophelia felt every bit as giddy as I did, with all these startling revelations to comprehend.

So, Jonathan had been not so much protecting his monster of a father, but his own financial interests. That didn't come as any great surprise from what we had come to learn about him. Someone who could deliberately attempt to frame a young and pregnant woman, attacked by his own monster of a father, was capable of just about anything.

"Do you know what happened to this?" I asked, pointing to the tea set. "Did Briar and Ernest keep it?"

Carson replied that they sold it. "Well, they auctioned it, to be more precise." He picked up the innocuous folder again from the table and riffled through a few more pages.

There was a local newspaper article dated 13th September1902.

Carson showed his copy of the piece to us. The headline was **TEA SET RAISES CHARITY FUNDS.**

He read aloud from the piece:

"A stunning tea set crafted by the renowned local artist Ernest Telfer has been sold at auction.

"The tea set reached a staggering one hundred pounds when it was sold by Briar and Ernest Telfer at a specially arranged event organised by Mrs Telfer and held at Briar Glen's Glen Valley Church yesterday morning.

"It has been announced that half of the money raised will be donated to the local Salvation Army Society for Widows and Orphans and the other is to be held in trust for Mr and Mrs Telfer's son George until he reaches the age of twenty-one.

"Both Mr and Mrs Telfer were delighted by the enthusiasm which greeted the auction and by the generous bids made by members of the local community and beyond.

"It is understood that the successful bidder of the tea set resides in London and wishes to remain anonymous."

A lump of emotion sat in my throat and wouldn't move. "What a lovely thing to do."

Carson agreed. "It was. They might not have had the education and the privileges of the Gray family, but they could have taught them a thing or two about humility and class."

Ophelia pushed a chunk of silvery hair back behind her ear. "I wonder who the person in London was, who purchased the tea set for that amount of money? That was a considerable sum in those days."

Carson trained his glittery gaze on Ophelia. "Well, I took the liberty of searching out old auction records after I read that article. I was keen to try and find out too."

"Any luck?" asked Ophelia, intrigued.

Carson's attention drifted to me and back again. "The

buyer wished to remain anonymous, as mentioned in the newspaper article, but I did discover in the archives a set of initials."

He folded his arms and reclined back against his sofa. "The initials of the anonymous buyer were I. G."

There was a short, sharp pause before Ophelia's age-speckled hand flew to her mouth. "No! Oh goodness! Are you sure? I. G.?"

Carson smiled. "I'm positive. I can locate the copy of the sales invoice. It's somewhere in one of those files…"

"No, don't worry," stuttered Ophelia. She snapped her head towards me. "I. G. Isadora Graves. My great-aunt."

It took a few seconds for my brain to catch up. My lips parted in shock. "Wow! So, Isadora bought it." A surprised smile enveloped my face. "I wonder if Jonathan Gray ever found out his estranged wife purchased it?"

Ophelia blinked several times. "I'd like to think so. Talk about events coming full circle." She nodded to herself. Her voice was determined and laced with purpose. "That's what I'm going to do next. I'm going to see if I can find out what happened to Isadora."

I jerked my head down to the tea set. "And have you given any thought as to what you might do with this?"

Ophelia stared at me. "But I gave it to you. I didn't want it."

I flapped my hand. "It's yours. Isadora wanted it to do something positive. Now it's your turn."

Carson raised one of his bushy brows.

Ophelia eyed the strutting peacock. "I think I will enlist the help of that young man of yours – Xander."

The mention of his name gave me an involuntary start, which I hoped I'd managed to conceal. It had been great, being so busy and occupied with all of this. It had prevented my thoughts from dragging up images of him and Nadia. I cleared my throat. "Oh? Why's that?"

Ophelia pulled her eyes away from the tea set to Carson and me. "I've just had a thought. I've decided to auction it too and use whatever money it raises, to start The Annabel Crichton Fellowship, in honour of my late sister. It can encourage underprivileged young people who have artistic ability."

"That sounds wonderful," announced Carson with enthusiasm. "A set like this, with its unique design and slice of notoriety, would go for a pretty penny, I'm sure."

I leant over and squeezed Ophelia's arm. "Something tells me both Briar and Isadora would approve."

Chapter Forty-Six

O phelia and I were just giving effusive thanks to a blushing but delighted Carson when his wife arrived back from her book club.

She thrust a couple of paperbacks under her arm and locked the door of her white Corsa. "Dear me! My husband hasn't kept you all this time, has he? I do apologise."

Marion Gray was a small, chirpy woman with a puff of wavy blonde hair.

"Not at all," I assured her. "He has been wonderful and such a huge help."

Mrs Gray's waxed brows wiggled good-naturedly. "Carson can talk for Scotland when he gets going, especially if it's anything to do with ancestry or family trees."

Ophelia, standing beside me on the flower lined path, laughed. "Well, thanks to your husband's diligence and genealogical talent, he has been able to answer so many questions for us."

At this enthusiastic praise, Carson puffed out his chest and beamed.

"He won't be able to get his head back through that door now," joked his wife. She bid us a good evening and vanished inside.

Carson gave us a cheery wave,before disappearing back inside his house in a flash of dark brown corduroys and checked shirt.

My head reeling with relief and surprise, I climbed back into my car and waited until Ophelia secured her seatbelt beside me. I was just about to start the ignition when she mentioned Xander again. "Do you think you could give me the contact details for your young man, please, Sophie?"

I forced my face into a smile. "Oh, he's not my young man."

As Ophelia stared at my odd expression, I set my shoulders and hoped I looked nonchalant. "Of course. No problem."

I reached into the back seat where my handbag and the tea-set case were nestled side by side. I retrieved my phone and searched my contacts list. I found Xander's mobile number and email address and pinged them to Ophelia. Then I shoved my phone back into my bag.

Ophelia continued to study my profile. "Thank you. Are you all right, dear?"

I eased away from the kerb, indicating right and out onto the main road. The sky was a mish-mash of hot mid-July shades of burnt orange and dayglo pink that were seeping over the roofs and tree tops of Briar Glen. "Yes," I answered a little too brightly. "I'm fine, thank you. Why do you ask?"

Ophelia's hands rested together in her lap. She angled her

head to one side. "You can tell me to mind my own business if you like…"

I trained my eyes ahead, as the lazy evening light glanced against my windscreen.

"But when I mentioned that young man's name, there was a look that passed across your face."

I felt my back stiffen. "What sort of look?"

Now it was Ophelia's turn to stare ahead. She aimed the tiniest glance at me out of the corner of her eyes. "One that I had on more than one occasion in my younger days. A trouble-of-the-heart look."

I was determined to continue driving and drop Ophelia home, but she maintained her concerned air. In the end, I found myself turning into the entrance of Briar Glen Park, with its wooden picnic benches.

Ophelia unfastened her seatbelt and angled herself round, so that she was facing me. I switched off the ignition and watched the dappled light reach down through the network of tree branches like golden fingers.

I didn't want to talk about Xander. I didn't want to think about his sea-coloured eyes or his lopsided grin. Or the way his expression twinkled when he talked about his favourite paintings. But there was something hypnotic in the way Ophelia was waiting for me to speak that lulled the words out of me before I could pull them back.

And so, as the noise of children laughing and the fizz of birdsong rang out around my car, I blurted out everything to Ophelia: how my feelings for Xander had crept up on me; his rivalry with Jake Caldwell over Nadia; his reaction to seeing me out for dinner with Jake and then Jake snatching a kiss from me and his petty behaviour.

Then I told her about Saffy Clements coming to see me at The Cup That Cheers.

"It's obvious Saffy adores Xander," I continued, a sense of relief in my chest at being able to open up, "but she told me that she wanted me to know the truth about him – about what a decent, good man he is."

Ophelia shifted further round in the passenger seat. "And?"

My fingers tapped around the circumference of my steering wheel, while a young couple pushing their sleeping baby in a buggy ambled past, sharing an intimate moment. "I rang Xander after Saffy came to see me. I wanted to tell him how I felt. I also wanted to apologise for believing Jake's warped version of events but he didn't answer the phone. Nadia, his ex-girlfriend, did."

I ran a frustrated hand over the top of my hair, before it slid down to fiddle idly with my ponytail.

"You're making a number of assumptions," responded Ophelia.

"Maybe I am," I admitted, "but he was crazy about her. When she went off with Jake, Saffy said he wasn't in a good place for a long while."

"That doesn't mean he has forgiven her," pointed out Ophelia.

I felt despondency building up inside of me. "I beg to differ on that one. She described herself as his girlfriend on the phone last night."

I reached forward for my car keys dangling out of the ignition. My keyring, a glittery pink heart which Mum gave me, swung this way and that. "It's all too messy," I protested, despite my heart screaming otherwise. "There's no way I would be prepared to be a substitute. for Nadia." I fired up the ignition, a strange combination of relief and melancholy settling on my shoulders.

"So," I exclaimed with fake brightness, "let's get you home, otherwise Hal will think we've gone clubbing."

Ophelia laughed. "Chance would be a fine thing." But she carried on eyeing me as we drove back.

Chapter Forty-Seven

Tuesday morning felt odd, like a severe anti-climax.

After last night's series of startling revelations about Jonathan Gray and his monstrous parents, it was as if all the loose ends had come together at last and arranged themselves into a huge, pretty bow.

Nevertheless, I still felt like I did when 27th December came around – deflated.

We had discovered Briar had spent the rest of her days happily with Ernest Telfer and George and that Isadora had purchased the tea set at auction, quite likely as an act of defiance and an almighty "Up Yours!" to her estranged husband.

When I'd dropped Ophelia back home last night, she had taken the tea set. I knew she was going to contact Xander and tell him what had happened and about Carson Gray being able to answer all our questions.

The tea set belonged with Ophelia, but she wanted to do something positive with it and auction it, which I thought was a wonderful idea. Establishing an organisation in her late sister's name to encourage and support arts students from underprivileged backgrounds would be such a fitting tribute. And if anyone could ensure that the peacock tea set created a stir and sold for a handsome sum, it would be Xander.

I pushed him to the edges of my mind. There was nothing I could do, if Xander was unable to fight his feelings for Nadia and if he was capable of forgiving her over Jake. If anything, that stoked my emotions for him even more. It said so much about his character, if he believed they could put the past behind them and have a future together after all.

Cass wasn't silly. She had noticed I wasn't my usual self and, when she thought I wasn't looking, insisted on giving me long sideways glances across the shop. She didn't mention Xander by name, but emphasised that if there was anything I wanted to talk about, she was there for me.

Keeping occupied was the answer and so I was relieved when there was a flurry of customers mid-morning, followed by a delivery of craft products I'd ordered online for our autumn window display.

There was everything from pretty leaf stencils to rolls of crepe paper in burnt copper and russet, as well as the Halloween items I'd ordered. They consisted of small glittery pumpkins, witches' broomsticks, flying bats, black and orange crepe paper and sparkly cotton spider webs.

"You're organised!" grinned Cass, picking up one of the little pumpkins and admiring it.

"The early bird catches the worm," I smiled. "Also, there was a ten per cent discount on this lot if you ordered now."

I set aside the autumn leaves and complementary colours

of crepe paper in one box, while switching the Halloween paraphernalia to another. "I thought we could make a start on ideas for the autumn display next week," I called over my shoulder as I carried both boxes and manoeuvred them into the store room.

Cass agreed that was a good idea.

I heard the shop doorbell ring out and dusted down my hands before making my way back out.

It was Ophelia.

"Good morning," I said, smiling at her, before bundling her into a fond hug. She smelled of lemon shampoo. "How are you today?"

She hugged me back. "I'm good. Very good. And you?"

I examined her. The edges of her face were taut. "Are you sure?"

"Of course," she barked through strained laughter. "Why wouldn't I be?"

I glanced across at Cass, who raised her eyebrows an inch.

"So, what can I do you for?" I asked her.

She glanced down at her wristwatch before fiddling with her dandelion chiffon neck scarf. "Oh, I thought I might as well just drop by and say hello, even though I'm busy. Well, very busy actually. You know how it is. You retire and then find you have no time! Well, you don't actually know, do you, seeing as you're still only a young thing… Ha!"

I blinked at her. "Oh. Okay." I watched her shuffle from foot to foot. There was something preoccupying her. She was rambling and fidgety. "Ophelia, are you sure you are feeling all right?"

She had been studying a nearby gold and white Sara Miller

Portmeirion porcelain cup and saucer set, inscribed with two love birds. She snatched her eyes away. "Oh, yes. Totally. Absolutely. I just dropped by to tell you that I spoke with Xander last night and he was more than happy to arrange the auction of the tea set on our behalf."

I forced a smile. "Good. Great. That's great." Now that the tea set was back in Ophelia's possession, I considered it unlikely that I would have to have much contact with him. I hoped not. The more space I could put between us, the better it would be, and I could just press on with concentrating on The Cup That Cheers.

Ophelia carried on chatting and I forced myself to concentrate on what she was saying.

"Xander is certain that with its chequered history, the tea set will sell for a significant amount of money."

"Well, that's great too," I answered. And I meant it. "It will help you to get Annabel's fellowship well established."

Ophelia continued to hover.

I eyed her with renewed suspicion. She kept glancing out of the shop window, a pained expression flitting across her features.

"Are you waiting for someone?"

She whipped her head to me. She was sporting a maniacal grin. " Waiting for someone? Like who? Why would I be waiting for someone?"

I cocked my head at her. "Well, if you aren't waiting around for someone, there's something up. This isn't like you."

Ophelia waved away my concern. "What isn't like me? Nothing's wrong. Nothing at all. Everything is fine. Great."

She swivelled her attention to a puzzled Cass. "I have a few minutes to spare, so I thought I'd browse."

"Right. Of course. Feel free."

I shrugged my shoulders at Cass in a helpless gesture while Ophelia wandered off.

The office phone rang and so I excused myself to slip away and answer it, but it turned out to be a cold call for double glazing. "That's the third time in the last few days that lot have called," I moaned, making my way back out to the shop at the sound of the dinging doorbell.

Oh good. Another customer.

I drew up. My heart somersaulted.

It wasn't another customer.

It was Xander.

Chapter Forty-Eight

C ass and Ophelia lingered behind Xander.

Ophelia had guilt scrawled all over her face.

Xander remained by the counter, regarding me out of his hypnotic eyes. "Hi there."

I realised my mouth had flopped open. It must have looked attractive. I clamped it shut again. "Hello."

What the hell was going on? Why was Xander here? And why was Ophelia looking like a child caught stealing biscuits from a cookie jar? She was shuffling towards the door in her snazzy trainers.

"I had better be off," she blurted, her hand shooting out for the handle. "Things to do; people to see. You know, you think you're going to take things easier when you retire…"

Her odd behaviour and constant vigilance at the window were beginning to make sense. I crossed my arms. "Wait a moment, Ophelia. What have you been up to?"

But she fluttered her fingers in a breezy goodbye wave and darted off into the village.

Cass let out a self- conscious cough. "I'll just be in the store room." She slithered past me.

Xander glanced down at his desert boots and then back up at me. A lock of black hair tumbled forwards onto his brow and he pushed it back. "Well, I'm so glad this is in no way awkward."

I was doing my best to control the swirling sensations in my stomach. "How can I help you?" I asked in a strangulated voice that didn't sound like me. I cringed. Good grief! I sounded like a sales assistant from the 1950s. I wrapped my arms around myself. "Look, Xander, I don't know what Ophelia told you." I found myself looking past his shoulder, wondering if Nadia was with him.

"She said a lot actually," he confessed, taking a step towards me. "She's a very wise lady."

I found myself lacing and unlacing my fingers in front of me. When I did it for what felt like the twentieth time, I thrust my hands behind my back like I was Prince Charles. "Oh?"

I indicated the array of crockery set out on the shelves. "So why are you here, Xander? Is it to buy a gift for Nadia? Because we have just had a delivery of gorgeous Portmeirion porcelain…"

Xander moved closer still. His thick, dark brows gathered in confusion. "Nadia? Why would I be buying something for her?"

Before I could answer, Xander's expression cleared. "Ah. Of course. That's because she answered my phone when you rang the other night. Ophelia mentioned it." A small, hesitant smile tugged at the corners of his generous mouth.

Ophelia had mentioned it?

I wrapped my arms around myself again for something to do. My cheeks were stinging from what felt like forty-degree sunburn. "Look, I have no idea what Ophelia has and hasn't told you. She probably meant well, but she shouldn't have said anything."

Xander towered over me in my little shop. "Oh, Ophelia told me rather a lot."

I waited for him to elaborate, but he didn't.

I tightened my grip around myself, worried that at one point I might restrict my own breathing. He wasn't making this easy for me. I hoped my expression didn't reveal the tumult inside me. I felt as if I was riding the world's most thrilling rollercoaster. "And what exactly did Ophelia say?"

Xander flicked me a look from under his blueberry-black lashes. "That you thought, because Nadia answered my mobile, we were back together."

Oh, Ophelia! What did you think you were doing? "It's none of my business," I answered, my face flaming.

"Isn't it?" he asked, moving closer.

"Of course not," I answered crisply. "What you do and who you are with have nothing to do with me."

His eyes churned like the sea. "I don't think you mean that."

I swallowed and fiddled with the cuffs of my shirt.

"Nadia did come round to see me and yes, she did want to try again, but I made it clear I wasn't interested."

My heart felt like it was turning inside out in my chest. I cleared my throat. "Right. I see."

"She's just like Jake, always playing mind games and thinking she has the upper hand." Xander stood there, studying me. He waited for a few moments. "Aren't you going to ask me why?"

I couldn't tear my eyes away from him. A basket of butterflies exploded in my stomach. "Why what?" I managed.

"Why I told Nadia I wasn't interested in trying again?"

In two long strides, Xander was in front of me, looking down and reading my expression. I felt a whisper of breath stick in my throat, as I watched him lift his hand and push a stray lock of my hair back from my cheek. "Because, Sophie, Frozen North has finally melted."

My chest rose and fell. I gazed back up at him. I had to hear it from his own lips. I needed to.

When I didn't say anything, Xander lifted both hands and placed them gently on the tops of my arms. The sensation of his fingers seared through the sleeves of my shirt. "Do I have to spell it out?"

It struck me that I had never seen him like this before. There was a vulnerable edge to his voice.

"I'm sorry, Sophie. I'm so sorry. I jumped to all the wrong conclusions. When I saw you with Jake, it just brought everything back about what happened between him and Nadia."

Xander's eyes locked with mine. "When I called you that evening on your mobile and Jake answered, I assumed I was losing you to him as well."

I stared up at him. "What evening?" Then a thought bolted through my mind. "Hang on. That must have been the evening he brought a take-away round. I thought I heard my phone ring from the sitting room, but when I went to answer it, he assured me it was his phone ringing and not mine." My resentment fired up. "He told me we must have the same ringtone." I shook my head with rising fury. "The lying cretin! So it was you who rang me and he deliberately answered."

Xander nodded. "He took great delight in letting me know he was with you."

I could feel my eyes searching his face. "But it isn't what you think, Xander. Yes, I will admit I was flattered that he asked me out, but that kiss... He engineered it for your benefit. In fact, when he found out I knew you, he engineered everything. That's so obvious now."

Xander's expression morphed from tenderness to rising anger, before softening again. He gazed down at me. "That's what Saffy told me too. She said she came here to speak to you."

I allowed my fingers to run up and down the sleeves of his black jacket. "Jake lied to me from the start. He told me Nadia wasn't happy with you and that was why she started seeing him. You became so jealous, you carried out a vendetta against his artwork and his career suffered."

I reached up one hand and caressed his stubbly cheek. "It was never him, Xander. Ever." I cleared my throat, hoping I could locate the right words. "It was Saffy who told me the truth. She explained what really happened with Nadia and Jake and about him ripping off another artist's work, when he was James Deighton."

My eyes fused with his. "Saffy cares about you a lot, Xander."

"I know she does. She's a good friend and always has been, but there is nothing more to it than that."

I digested this. "I'm so sorry about what happened between you and Nadia. It must have hurt so much."

"It did," he admitted after a few moments' consideration. "I guess my pride took an enormous hit as well. But then I met you and…" He sought out what to say next. "What I'm trying to say," he managed through a half-laugh, "is that what I had with Nadia was a perfect illusion. I was imagining how great things were between us. What I had with Nadia didn't feel real; not like this."

He ran a finger down the length of my nose, which made me grin. "I thought it was at the time, but then when I met you and my feelings for you started creeping up on me … well, I realised what had been between Nadia and me was a pale imitation." His cheekbones coloured. "Then when I saw you and Caldwell together, I thought it was Groundhog Day and I just couldn't face the prospect of losing you, let alone to someone like him again."

My heart throbbed in my ribcage. "Well, I can assure you it wasn't. When Jake asked me out, I wasn't all that bothered about going. I'm still not sure why I said yes." I offered him a small smile. "To be honest, I think I only agreed to go out with him because I thought you and I were a non-starter." Xander's words of only a few moments ago flapped around my head like twittering birds.

I failed to conceal a gasp as Xander's fingers reached down and stroked my ponytail. "So, Ms Harkness, what do you suggest we do now? We've wasted so much time waltzing around each other."

My chest felt as if it were about to erupt. "Well, I was going to say that perhaps we could arrange our first date?"

He gave me that smile again, the one that made my knees buckle in my flared trousers. "That sounds good. In fact, it sounds wonderful. But I was thinking of something else."

"Oh?"

Xander took a step closer, so that the curve of his lips were inches from mine. "This." He took my lips with his and I pressed myself against him. We held one another, our mouths moving together slowly at first, before becoming more urgent and greedy.

My stomach swooped and dived. Xander let out a tiny moan from the base of this throat, which sent my heart cartwheeling. I held him tighter, feeling the broad solidity of him against me. His scent of cedarwood body wash and the sensation of his dark stubble against my skin sent my thoughts in a spiral of joy and emotion I was struggling to control.

As my nerve endings sizzled and Xander stroked my hair, I was sure I heard a triumphant giggle and a hiss of "Yes!" from Cass in the store room.

Chapter Forty-Nine

13th October, Glasgow Art Gallery Auction Hall

Halloween was only a couple of weeks away.

Copper leaves spun from the trees and tumbled over the pavements; shop windows were crammed with pumpkins and the air was laced with woodsmoke.

The Cup That Cheers continued to attract an increasing stream of customers.

The sale of Gran's house had been completed and a young couple with their baby had moved in last month. Whenever we passed by, we were reminded of my late grandma's teasing blue eyes and raspy, mischievous laugh. That would never change.

For today's auction of the peacock tea set, I had treated myself to a new dress in town. It was a bright blue polka-dot affair with a white collar and I'd matched it with my long navy suede boots.

Today seemed to be a culmination of months of

speculation, investigation and deliberation, so in my mind it was an important milestone.

The granite steps of the Glasgow Gallery were damp from an earlier downpour.

Xander parked his car over by the trees in the rambling grounds and took hold of my hand. I lingered by the passenger side door, huddling into my swing coat. "I hope after all this that the tea set sells for what it's worth. I will be so disappointed for Ophelia if it doesn't." I blew out a cloud of anticipatory air. "It would give such a decent kick-start to Annabel's foundation." I felt Xander's warm fingers clasp tighter around mine. I pulled my eyes away from the striking Georgian architecture, with its arched windows and sharp spires.

"Stop worrying. You've seen yourself what major interest there is in the tea set. Look." Xander jerked his head to the right. Several feet away, a cluster of journalists and photographers were nursing takeaway cups of coffee and shuffling from foot to foot as the stiff breeze whipped amongst them.

Xander's hawkish, handsome features broke into an encouraging grin. "Come on. We don't want to be late."

A security guard checked our IDs before we were directed through an archway on the right to a huge auction room, which possessed an impossibly shiny wooden floor and rows of high-backed velvet and gold chairs.

Stern portraits of important-looking individuals examined us as another art gallery official guided us to our seats up a short flight of stairs and into a balconied area overlooking all the action.

Ophelia and Hal were already seated, as were my parents, Cass, Ivy, Carson Gray and his wife. We all exchanged nervous, excited smiles and pleasantries.

The chairs below were filling up fast with intended buyers. A sea of people flowed in, adorned in everything from bow ties and trilbies to expensive jewellery and vintage coats.

Xander seemed to know who everyone was, or at least who they were here to represent. "The lady in the pink leather boots and fascinator is Melody Vincent. She is like a freelance bidder for some of Scotland's richest families. And if you look to her left, there's a guy wearing red spectacles. He's Albie Cyrus-Hughes."

The name was familiar. "Is he connected to the Cyrus-Hughes family that own that wildlife park?"

Xander nodded. "He's their eldest son. Apparently, Albie is a bit of a wheeler-dealer."

Up on the polished dark wood platform, a serious man in a loud checked suit appeared from behind a billowing black curtain. Autumn light was pouring in through the floor-to-ceiling windows and glinted off his balding head. He reminded me of an egg. On a nearby table was the tea set, concealed beneath a red cloth. My stomach performed an impressive forward roll and I swallowed.

To my surprise, the auctioneer's severe expression broke into a wide smile. He thumped his gavel on his wooden platform. "Good morning, ladies and gentlemen. I hope you are all well on this rather dreich October day. Welcome to this very special auction of the Ernest Telfer peacock tea set."

I shot a charged glance at Xander sat beside me in his smart dark three-piece suit. His steel-coloured shirt and ghost-grey silk tie highlighted the Mediterranean shades in his eyes. "Stop worrying," he urged me with mock exasperation and squeezed my fingers.

The auctioneer, who introduced himself as Raymond Curtis, must have made a witty remark, because there was a ripple of laughter and a couple of bouts of applause. "Raymond Curtis is the best auctioneer in Scotland," muttered Xander into my ear. "Do you remember all that fuss about eighteen months ago, when a brooch belonging to a Scandinavian queen was discovered on a Norwegian beach?"

I nodded, recalling the news story being covered here.

Xander gestured to Raymond Curtis. "Raymond was asked by the Norwegian authorities to conduct the auction over there. He's a legend in the art world." He twisted himself round in his chair and offered a smile of reassurance to a pensive Ophelia along the row of seats. "Your tea set couldn't be in better hands."

A hush fell across the crowd downstairs. From this view, it was like a child had upturned their dressing-up box, what with the extravagant hats, splashes of paintbox jackets and garish shoes.

Xander sat up straighter. "Oh, here we go."

Raymond Curtis gave his gavel another thump. "Right, ladies and gents, let's get this show on the road." He nodded to a young man on his right, who stepped forward and tugged away the red cloth. The tea set glowed in its open case in all its rainbow greens and golds.

I shuffled to the edge of my chair. Even though I had looked at the tea set countless times, it seemed more regal now somehow, more mysterious, as it sat there, presented in all its porcelain glory.

I couldn't help wondering what Briar and Ernest would have made of all this. The cluster of reporters and photographers outside; the heavy security to gain access to the gallery; the buzz from the potential buyers. It was quite surreal for me, so goodness knows what they would have thought.

Mum, Dad, Cass and Ophelia delivered encouraging smiles down the row of seats to Carson as Raymond Curtis beamed. "Let's begin with a bid of £5,000. Come on, ladies and gents. Don't be shy. Ah, thank you, Sir."

I peered down over the edge of the balcony, catching a glimpse of a tall, thin man in round spectacles putting forward the first bid with a sharp nod.

And so, it carried on. Nods; blinks; flicks of hands. I sat rigid, clutching Xander's hand as the bids grew larger and more ambitious.

When the amount climbed to £25,000, I couldn't help letting out an audible gasp. A couple of heads down in the auction seats jerked up to frown. Xander stifled a laugh. "Be careful, otherwise you'll find yourself putting in a bid."

I craned my neck to have a look at the bold bidder. She was a hard-faced older woman, with bright red lipstick and severe black hair skimming her shoulders. "Who is she?" I asked Xander under my breath.

He frowned and narrowed his eyes. "I've no idea. I've never seen her before."

"New money?" hissed my dad down our row.

Mum rolled her eyes beside him." You've been watching too many repeats of *Upstairs, Downstairs*."

Xander grinned and angled his body more towards the balcony edge to get a better view of the mystery bidder. "She's talking to someone on her mobile. She must be representing someone and bidding on their behalf."

There was a ripple of surprise as the woman put in a further bid of £30,000.

Xander continued to study the woman in silence, before shooting me an unreadable look. He jumped out of his seat as the murmurings of the auction played out down below. "I'll be back in five minutes."

"Where are you going?"

He tilted up my face to his and kissed me, but didn't answer.

While Xander was gone, the rest of us watched with fascination as the stranger with the bright red lips batted away counter bids for the tea set, like they were annoying flies interrupting her picnic.

Heads turned to stare, gasps rose and whispers ensued.

"She seems very intent on buying the tea set," I whispered across Xander's vacant seat to Mum, Dad, Cass, Ophelia, Hal and Ivy. Behind me, Carson and his wife let out murmurs of agreement. The bid amount had now reached the dizzying heights of £45,000.

"Whoever she is, she must be loaded," observed Dad, smoothing down his stripy tie.

"Or her client is. She must be receiving instructions from someone." Mum shrugged her shoulders casually. "I've watched so many episodes of *Bargain Hunt*, you get to know these things."

Cass and I swapped smiles.

There was a sudden flurry at my shoulder. It was Xander returning.

"The bid has increased to £45,000," I burbled to him, unable to conceal my excitement. "Isn't that great?"

I peered back down at the woman, who had her coat collar up and her mobile clamped to her ear. I dragged my attention away from the dramatic scenes playing out downstairs.

Xander's expression was thunderous.

"Xander? What is it? Where have you been?"

He didn't answer. He just sat there, grim-faced, on the edge of his chair. "Xander? Are you okay?"

His attention was locked on the black-haired woman. I followed his gaze. "Xander. What's going on?"

The voice of Raymond Curtis rang out like a rusty church bell. "So, we now have a bid of £45,000. Do I hear £50,000?"

There was a growing buzz amongst the bidders. We could hear the intermittent scraping of chairs, as the other attendees turned to examine who was controlling the bidding war with such ease.

"Come on, ladies and gentlemen. Take a look at this beautifully crafted tea set again. It possesses a history no author could have dreamt up in their imagination. An Ernest Telfer original of the finest porcelain. Now, do I hear £50,000?"

I watched wide-eyed as the woman with the scarlet lips muttered into her raised mobile. She gave a definite nod.

Raymond Curtis couldn't disguise the thrill in his voice as the mysterious woman increased her own previous bid. "Thank you, Madam. That's £50,000 bid. Do I hear any more?"

The silence throbbed. I held my breath. Mum and Dad clung to each other, while Cass, Ophelia, Hal and Ivy looked like they had just been confronted by a hungry werewolf. Carson sat behind me, clasping his wife's hand.

"So, no more bids on £50,000?"

Silence greeted the auctioneer. "Going once… going twice…."

The dark-haired woman sat steadfast, a slight twist of triumph lurking at the corners of her mouth.

"£55,000!" roared a deep voice I knew so well.

I blinked down at the audience, before realising the vocal eruption had come from the chair right beside me. Cass gasped, Mum and Dad turned to stare at each other, Ophelia flopped back in her chair, while all Hal and Ivy could do was open and close their mouths.

"What are you doing, young man?" hissed Carson.

"£55,000," repeated Xander towering beside me. All heads below swung round to look up at where we were sitting.

Xander challenged the icy glare of the dark-haired woman with one of his own. "I'm bidding £55,000."

Chapter Fifty

I shot out of my chair and grabbed at Xander's suit sleeve. "Xander! What the hell are you doing?"

Xander contorted his mouth and hissed out the corner. "Don't worry, Soph. I know what I'm doing."

"But … but you can't know! You're bidding a huge amount of money."

Xander was too preoccupied with the glowering woman in the gallery below. She was twisted round in her chair and delivering the full force of her ire at him.

I turned helplessly to my parents. I knew Xander possessed an impressive private art collection. Surely he wasn't planning on selling one of his treasured paintings to buy the tea set?

My heart lurched with love and gratitude for his kind and well-meaning action, but there was no way I was prepared to let him do that. I thrust out my hand again.

Raymond Curtis couldn't contain his delight at the dramatic events unfolding before him. The auction hall had erupted. He looked like a six-year-old boy on Christmas morning. "Please, ladies and gentlemen. We must resume the auction. Now, £55,000 bid by the gentleman in the balcony. Do I hear any increase? Madam, can you be tempted?"

He turned again to the mysterious brunette. Her slash of red lipstick remained frozen.

"Xander," I said in as measured tones as I could muster. "I know what you're trying to do and I love you for it. But please. Don't spend all that money."

"I agree," implored Ophelia from her seat. "It's so wonderful of you to consider doing this, Xander, but…"

Xander shook his head. "You don't understand."

An expectant hush fell across the auction attendees. The dark-haired woman's eyes were like chips of ice. From our view in the gods, I could see her snarling into her mobile. Whoever she was talking to, they appeared to be having some sort of heated exchange.

I was at risk of dislodging my French roll as I snapped my head between the woman, Xander and the shocked entourage seated with us.

A sound like wind rushing through autumn branches escaped from everyone when the woman eventually gave the briefest shake of her head, to denote she wasn't prepared to increase her bid.

"Sold!" exclaimed Raymond Curtis, with the most dramatic thump of his gavel. "For £55,000 to the smartly dressed gentleman up in the balcony."

A gush of relieved air escaped from Xander, before a slow smile spread across his lips.

Before I could articulate anything, he scooped me into his arms and snatched my mouth with his in a fiery kiss.

I didn't complain, but I was still confused. "Will you please tell me what the hell is going on here?"

Ophelia looked dazed, while Mum, Dad, Cass and the rest of our party looked like they had just woken up from hibernation.

Xander slid an arm around my waist. "That woman," he began to explain, as chairs scraped along the wooden floorboards and the auction attendees filed in the direction of the function room for brunch. "Her name is Cameron Lomax. She's American."

"Okay," I answered, wondering where this was going. "Did you recognise her after all?"

"Not at first. Then it started to bug me that she seemed vaguely familiar." Xander trained his attention on everyone. "You've probably guessed by the way she has been clamped to her mobile phone for all that time that she's here at the auction representing someone who wanted to buy the tea set."

"A Russian oligarch?" piped up Dad. "Or an Italian mob boss?"

Mum dug her elbow into Dad and he winced. "Kenny, for goodness' sake! Let the young man speak."

Xander's mouth twitched with amusement. "Almost as exciting, but not quite." His warm aquamarine eyes travelled across the sea of rapt faces, including mine beside him. "I disappeared, so I could ask around and see if anyone knew anything about her. A friend of mine who heads up the security team working here today owed me a favour."

"Go on," I urged, my head rattling with questions.

"Tony told me this Cameron Lomax is hoping to make a name for herself as a controversial art critic in the States. She was married to some wealthy industrialist, but they divorced last year."

Cass was enthralled. "This sounds like a Jackie Collins plot."

Xander pointed to where Cameron Lomax had been sitting only moments before. Her chair was empty, as were most of the others now. "Tony was reluctant at first to tell me who she was, but he said if I happened to read his computer screen at an opportune moment, there wouldn't be much he could do about it."

He gave a wry smile. "Tony and his team were tasked with undertaking security checks for all the attendees at this morning's auction, because it was such a high-profile event. During their investigations, they found out that Ms Lomax has a new, younger man squiring her about town. He was the one so very keen to acquire the tea set."

"Lucky her!" joked Mum. Ophelia chuckled, whereas my dad and Hal frowned with disapproval.

"So do you know who this guy is?" I asked. "And why he was so keen to have it?" Why would some young Lothario be so adamant about buying a vintage tea set?

Xander turned to me. "The reason he wanted it will become all too apparent when I tell you who Ms Lomax's new boyfriend is."

He let out an almost disbelieving laugh.

From the direction of the function room, we could hear barks of laughter and clinking teacups.

"She's in a relationship with Jake Caldwell. He's the one who was at the end of the phone, talking to her."

Chapter Fifty-One

"You are kidding?" said Dad. "Not that jumped-up little shit who our Sophie had that disastrous dinner date with?"

"Thanks, Dad," I muttered, reddening.

Xander's hand held my waist a little more firmly. "The very one."

Cass folded her arms across the front of her beige woollen dress. "But I thought Jake Caldwell lost a lot of his sales and credibility, after you revealed he had been ripping off deceased artists' work?"

"He did," agreed Xander. "I strongly suspect that all that money he was bidding with wasn't his. It was hers."

"And he wouldn't come along here in person, because he knew we would be here," I realised with a mixture of resentment and relief.

"But why would he be so hell bent on getting hold of that tea set?" asked Dad, shooting inquiring looks at Xander and me.

"Because he's a petty, nasty piece of work?" suggested Cass.

Xander agreed. He reached inside his silk suit and tugged out his mobile. He jabbed a few keys and pulled up some images on his screen. "After Tony gave me that information, I googled Cameron Lomax. Here."

I accepted the phone from him and read the article from a newspaper gossip column that was shining up at me from the illuminated screen.

"Cameron Lomax received a generous divorce settlement from her ex-husband," explained Xander." But it would seem Jake has plans on how he is going to spend it."

"Good grief," I murmured, reading the lurid details of the divorce case, before handing back the phone. Xander tapped at the mobile screen again and fetched up another article. "Now read this."

It was in the latest society column from some gossipy magazine in the States;

LOMAX'S NEW ARTIST LOVE HAS DESIGNS ON HIS OWN MUSEUM

Jake Caldwell, the handsome British artist now accompanying Cameron Lomax around town, has made it plain he wants to launch his own museum.

Caldwell (36), whose reputation as inventive artist James Deighton was tarnished when respected art critic Xander North alleged a series of plagiarism misdemeanours, is attempting to relaunch himself into the artistic establishment, by having his own museums in both the UK and the States.

Caldwell, born and raised in Edinburgh, has admitted that following his fall from grace, he is keen to establish at least two museums, housing a variety of unique British art and ceramics, that would enchant visitors from across the world...

Fury and disbelief seized me. Jake wanted the tea set, not because of any legitimate reason or passion, but just to spite Xander and me. Of course, if he had been successful, he would have tried to deny it – at least for a little while – and then the temptation to gloat would have proved too much for him.

I read the article aloud to Mum, Dad and the rest of our assembled clan. They emitted a series of dismissive snorts and rude words.

So Cameron Lomax had been bidding her own money, manipulated by Jake.

Xander pointed at his phone still in my hand. "I expect it was her who decided not to bid any more of her cash. You can bet your life Jake was barking down the line at her, trying to persuade her to increase that bid to goodness knows how much." He allowed his sexy mouth to break into a smirk. "I should think Jake was livid when she refused to top my bid."

I allowed all of these thoughts and revelations to settle in my mind. I turned to Xander and gazed up at him. "And that's why you stepped in."

"There's no doubt in my mind, if he had had his way, Ophelia's tea set would have been winging its way to New York now and being touted around by Caldwell like some shabby novelty," said Xander. "He didn't want to acquire it for the right reasons."

Ophelia shook her head. She moved forwards, gazing up at Xander. "But the amount of money you've paid for it…"

Xander brushed aside her concerns. "Please don't concern yourself with that. I'm just about to close a deal on a Banksy."

Ophelia's eyes almost popped, as did mine. She reached up and planted a grateful kiss on Xander's cheek. "Thank you. I don't know what to say. That is so generous. That amount of money will be of such assistance in setting up Annabel's fellowship project…"

"Then please don't say anything." He smiled, blushing. "I'm planning on donating the tea set to the Glasgow Museum. It will stay in Scotland and close to Briar Glen, where it belongs."

As we all filed down the short staircase that would take us to the function room for brunch, I held Xander back for a moment. I greedily drank in his aquiline nose and arched, dark brows. "You never fail to surprise me, Mr North."

He bathed me in that smile that triggered fireworks in my chest. "And I intend to keep it that way, Ms Harkness."

We shared another lingering kiss, smiling against each other's mouths.

"Bugger!" I said, annoyed with myself. "I've just remembered I've left my mobile back in the shop. I was so preoccupied this morning about the auction…"

"Don't worry," Xander reassured me. "Let's go and grab something to eat downstairs and then we can pop back and get it. I know you. You'll start suffering withdrawal symptoms if you don't have it with you."

I pulled a sarcastic face. "Thank you. I think."

We enjoyed a delicious buffet of seafood canapes before excusing ourselves and driving back in Xander's car to The Cup That Cheers to collect my mobile.

We had decided to close for the rest of the day, so we could all truly celebrate the event of the auction.

I unlocked the shop door and Xander hovered in the doorway. He performed a theatrical shiver. "Don't be too long, will you, Sophie? It's not exactly tropical out here."

There was a brisk October wind today, sending the leaves cartwheeling like Olympic gymnasts through the street.

I rolled my eyes good-naturedly. "Don't worry. I remember where I left it. In the store room."

I hurried through the shop and clicked open the store room door. I cast my eyes about, before spotting my phone sitting on one of the closed boxes of newly arrived stock.

I snatched it up and started to close the door behind me, when a sudden whirl of wind travelled in through the shop. I managed to clamp my free hand down on sheets of tissue paper piled high on a nearby Formica table. They would have caused a right mess if they had gone spinning everywhere.

But as I moved to leave, something glittery lying on the floor drew my eye.

I crouched down and picked it up. What was it? It looked like it must have got blown out from under one of the shelving units.

I set my phone down by my feet. It looked like an old Christmas gift tag in the shape of a snowflake. It had shed most of its silver glitter, but there were still a couple of little clumps hanging determinedly on. I turned it over and let out a stunned gasp. I recognised my grandmother's handwriting straightaway, all gracious loops.

It said:

To Chris,
Hope you don't lose this one!
Love always, Helena XX

I stared down at the gift tag in my hands, drinking in my gran's writing. Who was Chris? I couldn't recall her speaking about someone with that name before.

And what had she meant by "Hope you don't lose this one"?

I ran one finger over the writing, as though connecting with her again. My heart jolted in my chest.

"Sophie?" called Xander from the doorway. "Have you found your phone yet? Please say you have. I'm losing all feeling in my legs!"

My face broke into a smile as I slid my phone and the gift tag into my bag for safekeeping. "On my way now," and I clicked the store room door closed behind me.

Epilogue

Six months later

A lot changed after Xander's surprise acquisition of the tea set.

As we had hoped, it found its way into a specially designated display at the Glasgow Museum, alongside a flashy electronic information board, detailing its rollercoaster journey from being presented to Leonora Gray as a birthday gift in the early 1900s, through to its exciting appearance at the auction.

There were images on the information board of Castle Marrian and Briar Glen as they used to be, with cobbled roads and oil streetlamps dotted everywhere.

Unfortunately, we couldn't find any surviving photographs of Briar Forsyth, but the local artist who made the Briar Glen tea set used his imagination and produced some lovely pencil drawings of what he thought she would have looked like.

Xander commented that he thought she carried a passing resemblance to me and I was secretly delighted. Being compared in even a small way to such a strong, brave and determined young woman was a compliment in itself.

As you might imagine, the tale of the peacock tea set triggered an increase in visitors to Briar Glen.

Not long after Xander's purchase of it, we learnt through the gossip columns that Cameron Lomax had dumped Jake. What with the US papers getting hold of the fact that he was the former disgraced artist James Deighton, things were getting too uncomfortable for Jake to handle over there.

We also were told by a couple of Xander's art contacts that Jake had returned to Scotland, after Cameron tired of him sponging on her and insisting that he could be the next John Paul Getty, if only she would just support his plans for a world-dominating chain of Caldwell Museums.

The last Xander heard, Jake had returned to Edinburgh and was eking out a meagre living as a nude model for still life evening classes.

The Cup That Cheers continued to flourish and on what would have been Briar Forsyth's birthday, 31st May, I dressed the shop window with artificial blue roses, one of the illustrations of her and two of the Briar Glen tea sets, which were very popular.

And as for Xander and me… I glanced down at my ring finger. My engagement ring, fashioned from vanilla gold and blueberry sapphires, glowed against my skin. Xander had made sure the stones were crafted into the shape of the mystical blue briar rose.

If it hadn't been for Ophelia depositing the tea set and fleeing like she did last year, I would never have got to know Xander, or the truth about a resilient young woman who, despite everything, made sure she carved out a decent life for her and her little boy.

The shop bell gave its familiar merry waltz, bringing with it a couple more customers, their faces lighting up with admiration at the selection of ceramic and porcelain teapots and tea sets, waiting to be admired and taken to a new home.

Thank you, Grandma, for believing in me.
I hope I've done your dream justice.

---

12 The Steadings, Briar Glen. One year later.

Using a garden trowel, I was overturning the generous beds of rich chocolate earth in the back garden.

The sky was shifting overhead, a blanket of soft cloud and April sunshine. I huddled a little tighter in my warm pink fleece and rearranged the sparkly crocheted hat on my head.

I finished removing a couple more weeds and plopped them into a small bucket by my feet. It was fortunate that the former owners, Keith and Andrew, had been very green-fingered.

I rose and straightened, pressing my garden-gloved hands into the base of my back. From beyond our back garden, the hills of Briar Glen swooped and dived, clotted with wild heather, and the buttery brick of our new home glittered in the sleepy sunshine.

It was as I turned towards the back door that I noticed a tiny flutter of something in one of the beds running up against the wooden fence.

I stepped over my abandoned trowel and orange bucket to go and investigate. Was it a new flower? There weren't many appearing yet, apart from the odd brave daffodil.

I trod over the neat, manicured square of acid-green grass and angled my head as I moved closer. I blinked, trying to reconcile what I was seeing. It was a rose, coiling upwards against the fence with its proud stem.

But it wasn't just any rose.

I clapped one delighted hand to my mouth, appreciating the scalloped, dusty powder-blue petals as they waggled in the breeze. My breathing picked up an excited pace. "I don't believe it!"

I took a few steps backwards, keen not to turn my back on it in case I was imagining it. "Xander! Xander!" I yelled towards the open patio doors.

Xander was in the dining room, rigging up a set of chrome spotlights we had just bought. He jerked his head round. "What is it, Mrs North?" His wide mouth broke into a lazy smile.

"Come and see this!" I gasped, staring wildly over my shoulder for fear it wouldn't be there when I looked back. "You know how you said the blue Briar Glen rose doesn't exist…?"

Acknowledgments

Thank you so much to my wonderful editors Jennie Rothwell, Nicola Doherty, Dushi Horti and Tony Russell at HarperCollins for their enthusiasm, creativity and insightful editing suggestions, as well as all the rest of the team who make not only the publishing process but also reading in general, such a magical experience. I couldn't be more grateful.

Huge thanks also to my amazing agent Selwa Anthony and to Linda Anthony. It is an honour to know you both.

As always, all my love to Lawrence, Daniel, Ethan and Cooper.

And finally, to my late mum Ellenor Trevallion, who taught me that dreams can and do come true and to never give up.

I love you and miss you always.

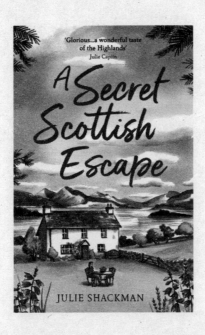

'Glorious...a wonderful taste of the Highlands'
Julie Caplin

A Secret Scottish Escape

JULIE SHACKMAN

When Scotland's sleepiest hamlet becomes the centre of hot gossip, Layla Devlin finds herself caught in a mystery…

When Layla's fiancé has an unexpected heart attack and dies – in another woman's arms, no less – Layla is determined to pack up and leave Loch Harris, the village she's always called home. But an unexpected inheritance and love for her quiet corner of Scotland send her down a new path.

Rumours swirl that a celebrity has moved into Coorie Cottage and Layla is determined to have him headline her opening night at local music venue The Conch Club. But the reclusive star is equally determined to thwart Layla's efforts. Rafe Buchanan is in hiding for a reason, and soon his past comes to Loch Harris to haunt him…

YOUR NUMBER ONE STOP

ONE MORE CHAPTER

FOR PAGETURNING BOOKS

One More Chapter is an
award-winning global
division of HarperCollins.

Sign up to our newsletter to get our
latest eBook deals and stay up to date
with our weekly Book Club!
<u>Subscribe here.</u>

Meet the team at
<u>www.onemorechapter.com</u>

Follow us!
🐦 <u>@OneMoreChapter_</u>
f <u>@OneMoreChapter</u>
📷 <u>@onemorechapterhc</u>

Do you write unputdownable fiction?
We love to hear from new voices.
Find out how to submit your novel at
<u>www.onemorechapter.com/submissions</u>